D0742402

AUG 2019

THE DAUGHTER of SHERLOCK HOLMES

Center Point
Large Print

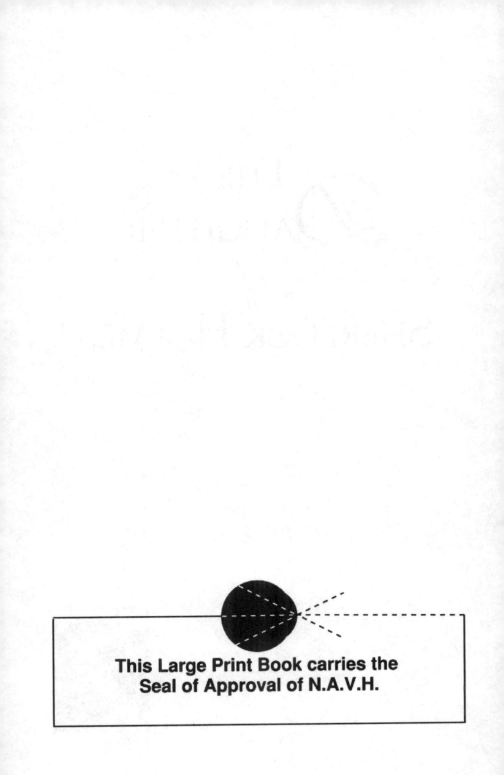

**This Large Print Book carries the
Seal of Approval of N.A.V.H.**

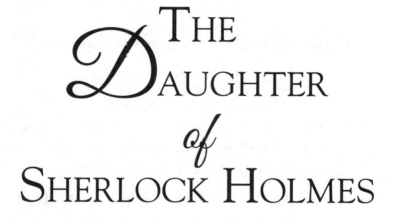

THE DAUGHTER of SHERLOCK HOLMES

Leonard Goldberg

CENTER POINT LARGE PRINT
THORNDIKE, MAINE

This Center Point Large Print edition
is published in the year 2019 by arrangement with
St. Martin's Press.

Copyright © 2017 by Leonard Goldberg.

The text of this Large Print edition is unabridged.
In other aspects, this book may vary
from the original edition.
Printed in the United States of America
on permanent paper.
Set in 16-point Times New Roman type.

ISBN: 978-1-64358-288-7

Library of Congress Cataloging-in-Publication Data

The Library of Congress has cataloged this record
under Library of Congress Control Number: 2019942051

In memory of Rachel,
who gave so much and asked for so little

CONTENTS

We are all prisoners of our past.
It shapes and defines us and can
no more be forgotten than changed.

INTRODUCTION

I am John Watson, Jr., M.D., the son of the close friend and longtime associate of the famous Sherlock Holmes, who passed from this earth in the year 1903, while tending bees on the Sussex Downs. To this day my father still resides in rooms at 221b Baker Street and can attest to the truth of the story I am about to record. It was his hand that guided us through this criminal maze and the terrible dangers it contained. He alone could serve as guide, because portions of the drama you are about to read transpired before, with the very same players he and Sherlock Holmes had encountered near the turn of the century.

How can this be, you ask?

Are not most of the people involved—Holmes, Moran, Lestrade—long dead?

Yes, indeed they are. But their genes live after them, and have endowed their offspring with many of the same features that the parents themselves possessed. When Shakespeare—in his play *Julius Caesar*—wrote, "the evil that men do lives after them," I wonder if he was in some measure referring to the master criminals and their offspring, and to the despicable deeds they would continue to do. I suspect this was Shakespeare's intent, but the reader can draw his own conclusions in this matter. I searched at length for a title to the story I am about to tell, but could not find one that fit well. So I turned to my father, who was the most excellent chronicler of the Sherlock Holmes mysteries. He smiled at his only son's predicament, and in an instant jotted down a perfect title: *The Daughter of Sherlock Holmes*. As he did, there was a definite twinkle in his eyes, and for once I thought I could read his mind. He was thinking that Sherlock Holmes was, after all, still with us.

1

The Game Is Afoot

As was my custom, I visited my father, Dr. John H. Watson, every Friday to make certain he was comfortable and not in need. His general health was slowly deteriorating and he was being deprived more and more of the simple pleasures of life. But he never complained and always greeted me with a warm smile and a wave. This Friday in the early spring of 1910 I found him standing at the window of his rooms at 221b Baker Street and staring out at a cold London morning. He continued to turn his head from side to side as if he were following some object in motion. He was attired in a tattered, maroon smoking jacket that was so badly worn it was threadbare at the elbows. I had offered to purchase him an identical replacement, and last Christmas had even given him one as a present. But he would not wear it, preferring to hold on to the old smoking jacket that was the last vestige of his happier, exciting days with Sherlock Holmes.

"Good morning, Father," I said cheerily. "I trust your cold is better."

"Some," he replied with a raspy voice, before

taking another puff on his favorite cherrywood pipe.

"You really should not be smoking," I advised. "It will only worsen the inflammation in your bronchial tubes."

"I will make a note of that," he said, his gaze still fixed on some object in the street below.

I groaned to myself and thought how foolish my comment was. Here was I, a young physician at thirty-two, giving advice to an esteemed, now retired doctor who had more medical experience than all my living years put together. But I cared for the man far more than I would admit, so I added, "At least promise that you will limit yourself to two pipefuls each day."

"Why give a promise that I have no intention of keeping?"

"To make your son feel better."

My father nodded slowly before saying, "A warm lie is much preferred over a cold fact, isn't it?"

"In your case, no."

He flicked his wrist, which was his way of ending a particular topic of conversation. In the morning light I could clearly see the toll the advancing years had taken on my father. Now he was a quite thin man, bent at the waist, with deeply grayed hair and mustache. His once strong jawline was partially hidden with hanging jowls. But his eyes were clear and his vision good despite the years. At length, he asked me, "How goes your work at St. Bartholomew's?"

"It is satisfactory," I answered, but my tone of voice said otherwise.

For the past five years I have been employed by the pathology department at St. Bartholomew's Hospital, where my workload is heavy and never ending. But it was stimulating and I held the highly regarded position of assistant professor. Nevertheless the head of the department, Dr. Peter Willoughby, made life unpleasant for those who were associated with him. He covered his shortcomings with a mean bark and an even meaner bite. "There are moments when I wonder if I have chosen the best place to practice my skills."

"Your day will come," my father prophesied. "Bide your time. Willoughby's type always fades and brings about his own end."

"The waiting is difficult."

"It always is."

Suddenly my father tapped his pipe against the window and pointed to the street below. "Ah! Now she makes her move!"

I hurried over to the window to see what had so aroused my father's interest. It was a veiled woman, dressed entirely in black, alighting from a horse-drawn carriage. She appeared to be studying the street address above the door, yet at the same time she glanced over her shoulders.

"What do you make of that?" my father asked.

"She is looking for an address."

"She knows the address already."

"How can you be so certain?"

"Because the very same carriage she rides in has stopped briefly in front of this front door three times, only to drive on and return shortly."

"Perhaps she was unsure of the address."

"Three times?" My father shook his head. "I think not. She knew exactly where she wished the carriage to go, having given the driver a precise address. That is why the carriage stopped momentarily in front of our very door."

"If that is the case, why did she not step out earlier?"

"Because she is uncertain as to whether or not she should bring her problem here."

"And the way she glances around makes me believe that she envisions herself being followed by someone."

"Possibly," my father said. "But unlikely. If she thought she was being followed, she would not keep returning to her destination three separate times in such a short period. More likely, she wishes to satisfy herself that she is not seen entering this well-known address because her problem is so delicate."

"How do you know her problem is delicate?"

"The death of a close family member always is."

It required only a moment to follow my father's line of reasoning. "The black dress and veil! She is in mourning."

"Exactly."

I could not help myself as I placed my hand on his shoulder and gave him a gentle squeeze. "I can see a bit of Sherlock Holmes in you."

"Pshaw! I am a rank amateur compared to Holmes. By now he would have given us all the details about this woman, including who she is, where she lives, and what her social standing is. He would even know the nature of her problem and why she is bringing it to 221b Baker Street. And if it was of interest to him, he would have answers to her dilemma before she entered the room or spoke a word."

"Oh, come now!"

"I do not embellish," my father assured me.

"How in the world could he accomplish this?"

"Because Holmes not only saw things as we do, he carefully observed them as well. He would then connect these observations to his vast knowledge on any number of subjects, which in this particular case happens to be the city of London." He paused briefly to watch the veiled woman, who was now chatting with her driver and still glancing about. "Allow me to give you an illustration. Did you notice the emblem on the door of the carriage that brought her?"

"Yes. But it has no special meaning to me."

"Nor to me. But to Holmes it would represent a treasure chest of information. He would have recognized the emblem and known the exclusive area of London it served. And since the carriage is obviously an expensive one and no doubt serves a very pricy clientele, Holmes could have pinned down the woman's address to a four-square-block area in West London."

"And her elegant attire attests to the fact that she is a woman of means," I added. "But how would Holmes be aware of the nature of her problem?"

"He would instruct us to reason backward, for that is how most such puzzles are solved. The most conspicuous clue in this case is her black dress and veil, which indicate she is in mourning for a close and loved relative. In all likelihood it is the recent death of this beloved one that brings her here. And there is an unpleasantness to this death, perhaps some scandal. That is why the woman is so hesitant to approach us with her problem and why she does not wish to be seen doing so."

"Father! Your mind seems so keen here."

"Not really." He downplayed his deductive achievement. "I witnessed Sherlock Holmes performing a similar feat many years ago when a veiled woman came to us in distress."

"But a scandal, you say."

"Quite."

"Do you know what the scandal is?"

"I have no idea, but Holmes would have arrived at the answer in a matter of minutes. Say, for example, the woman's address would be Belgravia, where the aristocracy live and where the scandals are the juiciest. The unpleasant death would have been covered extensively in the newspapers, all of which Holmes read on a daily basis. As a matter of fact, he kept copies of these newspapers for a week in case an article he had skimmed took on sudden significance. Holmes would have consulted these papers and quickly known the woman's family, the unexpected death, and the reason for her visit." My father paused to relight his pipe before concluding, "Putting all these clues together, he, like I, would rightly assume this woman brings with her a most delectable tale."

I applauded gently. "Holmes would be proud of you, Father."

My father shrugged. "He would have simply said, 'The clues were waiting there to be read, my dear Watson.' "

There was a soft knock on the door.

"Yes," my father cried out.

The door opened and Miss Hudson appeared, she being the daughter of the late Mrs. Hudson, the housekeeper who served Sherlock Holmes and my father for so many years. "There is a young woman downstairs who wishes to see you, Dr. Watson. Shall I show her up?"

"By all means."

As the door closed, I asked my father, "It seems strange that they continue to bring their problems here, does it not?"

My father nodded. "As if Sherlock Holmes was still alive."

"Are you able to help them?"

My father shrugged. "To the smallest extent. I give them guidance and hope for the best."

"That is most kind of you."

He shrugged once more and said, "I am merely an old man trying to remain relevant."

We heard soft footsteps coming up the stairs. Abruptly my father straightened up from his stooped posture, then ran a quick hand across his silver-gray hair, and smoothed out his thick mustache. "Do not pry until she has given us her entire story."

There was another tap on the door and Miss Hudson showed in a young woman, dressed from head to toe in black, with no adornments what-soever. She was small and thin and, as she raised her veil, we could see she had large, doelike eyes that were reddened and sad.

She spoke directly to my father. "I am at my wit's end and can only pray that you will be able to assist me, Dr. Watson."

"I shall try," my father said, and beckoned to a large, comfortable chair by the fireplace. "This is my son, the junior Dr. Watson, who is often of assistance to me. Please tell us who you are and the nature of your problem."

"My name is Mary Harrelston," she said with a quivering voice. "And I am here because of my brother's recent, tragic—" Before she could speak further, tears streamed down her cheeks. She quietly sobbed for several moments, then dabbed away the tears with a handkerchief she kept in her sleeve. "Forgive me," she began again, "but you will understand my sorrow and distress once you hear my story."

"Take your time," my father said gently. "And tell us in detail about your brother's heart-breaking death."

Mary Harrelston's eyes widened. "You knew my brother?"

"Only from a very brief account in the news-paper."

"Of course," she said, with an understanding nod. "They say his death was a suicide, but that is something my brother would never consider despite the depth of his woes. He was deeply indebted to a friend, Christopher Moran, and had even lost more while gambling with this friend on the afternoon of his death. When Moran left the room momentarily, it is said my brother was so consumed with despair that he leaped from a window to his death. This, Dr. Watson, would be impossible, for my brother was now the leader of our family and all of us—my father, my mother, and I—depended on him and his strengths greatly. Although his gambling was a weakness, he was so strong in every other aspect of life. And he continued to assure us that he had a definite solution to our financial woes, which would be forthcoming shortly. These are not the words of a man about to take his life."

My father squinted an eye, as if trying to recapture an old memory, then asked, "Did you say that the fellow gambler's name was Moran. M-O-R-A-N?"

"Yes," she responded. "That is how I believe he spells it."

"Curious. Very curious," my father remarked. "Pray continue."

She paused and dabbed at her cheeks once more, then added, "A strong man would have never done this."

"Perhaps you overestimated his strengths," I thought aloud.

My father gave me a disapproving look, for I had interrupted her story with an assumption.

It did not bother Mary Harrelston in the least. She promptly went on. "My assessment of his strengths is not simply based on the love I had for my brother, but on his exploits outside the family. He was commended for his bravery in the Second Afghan War, where he along with several other officers were taken prisoner by the enemy. It was he who was instrumental in planning and executing their escape. His medals and ribbons would easily fill the chest of any military coat. This was not a man who takes his own life when faced with a great challenge."

"Indeed," my father agreed. "Yet the newspapers said there were witnesses to this tragic event."

"There were two, but with differing accounts," she said. "A gardener working down the way swore that he saw my brother leap wildly out of the window, while a ten-year-old boy, who was walking by with his mother, claims my brother appeared to float down motionless from the roof."

"Float down from the roof, you say?" my father questioned at once.

She nodded firmly. "Those were the young lad's exact words according to Scotland Yard. They of course discarded his testimony and believed that he was simply embroidering the event with his own imagination. So we have two varying accounts of the same event. And there is an obvious difference between *leaping wildly out of a window* and *floating down from the roof.*"

"Which do you believe is correct?" I asked.

"Who can know the truth?" she answered back. "All I know is that I have a dead brother and that my family's reputation is stained forever because of the recounting of a nearby gardener and a young boy who happened to glance up as my brother fell." Her face suddenly hardened and she added, "It is not fair, Dr. Watson. It is not fair or just."

"What would you have me do?" my father asked.

"Why, investigate! Clear my family's good name by finding out who was responsible for my dear brother's death."

My father's expression told me that he had scant interest in the case and would have little to offer this poor woman.

"Perhaps I could make some inquiries to Scotland Yard on your behalf," he proffered.

"They will not help," she said. "I must confess that earlier I consulted a private detective who did just as you proposed. Scotland Yard told him in no uncertain terms that they would not bother Mrs. Blalock or her son or the gardener again. Their statements had been taken and the case closed."

My father sprang from his chair and stared down at the woman. "Are you telling me that one of the witnesses was Joanna Blalock?"

"Yes," she replied. "It was Mrs. Joanna Blalock who was walking with her son, and it was her son Johnnie who witnessed my brother's fall. She vouches for the accuracy of a portion of his account."

"This Mrs. Blalock being the daughter-in-law of Sir Henry Blalock, who resides in Belgravia?"

"The same."

"You are certain?"

"Positive, sir."

"Then we shall look into this matter," my father said with authority. "We shall investigate every aspect of this tragic happening for you."

"Oh, thank you," she said gratefully. "I feel as if a great weight has been lifted from my shoulders." She extended her hand and my father assisted her to her feet. Walking to the door, she asked a final question. "Where will you begin?"

"With the witnesses."

"Then you must avoid one Inspector Lestrade. It was he who insisted that Mrs. Blalock and the gardener not be bothered again."

"That is where the case starts. That is where we will go," my father said, undeterred.

"If there are any expenses incurred, I will—"

My father waved away the offer. "We shall keep you informed."

Mary Harrelston quickly left the room, taking with her what little hope my father could provide.

Once she departed, I noted that my father's entire demeanor had changed. He rubbed his hands glee-fully together while he paced, his posture upright and straight, a decided bounce to his step.

"What is the reason for the sudden joy and excitement I see in you, Father?" I inquired.

"Because, my dear John," he answered, refilling his pipe, "the game is now afoot!"

2

Joanna Blalock

The next morning my father and I found ourselves in the library of Sir Henry Blalock's magnificent house in Belgravia. The library was most generous in size with a large, brick fireplace and well-polished mahogany furniture. All of its walls were lined ceiling to floor with countless numbers of leather-bound volumes. There were rich Italian tapestries hanging near a bay window that overlooked a fine garden. I thought the room reflected the qualities of the man—elegant and dignified, yet formidable—for Sir Henry was an esteemed statesman who had once held the offices of Chancellor of the Exchequer and Home Secretary. As the morning air held a chill to it, we gathered around a crackling fire and warmed our hands. Sir Henry, like most Londoners, wished to talk of my father's past adventures with Sherlock Holmes, but Father deftly guided the conversation to the purpose of our visit.

"We are grateful, Sir Henry, for allowing us to visit on such short notice," my father said. "We know this must be an inconvenience."

"Not at all," Sir Henry said. "I only hope that

we can be of some assistance in this dreadful matter. The poor Harrelstons are absolutely devastated by their son's death. And it could not have happened at a worse time."

"How so?"

"They are a storied and distinguished family, Dr. Watson, with a line of descendants that would make any man proud. But now they have suffered severe financial reverses that threaten all of their holdings."

"So their misery is multiplied."

"Many times over," Sir Henry said. "Let us pray that your investigation brings them some comfort."

"I hope that your daughter-in-law can give us much-needed insight into this matter." My father reached for his cherrywood pipe and struck a match. "Do you mind?"

Sir Henry gestured his permission. "I am certain that Joanna will be more than pleased to aid your investigation."

"As you have no doubt surmised, the details in this death are quite gruesome, so I shall try to be brief and not unnecessarily graphic when speaking to Mrs. Blalock. I suspect the event has been quite upsetting to her."

Sir Henry smiled, which for the moment seemed out of place. "There is no need to be brief or delicate with Joanna. My daughter-in-law is looking forward to your interview, for she

27

is fascinated by such events. As a matter of fact, she has delved deeply into the subject of suicide for the past several days and has read every book, text, and monograph she could find that deals with this unpleasant act."

"Reading about a mangled body and looking at one are two different things, Sir Henry."

"Not to worry," Sir Henry said easily. "Joanna was once a practicing nurse, you see."

"But I must question your grandson as well," my father informed him. "Here I must carefully craft my words so as not to upset the lad. Surely you would agree with that, do you not?"

A smile again crossed Sir Henry's face. "You are about to be greatly surprised, Dr. Watson."

We turned as the door to the library opened.

"Ah," Sir Henry said. "Here is my daughter-in-law."

Sir Henry made the introductions, but I was so captivated by the woman's lovely appearance that I barely heard his words. Joanna Blalock was tall, only a few inches shorter than I, with soft patrician features and sandy-blond hair that was pulled back severely and held in place by a silver barrette. She had inquisitive deep brown eyes that seemed to study rather than just look at you. Her figure was quite trim beneath a long black dress, which had a white collar that came up to her chin.

Looking directly at me she said, "I have

admired your skills at St. Bartholomew's, Dr. Watson."

I was caught entirely off guard. "You were in the pathology department?"

"Only when a patient I had served died," she replied. "I would attend the autopsy in hopes of learning the exact cause of death. I was a great admirer of yours, as was my deceased husband, Dr. John Blalock."

"I remember your husband," I said, thinking back. "He was considered the very finest of surgeons. What a shame that he was struck down in his prime by King Cholera."

Joanna Blalock glanced away, as if to control her composure. "And we tried so to prevent it. We did all the right things and took every precaution. All the drapes and curtains were covered with lime, and we even placed some on the windowsills, but still the cholera came."

"A tragic loss," I consoled.

"In more ways than I can count," Joanna Blalock said softly, then turned to my father. "But my loss is not the purpose of your visit, is it?"

"Indeed it is not," my father replied. "We are here on a somewhat delicate matter."

"You are here to investigate the murder of Charles Harrelston," she said straightforwardly.

My father parted his lips in a thin smile. "What brings you to that conclusion?"

"Because you are here, and the famous

associate of Sherlock Holmes would have little interest in suicides. As you no doubt know, there are only four general causes of death, Dr. Watson. Natural, accidental, suicidal, and murder. Charles Harrelston's death was obviously not natural, nor could one envision him tripping over himself and falling three stories to his death. Which leaves us with suicide or murder. Since you are here, I think it fair to assume that you are not at all convinced the man committed suicide. And that leaves us with murder. And you are here in an attempt to prove it."

"What do you believe is the case?" my father asked.

"Only what the facts will allow. So pray ask your questions and let us see where it takes us."

Sir Henry sighed resignedly. "Dr. Watson, I am afraid my dear daughter-in-law has spent too much time around the dead and dying, and far too much time reading detective mysteries. You will have to forgive her."

"There is no need." My father quickly waved away any apology. "Tell me, Mrs. Blalock, which detective stories do you favor?"

"I particularly enjoy the ones by Edgar Allan Poe that feature the very clever C. Auguste Dupin."

"Have you read the Sherlock Holmes mysteries that I chronicled some years ago?"

"I have."

"And what do you think of Holmes's methods?"

"They have some merit."

Sir Henry rolled his eyes toward the ceiling while my father and I suppressed our grins.

My father looked at Joanna Blalock admiringly and inquired, "Are you as observant as you are quick?"

"I think so," Joanna Blalock said, without even a hint of modesty.

"Then tell me exactly what you saw two afternoons ago on Curzon Street. I want every detail. Leave out nothing."

"It might be best for you to start with my son," she suggested. "It was he who first saw the man and brought him to my attention. I witnessed only the landing."

"Very well."

Joanna Blalock rose and said, "I shall go fetch Johnnie."

As she departed, my father turned to Sir Henry and quickly asked, "How old is your grandson?"

"He will be ten next month."

"Is he mature for his age?"

"Quite."

"Does he have a keen eye?"

"Remarkably so."

"And you are certain he will not be disturbed by the gruesome features in this case?"

"He is like his mother," Sir Henry said, with obvious pride. "Need I say more?"

"He does not sound like a lad of ten."

"I am reminded of that on a daily basis," Sir Henry went on. "Only yesterday I found him studying a text on human anatomy and asked him why. He told me he was trying to find the name of the skull bone that had been so badly disfigured in Harrelston's fall."

"Did he identify the bone?"

Sir Henry nodded. "It was the occipital. He wrote down the name a dozen times so he would not forget it."

"Well, well! We are dealing with something very special here."

Sir Henry nodded again. "Like mother, like son."

The door to the library opened and Joanna Blalock returned with her son. The lad was tall for his age, with a handsome, narrow face and a jutting jaw. His dark brown hair was long and tousled, but not overly so. Yet it was his eyes that caught your attention. They were half-lidded and gave him a serious, studious expression. If there was any uneasiness caused by our presence, he did not show it.

As Joanna made the introductions, I saw my father's complexion go pale. His mouth was agape, as if he were suddenly stunned. I rushed to his side and asked in a whisper, "Are you in distress, Father?"

His quiet words came slowly. "There is no distress."

"But you do not look well."

"I assure you I am," my father said as color returned to his face. "I—I was momentarily startled by the unexpected."

"What was so unexpected?"

"Later," my father replied mysteriously, and composing himself, began to interview the lad. "Johnnie, I hear that you have been studying anatomy."

"Yes, sir," Johnnie answered.

"Your grandfather informed us that you were particularly interested in the occipital bone," my father said. "Could you please refresh my memory and tell me where that bone is located?"

Johnnie's eyelids went up, as if letting the question into his brain and allowing it to register. In an instant he responded, "It occupies the entire back of the skull, sir."

"Very good! Thank you," my father said, and ran a hand through the lad's tousled hair, which put the boy at ease. "I have just a few more questions. Would you agree to answer them for me?"

"If you wish," Johnnie said, then glanced up at his mother who nodded back her approval.

Joanna Blalock seated herself in a high-backed leather chair, with her son at her side. "If you ask your questions in an adult fashion, he will reply in a like fashion."

My father pulled up a cushioned ottoman and sat leaning forward so that his eyes were on the same level as the lad's. "Now tell me, my good fellow, what did you see the other day when the man fell?"

Johnnie licked his lips and thought back. "The man fell from the roof."

My father's eyes narrowed noticeably. "From the roof, you say?"

"Yes, sir."

"Could he have fallen from the window?"

"The roof," the boy insisted.

"Was he by himself?"

Johnnie stared at my father, not understanding.

My father rephrased the question. "Did you see anyone else up on the roof with him?"

Johnnie shook his head. "Just the man."

"Then he fell and struck the ground. Correct?"

Johnnie nodded. "And bounced."

"How many times?"

Johnnie held up one finger. His expression stayed placid, his voice even. He appeared to be totally unfazed by the memory of the event.

"Did he cry out while he fell?" my father asked.

Johnnie hesitated, not sure.

"There was no cry," Joanna Blalock said. "He made no sound at all."

"He made a thud when he hit the street, Mummy," the lad recalled.

"Yes," Joanna Blalock said and smiled at her son. "Indeed he did."

My father leaned back and furrowed his brow

as he digested the new information. "How far were you away from the man?"

"Thirty feet at the most," Joanna Blalock answered.

"That was close."

"Quite."

"And you are certain he made no sound at all?"

"None."

"Could his cries have been obscured by the noise of traffic on the street?" I ventured.

"I do not think so," Joanna Blalock answered at once. "Only moments earlier I had commented to my son how clearly we could hear the chirping of nearby birds."

It appeared the lad was becoming bored or fatigued with the questioning and brought a hand up to stifle a yawn. My father's eyes widened as he pointed to a small star-shaped birthmark on the lad's wrist. "What a curious thing," he remarked. "It has the appearance of a star. It is so perfectly formed that it could be mistaken for a tattoo."

"Oh, no," Joanna Blalock answered. "It is a birthmark. Even when he was an infant, I could see its most unusual shape."

"How distinctive."

"Mummy says it will bring me good fortune," the lad said.

"Let us hope it does." My father gazed at the strange birthmark once more and for a brief moment I thought I saw a smile come to his face. Then his expression returned to the sordid business at hand. "I have one final question, Johnnie. What was the position of the man as he fell?"

Johnnie glanced up at his mother, confused by the question.

Joanna Blalock simplified the query. "When the man was falling, did it appear as if he was diving into a pool of water? Or did he look like he was jumping off a bed onto the floor?"

"He was on his side, Mummy," Johnnie replied.

Joanna thought back for a moment, then nodded. "He was definitely on his side, with his head a bit lower than the rest of him. I believe his head took most of the force because it was terribly disfigured."

"Did you—"

"And there was one other thing," Joanna Blalock continued on. "Despite the massive injury to his head, there was very little bleeding. I found that rather strange."

"Strange indeed," my father agreed and looked over to me. We exchanged knowing glances. It is a cardinal rule of pathology that dead men bleed very little, even after massive trauma.

Then my father came back to Joanna Blalock. "We briefly visited Curzon Street this morning, but unfortunately the street cleaners had already been there and scrubbed everything away. We could not re-create the prior event that had occurred there, which could be of utmost importance in our investigation. I wonder if you would be so kind as to accompany us to Curzon Street now and point out the critical landmarks at the death scene. We would be most grateful for your assistance."

"I should be glad to," Joanna Blalock said, and looked over to her father-in-law who gestured his approval. "Father, would you be good enough to look after Johnnie until the tutor arrives?"

"Oh, I believe I can manage."

Joanna Blalock affectionately ruffled her son's long hair before patting it back in place. "Then I shall fetch my coat."

As the library door closed, my father brought his attention back to Johnnie. "There is one more question I have. Do you think you might help me with it?"

"I shall try, sir," Johnnie said.

"Good." My father flattened his hand and held it up, then slowly let it descend. "As the man fell, did he move his arms and legs?"

"No, sir," Johnnie replied. "He was quite still."

"Thank you," my father said, and watched the lad run to the far side of the library where he began to spin a giant globe. "Observant little boy," he commented.

"And bright," Sir Henry added. "In many ways just like his mother."

"I hope you will forgive me for not seeking your permission before asking your daughter-in-law to accompany us," my father said formally. "I am afraid my mind is somewhat preoccupied this morning."

"No apology is needed," Sir Henry responded. "As a matter of fact, I'm delighted you have asked her to join you. You see, Dr. Watson, my daughter-in-law has been in the doldrums since the death of her husband two years ago. Her spirits have been rather low and she rarely goes out."

"A natural response to grief," I said in a clinical tone.

Sir Henry nodded. "I know. But it still hurts to see."

My father inquired, "You say she rarely goes out, yet she left the house a few days ago, did she not?"

"Only to visit an ill friend, Lady Jane Hamilton. Were it not for that, she would have remained at home here in Belgravia."

"And she goes out on a lovely day," I thought aloud, "only to see a most dreadful sight. She must have been distressed on returning home."

"Not in the least," Sir Henry said. "You must remember that Joanna was a highly trained surgical nurse, and during her time at St. Bartholomew's had no doubt seen far worse."

"Indeed," I concurred.

My father asked, "Please forgive my curiosity,

Sir Henry, but is it not unusual for a woman of your daughter-in-law's standing to continue being a nurse once she has married?"

Sir Henry sighed deeply. "There is nothing usual about my daughter-in-law, Dr. Watson. She is bright, headstrong, and does exactly as she pleases."

"So you had no objections?"

"Oh, I had objections," Sir Henry said. "But I also understand Joanna. She is very smart, ten times smarter than most men, with a mind that works like a steel trap. Once a fact enters, it never leaves. Now tell me, what would you do if she were your daughter?"

Sir Henry didn't wait for my father's response before answering his own question. "My daughter-in-law has an extraordinary mind that needs to be occupied and challenged. Otherwise her spirits seem to sink and she becomes moody. Nursing was the one profession open to her that could keep her mind in high gear. It was perfect for Joanna, so I agreed with her wishes. Her husband was strongly in favor as well, for he knew of Joanna's skills in the operating room. He actually encouraged her to stay on."

"A wise decision," my father remarked.

Sir Henry sighed again, this time unhappily. "I think her very best moments were when she was working next to my son at St. Bartholomew's. Of course, King Cholera ended all that."

"Your daughter-in-law was fortunate to escape the dreadful disease," I said.

"She did not escape," Sir Henry said. "She survived it. Joanna, you see, has a strong body to go along with her strong brain."

The library door opened and Joanna Blalock entered, now wearing a bonnet and cape. "I am ready," she announced.

After giving her son an affectionate hug, she led the way to the front entrance where a butler held the door.

Outside the day was gray and crisp, with a definite hint of rain in the air. We climbed into a waiting carriage and started off on the ride from Belgravia to Curzon Street. Traffic was light so we made good time.

"I should like to thank you for coming along to assist us," my father said cordially.

Joanna Blalock gave my father a thin smile. "If I am to assist you, Dr. Watson, then you must fill in the blanks for me."

My father's eyelids came up. "Which blanks?"

"The ones you left unsaid."

"Such as?"

"Such as the reasons you knew this was murder and no suicide before you even walked into the Blalock home."

My father glanced over to me as his lip curled in amusement. "This is not a woman to be trifled with."

"Perhaps she is only guessing," I suggested. "After all, the nature of your questions would indicate something sinister."

"It was not so much the nature of Dr. Watson's questions," Joanna Blalock explained. "It was the manner in which he asked them. He was a man looking to confirm that which he already knew."

My father chuckled briefly at me. "I warned you."

"So please be so kind as to fill in the blanks, Dr. Watson," she persisted.

My father took out his cherrywood pipe and nibbled on it without lighting it. "What I am about to tell you comes from the newspapers and from an informant at Scotland Yard who owes me a favor or two. First, let me give you what is known. The victim here is Charles Harrelston, the eldest child of Lord Harrelston. He was educated at Eton and Cambridge and accustomed to wealth and privilege. He moved in the right circles and belonged to the right clubs. At this point in his life, his record was unblemished. Then he volunteered and served with distinction in the Second Afghan War. When he returned he was a changed man. He became a womanizer and was heavily into drink and gambling. Then he straightened up and became solid again, except for excessive gambling. And that may have cost him his life."

"He found himself deeply in debt," Joanna Blalock surmised.

"Exactly," my father went on. "To the tune of a thousand pounds, which is a considerable sum, particularly to the Harrelston family that currently has overwhelming financial woes. Like all compulsive gamblers, Charles Harrelston thought he could gamble his way out of debt. So he visited the man he was indebted to, who happened to live on Curzon Street. Once there, he played a single hand of poker for a thousand pounds. If Harrelston had won, he would have been debt-free. If he lost he'd have owed two thousand pounds. Unfortunately, Charles Harrelston lost. The man he was playing poker with left the room briefly. When he came back the window was open and Charles Harrelston was nowhere to be found. The rest of the story you know."

"But my son distinctly told us the man fell from the roof," Joanna Blalock argued.

My father's eyes twinkled. "Yes. I do believe he did."

"And the man fell sideways, which is not the position a man jumping to his death would assume."

"That too."

"And he made no cry as he fell," Joanna Blalock recalled.

"Not a peep."

"My, my!" Joanna Blalock said. "Things are not fitting together well at all, are they?"

"And there is more," my father said. "Your son told us the man did not move his arms or legs as he dropped down."

Joanna Blalock gave my father a stern look. "I do not remember you asking my son that question."

"He volunteered the information," my father lied.

Joanna waved her hand, dismissing the explanation. "You asked the question in my absence so I could not prompt his answer."

"I confess," my father said with no remorse. "But you see how important his answer was."

"Quite," Joanna Blalock said before concluding, "So we have a man who falls through the air sideways, makes no cry, and does not move his arms or legs. Which means our falling man was either unconscious or dead."

She wet her lips, then continued on. "And neither unconscious nor dead men are known to leap from windows, are they, Dr. Watson?"

"Hardly," my father answered. "Assuming your son's observations are correct, Charles Harrelston did not jump to his death; he was pushed to it."

"My son's observations *were* correct," Joanna Blalock insisted. "Charles Harrelston was pushed to his death. There is no other explanation for the facts we have."

"But who would do such a foul deed?" I asked.

"Let us determine why," Joanna Blalock replied. "That will tell us who."

3

The Nearsighted Gardener

At noon our carriage arrived at the curb in front of a fashionable three-story house on Curzon Street. At the door stood a uniformed police officer who intently watched our every move, with an expression that said we were not welcome. He directed a particularly long look at Mrs. Blalock who returned it in like.

Helping my father down from the carriage, I asked, "If Scotland Yard is so convinced this is a suicide, why have they posted a bobby?"

"To discourage the curious, I would guess," he replied, and gazed up to the third-floor window, then brought his eyes down to the sidewalk directly beneath it. "Mrs. Blalock, please be so kind as to show us your exact position when you saw the man falling."

"If you wish," Joanna Blalock said. "But might I suggest we begin with the gardener, who gave such a vivid description of the fall?"

"We questioned him earlier this morning," my father informed her. "And he stood firmly by his account of the event."

"Then he will not mind telling it once more."

My father hesitated. "I must warn you that the gardener is a rather surly fellow. He will not take kindly to being questioned yet again."

"He may well refuse altogether," I interjected. "The man is that hostile."

"Yes, yes," Joanna Blalock said, not the least bit deterred. "But he is either a liar or has a colorful imagination."

"You will have to prove it beyond a reasonable doubt," my father said.

"That is my intent," Joanna Blalock told him. "Now please lead the way."

We walked nearly the length of the block before approaching a well-kept garden in front of a stately house. With each step I noticed Joanna Blalock moving her lips as she counted to herself.

"Why the counting?" I asked in a quiet voice.

"For distance," she answered. "I have a stride that measures just under two feet. Thus, I calculate the garden to be forty yards away from the crime scene."

"What is the significance of that?"

"Either everything or nothing."

Ahead we watched the gardener carefully clipping away at the top of a waist-high hedge. Deep-chested and bald, he had a ruddy complexion and a protuberant stomach that drooped over his beltline. Despite the coolness of the day, he perspired freely.

When he saw our approach, his face hardened.

"Not you again! I have told my story to the coppers and to you and to the newspapers, and I will not tell it more. So go away and let me work. A working man, I am, and I will not waste my time further."

The gardener turned away from us and returned to trimming the tall hedge. He kept its top smooth and perfectly even, and did so by eyesight alone. If there was a leveling instrument on hand, I could not see it. The gardener ignored us, as if we had suddenly disappeared.

"With your shaping of the hedge, will you not harm the surrounding flowers?" Joanna Blalock asked.

The gardener let out a most exasperated growl. "I have been at this for nigh on thirty years, madam. I can assure you I know my work and can trim without harming any flowers whatsoever. Now, that is the last question I shall answer for you. So go away and leave me be."

"Surely you can spare a few minutes," Joanna Blalock persisted.

"Madam! How many times must I repeat myself?" the gardener bellowed. "Time is like money to me, and I will not waste a farthing on your questions."

"And well you shouldn't." Joanna Blalock reached into her purse for a half crown and pressed the coin into the gardener's hand. "This will compensate you for your time."

"Oh, it will, madam! It will!" the gardener said excitedly. He was clearly astonished by Joanna Blalock's generosity and studied the coin at length to confirm it was genuine. Satisfied, he placed the half crown in a weathered wallet, then appeared to groom himself for his presentation. He opened his coat and dug into an inner pocket for a balled-up, soiled handkerchief. While extracting the handkerchief, he dislodged a set of spectacles that nearly fell from his pocket. He secured the spectacles, then went about mopping the perspiration from his head.

Joanna Blalock watched each and every move the gardener made. Her eyes stayed focused on the man's callused hands. She seemed to be studying his motions, but they had little meaning to me.

"Where should I start, madam?" the gardener asked, his tone now subservient.

"At the beginning," Joanna Blalock replied. "I would like you to show us where you were standing when you saw the man fall. Mind you, it has to be the precise spot."

The gardener moved to the side of an adjacent hedge and faced the length of Curzon Street. It afforded him an unobstructed view of the house where Charles Harrelston had gambled and lost. "Right here, madam."

"What were you doing at the time?"

"Finishing up on this hedge," the gardener

recalled. "I was making sure there were no rough areas at its top."

"So you were paying close attention to this task?"

The gardener nodded. "It had to be ever so even. Otherwise it's not a good job I've done and I've not earned my pay. Not a twig was out of place, I can tell you."

"Well put." Joanna Blalock seemed to approve. "That is exactly what you indicated in your earlier testimony."

"Indeed it is, madam. And I will not change a word, for everything I have told you is the truth," the gardener said. "I was just finishing the trimming when I glanced up and saw the man jumping from the window's ledge. It happened in a flash, but there he was, clear as day."

"So you actually witnessed his jump?"

"He took a leap, madam," the gardener said, nodding firmly several times. "The moment I looked up he jumped into thin air. I could not believe my eyes."

"Did he fall feet first?"

"Oh, yes, madam. Feet first, to be sure."

"Was he moving his arms and legs as he fell?"

"Like a wild man, he was."

"Dreadful," Joanna Blalock commented.

"Exactly so, madam. I ran to see if I could be of assistance, but I could tell there was no life left in him."

"How strange that such a well-to-do man would choose to end his life that way."

"It is far beyond strange, madam. A man has everything in the world and does that."

"And certainly the address of 28 Curzon Street would indicate a man of considerable means."

"So it would," the gardener agreed. "You were correct with that, but not with the address. The house he jumped from was 26 Curzon Street."

"Are you certain?"

"Yes, madam. I know this street up and down and every house on it, like the back of my hand."

"Then the article I clipped from the newspaper must be incorrect," Joanna Blalock said and opened her purse. She removed the clipping and pointed to the title of the article, which read SUICIDE IN MAYFAIR. "See, the first line states the address to be 28—"

"No, no, madam." The gardener interrupted and placed a dirty finger on the printed address. "It says that the address is 26 Curzon Street, not 28."

"Ah, you are correct. I misread the small print," Joanna Blalock admitted. "Thank you for making me aware."

"You are very welcome," the gardener said and straightened up, posturing like a man who had accomplished an important deed. "I shall never forget that address and the sight I witnessed there."

"I would wager you did not sleep well that night."

"I tossed and turned and never really closed my eyes."

"Well, let us hope the horrific memory fades."

"It cannot happen soon enough."

"Perhaps a pint or two after work might help."

The gardener smiled broadly. "It just might, madam."

"You look like a Guinness half and half man to me."

"It is my favorite," he replied, and licked his lips at the thought of the common beer served in pubs.

Amazing! I thought to myself. In a matter of minutes Joanna Blalock had converted this sour, rude gardener into a gentle, talkative man. They appeared now to be having a friendly conversation, both totally at ease, with the man readily answering every question in an unrehearsed fashion.

The gardener was pointing down Curzon Street, directing our attention to the cursed house. He made no secret of how much the event that occurred there had disturbed him. "I am afraid the terrible memory will stir every time I walk by number 26."

"It will pass," Joanna Blalock assured him, and followed his line of sight down the wide street. Raising a hand, she shaded her eyes against the sun, which was now breaking through the mist. "Oh! I believe our driver is motioning to us, but I cannot be sure. My vision does not allow it."

The gardener quickly reached for his spectacles and squinted at the carriage in the distance. "Yes, madam. He seems to be waving."

"Perhaps he is beckoning us," Joanna Blalock said, and thanked the gardener for his time and information.

"I hope I was of some help, madam," the gardener said, with a half bow.

"You were of great assistance," Joanna Blalock told him. "You have made things quite clear for us."

We walked away in silence until we were well out of the gardener's earshot. Even then I spoke to Joanna Blalock in a low voice. "Our driver was not waving. He was sitting motionless with his back to us."

"I know," she said.

"What does this signify?"

"It signifies that the gardener is a liar."

"Not so quick," my father cautioned. "Simply because he could not describe what the driver did or did not do does not invalidate his witnessing Charles Harrelston's fall. At that distance he might not be able to see the driver's arm, but he could surely make out a full-grown man in flight."

"Not without his spectacles," Joanna Blalock countered. "The gardener is nearsighted and that is why he could easily read the fine print of the newspaper article. But he cannot see at a distance and that is why he carries such thick spectacles. You must have noticed that he had to put on his spectacles only to make out our driver's image, and even then he could not tell us what the driver was doing."

"Perhaps the gardener had his spectacles on when Charles Harrelston fell," I argued. "Then he could have seen the man about to take flight."

"That does not fit with the story he told us," Joanna Blalock continued. "Remember his exact words. He was finishing the trimming of a hedge and making certain its top was smooth and even. Now we know his near vision is excellent. That is why he was not wearing his spectacles when we approached him a few minutes ago and why he did not have them on while trimming a hedge several days earlier. He only uses his spectacles for far vision and thus did not have them on at the moment Charles Harrelston fell."

"Could he have seen a figure on the ledge a moment before the fall and rapidly put on his spectacles?" I inquired.

"Impossible," Joanna Blalock said at once. "An object falling through space drops at a speed of thirty-two feet per second. Since that is the approximate height of a three-story building, the gardener would have been required to glance up from his work and see a man on the ledge, then put on his spectacles and focus his vision, all in one second. It cannot be done. Allow me to demonstrate." She turned to my father. "Do you have your reading glasses with you, Dr. Watson?"

"I do," my father replied.

"Excellent," Joanna Blalock went on. "On my request, I would like for you to glance up at the building, then reach for your spectacles and place them on and look back at the building. Your son will be our timer." She waited for me to take out my timepiece. "Everyone prepared?"

My father and I nodded.

"All right, then," she said. "On my signal."

I readied myself.

"Now!" Joanna Blalock called out.

In all haste my father glanced up at the building, reached for his reading glasses and placed them on, then looked back at the building.

"Done!" Joanna Blalock shouted, then turned to me. "How much time passed, please?"

"Five seconds," I reported.

"So my mathematics indicate that an object falling at thirty-two feet per second would drop one hundred sixty feet in five seconds," Joanna Blalock calculated. "Thus, the building at 26 Curzon Street could have been fifteen stories in height and the gardener still would not have witnessed Charles Harrelston's leap to his death. Which tells us the man's testimony was a complete fabrication."

"Why would the gardener invent such a story?" I asked.

"For public recognition, self-importance, and a dozen other reasons, none of which are relevant," Joanna Blalock replied. "What is relevant is that we can discard the gardener's account and trust my son's. With that in mind, I believe we can conclude that Charles Harrelston did not jump to his death, but was pushed to it."

"You do realize that this type of evidence will not hold up in court," my father warned. "For example, the gardener will claim to have had on his glasses for distant vision at the time he viewed the fall. A good barrister would so prepare him and it would be most difficult to dispute."

"It may not hold up in a court of law, but it will in a court of logical deduction," Joanna Blalock responded. "And in this case. that is what will lead us to the solution. Solving a crime is similar to disentangling a ball of yarn. One must find the free end and untangle the first knot one comes to. We have by logic untangled our initial knot."

We walked on silently toward 26 Curzon Street, but there were two questions that gnawed at me. "Pray tell, Mrs. Blalock, how reliable is this measurement that states a falling object descends at a speed of thirty-two feet per second?"

"It is quite reliable," she answered. "It is a rule of physics that is based on gravitational pull."

"How did you come by this knowledge?"

"I read it in a textbook of physics."

"So, you are good at that science?"

"Hardly. I simply remember facts that may be of importance in solving mysteries."

My father joined in. "I think the speed of a falling object you referred to is based on Newton's law of gravity."

Joanna Blalock shrugged. "Its discoverer is of little matter. Its accuracy is all that counts."

"I have one further question," I said. "What made you think beforehand that the gardener's vision might be impaired?"

A faint smile came to her lips. "What makes you believe I had that in mind?"

"A number of things," I replied. "But the newspaper article on Harrelston's alleged suicide that you had in your purse was a major clue. Its presence required forethought. And I much admired the way you guided him into reading the small print."

"I rather enjoyed that myself." Joanna Blalock beamed. "And of course you are correct in that I did think of the device beforehand. But the original idea was not mine. I had read about it previously in a French mystery novel. The detective's name was Delon and he too had to deal with an eyewitness in a murder case whose testimony did not fit the facts. He brought along a newspaper clipping so he could test the witness's near and far sight."

"But how did you know the gardener had such poor far vision? You seemed aware of this before the actual test."

"I did not know until I watched him read the clipping without using his spectacles," Joanna Blalock said. "Then it became a simple deduction. If a man has excellent near vision, yet carries around thick spectacles, he must have poor far vision."

Remarkable, I thought. Absolutely remarkable. Here we have a highly trained surgical nurse who dabbles in physics and seems to have a knack for uncovering clues in murder cases. I could not help but wonder how deep the well went in this most attractive woman whom I could not help but gaze at in my peripheral vision. And then a Mona Lisa–type smile came to her face, but I had no idea to what or to whom it was directed. Was it simply a show of confidence or was there some hidden mystery behind the smile? As I forced my eyes away, I was left with the thought that a man could become lost in such loveliness and never find his way out.

4

Christopher Moran

On our return to 26 Curzon Street, Joanna Blalock immediately moved to the sidewalk in front of the house and plunged into a study of Charles Harrelston's fall. With a careful eye she gazed up and down the building several times before focusing on the granite curb. Only after completing her scrutiny of the bloodstained curb did she stroll over to us and announce, "I was wrong. The body of Charles Harrelston was neither dropped nor pushed off the roof. It was thrown."

"But your son said it floated down," I argued.

"It did," Joanna Blalock said. "But only after being thrown."

"Where is the evidence for this conclusion?"

"Directly before our eyes." She walked to the edge of the curb and paced off the distance to the front wall of the house. "It measures a good ten feet. What do you make of that?"

My father and I had no answer.

"Come now," Joanna Blalock coaxed. "Look to the very top of the house and tell me what you see."

We strained our necks to find the clue Joanna Blalock had discovered. My father even stepped back to enhance his view before saying, "At the utmost height is a stone parapet that blocks our vision from the remainder of the roof."

"Which is an important observation I should have noted earlier," Joanna Blalock told us. "If Harrelston's body was simply pushed or rolled off the roof, it would have dropped straight down and landed only a few feet in front of the house. But in fact it came to rest a good ten feet away. Thus, some force had to lift and propel that body over the parapet for it to end up a distance from the building."

"It had to be the murderer," I concluded.

"So it would appear," Joanna Blalock agreed.

"Perhaps there was some structure protruding from the building that altered the body's flight," my father suggested.

"There is no such structure, which is the second important observation," she went on. "It is also worth noting that the murderer must be quite strong since it is no easy task to stand back and toss a grown man's body over the parapet. I suspect he was tall as well to give his throw that much arch."

It all seemed clear now that the essential clues were pointed out. I could even surmise how Joanna Blalock had discerned the murderer's position on the roof when he threw the body.

"And the perpetrator had to place himself well back from the parapet so as not to be seen from the street below."

"Which tells us the perpetrator knew his way around the entire building," Joanna Blalock said. "This was no spur-of-the-moment murder."

"But if Harrelston was already dead, as the evidence indicates, why did the perpetrator bother to throw him off the roof?" I pondered.

"To conceal his crime," Joanna Blalock replied. "Our assailant is not only tall and strong, he is also quite clever. He knows how to cover his tracks."

"Much to the benefit of our friends at Scotland Yard," my father added, with disdain. "They always search for the easy answer. And in this case, it would be suicide."

"Did they not note the small amount of blood the terrible head wound left behind, as Mrs. Blalock did?" I asked. "This would be an obvious indication that the victim was dead before he fell."

"If they noticed it at all, they chose to disregard the finding," my father said. "You see, it did not fit with their preconceived narrative."

"Surely they are not that shallow," Joanna Blalock reproved.

"As Sherlock Holmes would say, they are bunglers," my father said. "They depend almost entirely on paid informants to solve their cases.

It is not that they have no brains. It is that they refuse to use them."

"Ahoy, Dr. Watson!" a voice cried out.

As if on cue, Inspector Lestrade from Scotland Yard stepped from the front door and doffed his hat. I recognized him from a photograph in the newspaper I had seen earlier in the week. He was a tall, middle-aged man, with a pleasant face except for his eyes that seemed fixed in permanent squint. Other than a fringe of hair above his ears, he was completely bald and kept his head covered with a worn brown derby. The aforementioned article had noted that he was the son of the well-known inspector chronicled by my father in the Sherlock Holmes mysteries.

"I heard that you had visited earlier this morning," Lestrade said.

"And was refused entry," my father said irritably.

"For that I must take blame," Lestrade apologized. "An aristocrat's suicide always brings out the crowds, you see. So I left instructions to keep the area clear and permit no one entrance. I would have certainly made an exception had I known you were involved."

"Not to worry," my father said, and then gestured to Joanna Blalock. "Lestrade, allow me to introduce Mrs. Joanna Blalock who witnessed the man's fall. She has graciously agreed to reconstruct the scene for us. Next to her is my son, John."

Lestrade tipped his derby and said to Joanna Blalock, "And a dreadful sight it must have been."

"Yes," she said flatly. "Dreadful."

"I see no need to put you through that gruesome remembrance again," Lestrade went on. "All the evidence gathered thus far indicates that Mr. Charles Harrelston took his own life."

"So it was straightforward suicide, then?" my father inquired.

"I did not say that, for there are several features that do not fit here."

"Such as?"

"I found it strange that a fine gentleman like Mr. Harrelston would choose to end his life in this manner, with everything on public display," Lestrade said. "In my experience, the aristocracy prefer to do this sort of deed in private. And since Mr. Harrelston was once an officer in His Majesty's army, he was certainly familiar with firearms and could have easily ended it all with a single shot. So there are some unusual aspects to this apparent suicide."

"Indeed," my father agreed, "for we have been told there are eyewitnesses who contradict one another."

"Which is so on the surface," Lestrade said. "A gardener a half-block away stated that Mr. Harrelston leaped from the third-floor window, with arms and legs flailing wildly, while a young lad of ten told us the man seemed to float down."

"Which do you believe?" my father asked.

"Both," Lestrade replied promptly. "The gardener no doubt saw the man jump from the window, at which time his arms and legs were thrashing about. The boy viewed the very end of the plunge, when Mr. Harrelston was bracing himself at the last moment for final impact. This I believe explains their differing accounts."

"But there remains a contradiction that has not been explained," my father said. "The young lad insisted the man fell from the roof, and not from the third-floor window as described by the gardener."

"The inspector who questioned the boy did not consider his testimony to be reliable," Lestrade elucidated. "You see, the little boy was only twenty-five feet or so away from the end of the fall. Being of such low stature, the child would almost be required to be lying on his back to have a clear view of the roof. And of course the lad's story contradicts the other evidence we have at hand. Thus we concluded the gardener's observation was the more accurate one."

"Perhaps," my father said. "But you must admit it does raise some doubts."

"Oh, it did, Dr. Watson, but these doubts were swept away by the suicide note that was signed by Mr. Harrelston himself."

"I should like to see the note," Joanna Blalock said at once.

Lestrade's eyes narrowed noticeably. "Might I ask why?"

Joanna Blalock quickly covered her seemingly inappropriate request by saying, "I am a dear friend of the Harrelston family and I am certain they would appreciate this tragic chapter in their lives being brought to a final conclusion. Knowing their son's last words would do so and remove any unwanted speculation."

"You are most correct, madam," Lestrade agreed. "I shall allow you to see it."

"I will tell the family of your kindness."

Lestrade led the way inside and, talking over his shoulder, began to ascend the stairs. "You will have the opportunity to meet the gentleman who owns the house. He apparently was a close friend of the deceased."

"What is his name?" Joanna Blalock asked.

"Dr. Christopher Moran."

"A physician?"

"Of the highest caliber."

As we climbed the stairs, I was glad to be behind the others, for fear of showing the deep concern on my face. Joanna Blalock and my father had demonstrated some remarkable deductive skill in overturning the notion that Charles Harrelston had committed suicide. The evidence thus far surely indicated it was premeditated murder. But all that evidence was circumstantial and would never hold up at an official inquiry. A signed suicide note on the other hand was powerful proof and could not be explained or ignored. Such a note was strong enough to whisk away our observations, as if they were loose dust.

We reached the second floor of the row house and entered a reception area. A short, balding secretary sat at his desk and busily sorted through papers. He was obviously distraught.

Joanna Blalock stopped to study the man. "I take it you are Dr. Moran's secretary."

"Only until the end of the day," the secretary said. "For I have given notice. I do not wish to remain here longer."

"Because of Mr. Harrelston's death?" Joanna Blalock asked.

"That and other matters," he replied.

"Tell me of these other matters," she requested. "Please do not omit any details."

Lestrade stared at Joanna Blalock with a most perplexed expression. He was clearly surprised by the manner in which she had taken over the investigation. Rather than object, Lestrade gestured to my father for an explanation. My father held up a finger to indicate an answer would be forthcoming shortly.

The secretary was glancing around to make certain no one was close by, then spoke in a low voice. "There are strange doings going on in this house, madam. Death seems to come from nowhere. Like in Mr. Harrelston's and again in the case of Dr. Moran's dog, Punch, a friendly Jack Russell terrier loved by all. Only a week ago he was playing by my desk when he went into the parlor through a barely opened door. A moment later I heard him cry out, then he came back to me, limping and licking his paw. Within minutes the paw was swollen and red, and within a few hours the sweet dog was dead. That was most unnatural, would you not agree?"

Joanna Blalock nodded. "Most unnatural indeed. What did Dr. Moran say?"

"He believed that an infected rat had bitten the dog," the secretary replied. "On occasion I have been instructed to purchase several rats to be used for training the dog. Punch, you see, had become an excellent ratter."

Joanna Blalock's lips parted in the slightest of smiles. "A rat bite, you say?"

"So I was told." The secretary hurriedly placed his belongings in a leather case. "And if an infected rat could do that to a dog, it might well do the same to a man. In any event, I have given notice. I shall go someplace where death is not lurking about."

"Most interesting," Joanna Blalock said. "Your description of prior events has been very helpful."

"Then I shall be on my way," the secretary said and reached for his hat.

Joanna watched the secretary depart, and then

turned to my father and said, "Curious, is it not, Dr. Watson?"

"What is so curious?"

"The dog's death."

"With all due respect, madam," Lestrade interceded, "a rat bite can be quite nasty and quite deadly."

Joanna Blalock looked over to me. "Dr. Watson, you are a qualified pathologist, are you not?"

"I am."

"Then tell us, in all your experience have you ever heard, seen, or read about a rat's bite causing death for man or animal within a few hours?"

"Never," I answered. "It does not occur."

"That is what is so curious about the dog's death."

The stunned expression that came to Lestrade's face was indescribable. It clearly showed a man out of his depth. "Then—then what killed the dog?"

Joanna Blalock did not bother to answer. She walked quickly up the stairs to the third floor and entered a large parlor. Carefully she viewed the entire room, looking high and low for something to catch her eye. If it did, the finding did not register on her face. Next she busied herself gently tapping on the walls and listening for a returning sound.

Lestrade moved closer to my father and asked, "Who is this Mrs. Blalock?"

"It is not who she is, but what," my father replied.

"What is she, then?"

"She is London's first female detective."

Lestrade's jaw dropped. "Blimey!"

"Give her free rein," my father suggested, "and you will be amazed at what she comes up with."

"Well, let us give her a try." Lestrade walked to a large window that was open and overlooked the street below. He turned to Joanna Blalock and said, "Here is the place he leaped from. Be so kind as to tell us something we do not know."

Joanna Blalock went to the window and studied it at length. It was three feet wide at the most and perhaps five feet in height. There was a thick layer of dust and soot on the outer ledge.

She moved in closer and peered out. It was obvious something had caught her interest, and this enticed all of us to follow her gaze. The air was fresh and clean, so our view was unobstructed. Across Curzon Street we focused our vision on the third-floor window of the row house that was directly opposite us. Its drapes were open. A woman was speaking to someone.

"Well?" Lestrade pressed.

Joanna Blalock ignored the question and continued to study the house across the street.

"And here is the suicide note." Lestrade broke into her thoughts. "It is in the typewriter where he left it, so it would be easily seen."

Joanna Blalock went to the typewriter and examined the note that had been typed on Charles Harrelston's personal stationery. It read:

> I have disgraced my family and cannot bear to live with the shame. God forgive me and have mercy on my soul.
>
> CH

"And there you have it," Lestrade said with finality.

"It has been typed," Joanna Blalock said disdainfully.

"But signed," Lestrade countered. "And we made inquiries to determine if he signs all his correspondence with initials, and he does—or rather did. And that is his handwriting as well."

"His initials are written quite clearly," Joanna Blalock observed.

"He had good penmanship," Lestrade agreed. "We can say that for him."

Joanna Blalock smiled ever so slightly to herself. "Remarkably good, under the circumstances."

We heard footsteps behind us and turned. A tall, well-built man entered. He was in his middle years, with sharp features and a firm jaw. His hair was a reddish-blond color that seemed to emphasize his Teutonic blue eyes. He was very finely dressed with a black frock coat and pearl-gray trousers. In his left hand was a silver-headed walking stick.

"Ah, Dr. Moran," Lestrade said and formally made the introductions. He did not mention that Joanna Blalock was taking part in the investigation. She was only described as being a concerned friend of the Harrelston family.

"I have a most pressing engagement and wondered if my further presence will be required," Moran said.

"We are just tidying up a few last matters, Doctor," Lestrade replied. "We shan't delay you much—"

"I have a question or two," Joanna Blalock interrupted.

"Of course," Moran said easily, but his eyes narrowed into a frown.

"As I understand it," Joanna Blalock recounted, "you and Charles Harrelston were in this very room playing one last hand of poker for a thousand pounds. Correct?"

Moran nodded. "I tried to persuade him otherwise, but he persisted. I had no choice."

"And he lost?"

"He lost."

"What was his response?"

"He was badly shaken," Moran replied. "After all, he was now two thousand pounds in debt. He seemed to lose color and, appearing quite faint, requested a glass of water. I hurried out to my secretary, who was unfortunately away from his desk. I went for the water and when I returned Charles had disappeared. At first I thought he was playing some sort of prank. Then I saw the note and the open window. I dashed over to the window and looked down at the sidewalk. To my horror I saw the body of dear Charles, with a group of people gathered around him."

"And the housekeeper, Mrs. Lambert, can attest to this sequence of events," Lestrade added. "You see, she had come up to the parlor to inquire if the gentlemen required any refreshment. It was at this very moment that Dr. Moran rushed into the hall and, spotting Mrs. Lambert, asked that she go downstairs for a glass of water while he went to fetch his medical kit. Before rushing off, Dr. Moran called into the parlor and insisted that Charles Harrelston remain on the couch until he and Mrs. Lambert returned. Mr. Harrelston replied in a weak voice that he would adhere to the doctor's orders. The good Dr. Moran and his housekeeper were gone only a minute or so, and came back to find the room empty. I believe the rest is known to you."

"Oh, yes, I can assure you I know the rest," Joanna Blalock said, her face hardening for a brief moment. "Might I know the very last words Charles Harrelston spoke?"

"To what purpose?" Lestrade asked.

"He may have uttered a phrase or two that his

family would cherish," Joanna Blalock said. "Perhaps some word of farewell."

"Indeed," Lestrade said, with a nod. "You are very kind to think of that, madam."

"Not at all," Joanna Blalock replied.

Turning to Moran, Lestrade asked, "Do you recall the last words of Charles Harrelston?"

"Only that he would be fine until I returned," Moran said.

"Are those the same words Mrs. Lambert heard?" Joanna Blalock inquired.

"I believe so, but I have no objection to you asking her directly," Moran offered.

"Thank you," Joanna Blalock said. "We shall do so on our way out."

"I am afraid that will not be possible," Moran informed. "Mrs. Lambert was so badly shaken by the event that I deemed it best to send her home to recover and rest for the next several days."

"How thoughtful of you," Joanna Blalock said without inflection. Her eyes caught Moran's and held them for a moment before she continued. "Charles Harrelston's death must be very trying for you as well, for I am told that you two were good friends."

"Better than good," Moran said. "We served together in the Second Afghan War and have been close ever since." He shook his head sadly. "And now this. Had I known this tragic event might occur, I would have gladly forgiven the debt."

My father stepped forward. "I too was in the Second Afghan War. But I must say you look rather young to have fought back then."

"I volunteered on my twentieth birthday, while in medical school," Moran explained. "Much to my parents' dismay, I should add."

"I would imagine," my father said. "Might I ask what regiment you were assigned to?"

"I was attached to the Fifth Northumberland Fusiliers," Moran said proudly.

"Why, so was I!" My father extended his hand and shook Moran's vigorously. "But I am afraid I do not recall you."

"I was there at the beginning of '78," Moran said.

"And I in late '78," my father reminisced. "When I arrived in Bombay the regiment had already moved out and were pushing into the mountains, where the rebels were soundly defeated."

"We won," Moran said without emotion. "But at a terrible price."

"All wars are fought at a terrible price."

Moran nodded gravely and then reached for the gold timepiece in his waistcoat. "I hope you will excuse me, but I must be on my way."

"I should like to continue our conversation at another time convenient to you," my father said amicably.

"That would be my pleasure," Moran said, turning for the door.

"Before you leave, Dr. Moran, there are several points I need clarified for my final report," Lestrade said. "Might I impose a bit more on your time?"

"Certainly," Moran consented, but he looked at his timepiece again, as if to encourage Lestrade to hurry along.

"Some of my questions may have already been asked, but you will have to bear with me, for we must leave no doubts as to what happened here."

"Of course."

"To the best of your knowledge, did Mr. Charles Harrelston exhibit any erratic behavior in the past?" Lestrade asked.

"Not that I know of," Moran replied.

"Did he ever show a tendency to self-destruct?"

"Never."

"Or speak of wanting to end his life?"

"Not in my presence."

"In your professional opinion, would you say he was emotionally stable?"

"Quite so."

"Were you aware of any death threats he may have received?"

"None were ever mentioned."

"Had he enemies?"

"Not that he spoke of," Moran said. "I should tell you, Inspector, that Charles was well liked by all and his list of friends seemed endless."

"Was Mr. Harrelston in debt to any of these friends?"

Moran hesitated briefly. "That was possible, for he enjoyed gambling. But he never confided such information to me."

Lestrade opened a small notepad and studied it for a moment, then asked, "Were you aware that Mr. Harrelston had taken out a life insurance policy for five thousand pounds?"

"I was not. But surely Charles would not kill himself over such a modest sum."

"Desperate men commit desperate acts at times," Lestrade said.

Joanna asked, "When was the life insurance policy applied for?"

"Two years ago, with Mr. Harrelston paying all the premiums," Lestrade answered, then revisited his notepad. "Two years and two months, to be exact."

"In that case, his family may not be able to collect," Joanna informed. "Many life policies have a clause that states no payment shall be made if death by suicide occurs within three years of establishing the policy."

"Perhaps Mr. Harrelston was unaware of such a clause," Lestrade said, then came back to Christopher Moran. "While you and your house-keeper were scurrying about downstairs, were the doors to the house secured?"

"Front and back," Moran replied. "They are

kept locked at all times and no one enters without Mrs. Lambert's permission."

"Were any of the first-floor windows ajar?"

"They were tightly closed and latched."

"And you say that you and Mrs. Lambert were downstairs for only a minute or so?"

"It was surely under two minutes."

"And you, Mr. Harrelston, and the housekeeper were the only ones in the house at the time. Correct?"

"There were no others."

"Not even your secretary?"

"He had departed for lunch and to attend to some errands."

Lestrade closed his notepad and said, "Well then, I have all the information I need for my final report. Now, Dr. Moran, if you will accompany me downstairs, I will require your signature on the eyewitness account you provided."

"Of course. But we must hurry, for I have patients waiting at St. Bartholomew's."

"It will only take a moment for you to read and sign the document."

As the two men were departing, my father called after Moran, "I look forward to reminiscing about our days with the Northumberland Fusiliers."

"As do I," Moran said, and led the way out.

The door closed behind them.

"Liar!" Joanna Blalock spat at the door. "Every other word out of the doctor's mouth was a lie."

My father looked at Joanna Blalock with a stunned expression. "Surely you do not doubt his war record."

"It is the murder I am referring to, Dr. Watson."

My father's brow went up. "Do you think Moran is involved?"

"Up to his teeth. Why else would he lie?" Joanna Blalock stepped over to the open window and pointed to the sill. "Please note the thick layer of dust and soot on the sill."

"So?" My father was still confused.

"So, for the past three days the air in London has been fresh, with no pollution, and there has been no rain," Joanna Blalock went on. "Thus, this layer of grime has been on the sill for at least three days."

"And it is undisturbed," I observed.

"Precisely," Joanna Blalock said. "That is the important fact. It is undisturbed."

My father leaned over and examined the sill more carefully. "Why is the undisturbed dirt so noteworthy?"

"Because it is so revealing," Joanna Blalock elucidated. "We know that the grime on the sill has been there for at least three days, which means it was there when Charles Harrelston fell. Since the sill is over a foot in breadth, there is no way anyone could have jumped from this window without touching the sill and disturbing the soot."

My father nodded slowly. "Which proves that Harrelston did not go through the window."

"Which makes Dr. Moran a liar," Joanna Blalock concluded.

"I'm surprised that Lestrade did not make that observation," my father said. "It seems so obvious now."

"There is a great deal more that Lestrade did not observe," Joanna Blalock continued. "For example, Dr. Moran did not lean out the window and gaze down at the sidewalk, as he stated he did."

My father asked, "How could you possibly know that?"

"Would you be kind enough to look out the window and locate the spot where the victim landed?" Joanna Blalock requested.

"Of course." My father leaned out the window and stared down at the curb. "I can see it quite clearly."

"Excellent," she said. "Now could you show me your hands?"

My father held up his hands, palms out. They were covered with black soot. "By Jove!"

"By Jove, indeed. Had Moran leaned out the window, he too would have disturbed the grime on the sill," Joanna Blalock reasoned. "And since the grime was undisturbed, we can conclude he did not gaze down at the curb."

"Which makes Moran a double liar," I noted.

Joanna Blalock moved quickly to the typewriter on the desk. "And then there is the suicide note. It is so amateurish it is hardly worth our consideration."

"But it is written on Charles Harrelston's personal stationery," my father argued, brushing the soot from his hands.

"Stolen," Joanna Blalock responded.

"His initials, in his own handwriting," my father countered.

"Easily forged."

My father wrinkled his brow as he tried to think through the problem. "But these are suppositions."

"Indeed they are," Joanna Blalock said. "But tell me, Dr. Watson, is it not odd to find a typewriter in the parlor rather than at the secretary's desk and, even odder yet, for a gentleman to bring his personal stationery to a game of poker? And what kind of man would type a suicide note, take the note out of the typewriter to initial it, then return it to the typewriter?"

"Perhaps he initialed it while it was still in the typewriter," my father suggested.

"I do not think so." Joanna Blalock carefully removed the suicide note from the typewriter and inserted a blank sheet. Next she picked up a pen from the desk, dipped it in the inkwell, and gave it to my father. "Please sign your initials on the sheet in the typewriter."

My father did so and said, "There."

"Notice how uneven your handwriting is compared to that of Charles Harrelston's," Joanna Blalock pointed out. "That is because your hand was in an awkward position when you wrote. That would be the case with anyone who attempted to write a note while the paper remained in the typewriter. Thus, it is fair to assume that the note was taken out of the typewriter before it was signed, then returned."

"Also," I interjected, "a man about to commit suicide would be highly distraught. His writing would never be so even. In all likelihood, his penmanship would be little more than a scribble."

"Well put, Dr. Wat—" Joanna Blalock stopped in mid-sentence and said, "It is very awkward working with two Dr. Watsons, and having to address both the same. Would it be permissible for me to call you John and your father Dr. Watson?"

"Only if I am allowed to call you Joanna," I replied.

"That is my name," Joanna said, and gave me a warm smile, which I must admit almost caused me to blush.

My father added, "Let us not be so formal with my name. I too shall refer to you as Joanna and you must call me Watson, just as Sherlock Holmes did too many years ago."

We all nodded in mutual agreement.

"Now that we are on such informal terms, I must say I have major reservations regarding Christopher Moran's guilt," my father said frankly. "Despite the obvious misinformation the man gave us, there is no proof he actually committed the murderous act. Indeed, we cannot dismiss the housekeeper's eyewitness account, which would appear to clear Moran of any involvement."

"I am not dismissing it," Joanna said.

"But it points in every way to Moran's innocence."

"Only if one assumes the housekeeper's version of the event is accurate."

"But why would she lie?" I interjected.

"I did not say she lied," Joanna responded. "I simply said we have to verify her account, for it represents Moran's only solid alibi."

"But you are inferring that the housekeeper's testimony will differ from that given by Moran."

"I am inferring that Moran is a liar and only the housekeeper can provide us with the truth, and that is why it is so important we ascertain the veracity of her statement." Joanna glanced over to my father and said, "Please obtain Mrs. Lambert's address from Inspector Lestrade, but do not reveal the true purpose of our pending visit."

"What if Lestrade insists on joining us?" my father asked.

"I doubt he will bother," Joanna predicted. "Lestrade only sees what he wishes to see and for the moment considers this death to be straightforward suicide. Nevertheless, should he show any interest in joining us, we must dissuade him by promising to share any information we may gather."

"Surely he will not interfere with the interview."

"But he might unintentionally prompt the woman and it is her words we want to hear, not his."

In the next instant, Joanna returned to the business at hand, with the brain behind her lovely face shifting back into high gear. She rapidly looked around the room, then up at the ceiling. "Now, how did Moran move the body onto the roof?"

"There must be stairs up to the roof in another part of the house," I surmised. "Perhaps he used those."

Joanna shook her head. "He would not carry the body through the house on the chance the secretary might see him."

"The secretary might be in on it," I said.

Joanna shook her head once more. "I think that unlikely. Moran is not the type to trust his future to a servant. It would open him up to all sorts of unpleasant things, such as blackmail. I very much doubt that the secretary is involved here."

"That being the case," my father said, "why not

simply ask the secretary where the stairs to the roof are located?"

"Not a good idea, Watson," Joanna said at once. "The secretary may not be an accomplice, but he is a servant and thus would report anything we say or do to Moran. And at this point in the game, it is best the fox not know that the hounds have picked up his scent."

"It is still difficult for me to believe that Moran is involved in this nasty business," my father remarked. "Doctors are usually not murderers."

"But when a doctor goes wrong, he is the best of criminals. He has the nerve and he has the knowledge." Joanna's eyes went to a closed closet at the opposite end of the room. She walked over and peered inside. It was empty and contained no clothes, hooks, or hangers.

"Strange," Joanna said and was about to close the door when she abruptly stopped. She gazed back at the inner wall of the closet and noticed that it did not reach the floor completely. "There is something behind this back wall."

Joanna reentered the closet and thoroughly searched its entire structure. At the last moment she rose up on her tiptoes and discovered a small metal latch beneath a ceiling beam. Carefully she pulled it down. The back wall of the closet slowly opened.

"Hello! What is this?"

She entered the hidden room, with my father

and me a step behind. The secret room was windowless and empty except for a sturdy Chubb safe. Off to the left was a flight of stairs ascending to the roof.

"This is the way he went," Joanna said excitedly, and led us up the steps and through another door.

The roof was perfectly flat and surrounded by a parapet three feet high. In the distance we could see the spires of Westminster Abbey.

My father paused to catch his breath. "Why bother to carry a body up here? Why not simply toss it from the window?"

"Moran was afraid of being seen," Joanna replied. "The third-floor window of his parlor can clearly be seen from the row house across the street. I myself could see a finely dressed woman in the window across the way."

"But why would Moran kill Harrelston?" I asked. "After all, it was Moran who was owed the money."

"How do you know that?" Joanna challenged.

"Well, Moran said it."

"Moran said a lot of things."

My father fumed under his breath. "A doctor and a fusilier, and he turns out to be a cold-blooded murderer! He is a disgrace to the uniform and to his profession, and I would not mind in the least watching him being marched to the gallows."

"Murderers come in all stripes, Watson," Joanna reminded.

"But I defy you to find one who so wantonly kills a brother-in-arms." My father took several deep breaths and allowed his anger to pass, then brought his attention back to the crime scene. "So it appears the despicable Moran carried his victim to the edge of the roof and threw him off."

"The victim was not carried." Joanna corrected him. "The victim was dragged."

"Oh?" My father looked over to the place on the roof Joanna was pointing to. He saw a smear of blood there and another smear closer to the wall. There were brush marks through them, which indicated someone had tried to scrub them away. "There is definite blood here."

Joanna nodded slowly. "The blood drippings did not form spots or splatters, but only smears. That tells us the body was either rolled or dragged toward the parapet."

"And Moran no doubt stayed crouched down so as not to be seen," my father envisioned. "A clever jackal, this one."

"He is a beauty," Joanna agreed.

"But where is the motive here?" I asked.

Without answering, Joanna suddenly turned and hurried back down the stairs. My father and I were directly behind her.

In the secret room, Joanna took a magnifying glass from her purse and dropped to her hands and knees. She carefully examined every inch of the floor until she came to the area just in front of the safe. "And here is more blood," she announced. "Someone attempted to clean it up, but a small amount remains."

"Does it give us any clue as to the motive?" my father asked.

Joanna stood and brushed the dust from her long dress. "There is a long history between the victim and the murderer, Watson. And that is where the answer lies."

"Are you saying the murder was planned a long time ago?"

"I am saying these are very dark waters," Joanna said gravely. "Much darker than any of us might at first imagine."

5

Proof of Lineage

That evening my father and I dined on superb fillet of sole prepared by Miss Hudson, then settled in front of a glowing fire and sipped nicely aged brandy. Outside a fierce storm pounded down on London, so I agreed to spend the night in the bedroom of Sherlock Holmes. I had no idea how close to the famous detective I was about to become.

My father stared at length into the blazing logs before he spoke in a most serious tone. "I am about to tell you a story that goes far beyond your wildest imagination. It will astonish you in every possible way."

I leaned toward him, not wishing to miss a single word.

My father continued. "The story you are about to hear can never be repeated, for you and I will be the only two people on earth who know it, and it must remain that way. Thus, I must have your word on this."

"You do, Father," I said solemnly.

"This Joanna Blalock is a very remarkable woman," my father began. "You would agree?"

"Most certainly."

"Well, she is even more remarkable than you could ever imagine."

"How so?"

"She is the daughter of Sherlock Holmes."

"What!" I blurted out, stunned. "What did you say?"

"She is the daughter of Sherlock Holmes," my father repeated.

"How—how can this be?" I stammered.

"The story begins long ago." My father rose to fetch more brandy and replenished our Waterford snifters. "Prepare yourself for twists and turns that are stranger than any fiction you have ever encountered."

"Pray go on," I encouraged.

"It all dates back to one of Sherlock Holmes's most interesting adventures. Do you recall the case of *A Scandal in Bohemia*?"

"Not in detail," I admitted.

"Allow me to refresh your memory," my father said, and gazed out into space like a man about to relive an exciting episode in his life. "On one winter's night Holmes and I were visited on Baker Street by a most unusual man. He was over six and a half feet tall, with the chest and arms of a Hercules. The man was very richly dressed and wore a black mask to hide his identity. He was in fact the King of Bohemia, and had compromised himself by becoming entangled with an adventuress named Irene Adler."

"The operatic star?"

"The very same." My father went on. "During their romantic escapade, the king wrote some rather delicate letters to this woman, and now wished to have them back. In addition there were also some indiscreet photographs of the couple that could cause an immense scandal, for you see the king was shortly to become engaged to marry the second daughter of the King of Scandinavia. For obvious reasons he desired to have them destroyed as well. But alas, the Adler woman was still madly in love with the king and refused to return any of the items. And if the king were to proceed with his engagement to be married, Irene Adler threatened to send the letters and photographs to the royal family in Scandinavia."

" 'Hell hath no fury like a woman scorned,' " I uttered.

"Truer words were never written," my father agreed. "In any event, it was Sherlock Holmes's task to retrieve these items and return them to the king."

"I take it Sherlock Holmes was successful."

"He was not," my father said, with a half smile. "He was outsmarted by the most enchanting and beautiful woman he had ever seen."

"Sherlock Holmes, beguiled by a woman's beauty?"

"It was not her beauty that outwitted Holmes, but her brains."

"Was Holmes upset?"

"Not in the least. As a matter of fact he greatly admired her and always referred to her as *the* woman. In his eyes she eclipsed and outclassed the whole of her sex. But there was never any emotion akin to love for that would have been abhorrent to his precisely balanced mind." My father paused to sip more brandy before continuing. "At least that is what I believed, for Holmes always seemed to be a cold reasoning machine that was devoid of emotion. But all this changed when one evening he called me back to Baker Street to tell the most incredible story—which I am about to share with you."

I held up a hand. "So I take it that the letters and photographs were used in a most unpleasant manner against the king."

"They were not," my father replied. "But more about that later. Now here is the story Holmes related to me. Some years later there was a knock on the door to his rooms at 221b Baker Street. It was none other than Irene Adler, whose last name was now Norton. Shortly after her encounter with Sherlock Holmes she ran away to Paris with her new husband, a successful lawyer named Godfrey Norton. The marriage did not go well and her husband became a rogue, a gambler, and a philanderer with a string of mistresses. She tried desperately to change him, but he continued in his ways and became something she could not tolerate at all."

"An abuser?"

"Worse."

"What, then?"

"A bore," my father replied. "With her wonderfully sharp mind, nothing could have been more intolerable. Here was this woman with a finely tuned brain who was now hooked into a drunken dullard. Like most people of great intellect, she required mental stimulation to avoid misery. Her husband could not or would not provide it, so out of desperation she came to 221b Baker Street."

"How did Holmes receive her?"

"With delight. For his brain too required constant stimulation and her brain was a perfect match for him. They got along splendidly that evening, with long conversations on an endless variety of subjects, and all the while drank too much cognac and gave each other repeated injections of cocaine. And, believe it or not, they ended up in bed together."

"I say!"

"It is difficult to believe, but true."

"I simply cannot envision your Sherlock Holmes in a passionate position."

"I did not use the word *passion,* for there was none involved, at least on his part. He described the encounter in very clinical terms and told me the experience felt pleasant through his alcoholic and cocaine haze, but not particularly memorable. He thought it similar to foot-paddling a boat on the Serpentine Lake in Hyde Park. Enjoyable, but hardly worth the effort. In any event, the next morning she had gone without so much as leaving a note behind."

"I would surmise that Sherlock Holmes did not find this disappointing."

"If anything he was relieved because now he could focus his mind on a most perplexing case without interruption or distraction. He thought that was the end of their association, but he was wrong. Eight months later she returned to his doorstep, now very pregnant with child."

"Joanna Blalock!" I breathed.

"Yes," my father said, and took another sip of brandy. "As I mentioned earlier, Irene Adler's marriage was a loveless one. He was rarely home, and when he was it was to obtain money so he could continue in his selfish ways. Which meant the child was Sherlock's."

"But what proof?"

"Her word, which was as resolute as her mind."

"But still—"

My father waved away my interruption. "It would be wise to hold your reservations until you have heard the entire story."

"Forgive me for getting ahead of myself," I apologized. "Please continue."

"Sherlock rightly believed the child was his and offered to give whatever financial support was needed. But that was not the purpose of her visit. Although near penniless and deserted by her husband, Irene Adler's problem was far greater than lack of funds. She was stricken with severe toxemia related to the pregnancy and her life was now in peril. Her blood pressure was out of control and her kidneys were failing. As her condition worsened, it became clear she would not survive and needed someone to look after the child to be born. It was impossible to even entertain the thought that Sherlock Holmes might care for the newborn. He simply could not and would not do it. But in his incredible mind, there was no problem he could not solve, so he went about solving this, much to Irene Adler's satisfaction."

"Well, it could not have been an abortion."

"Obviously."

"What then?"

"An adoption," my father replied. "Sherlock asked me to have the newborn placed with a suitable family, and so I did. Irene Adler gave birth here in London at St. Mary's Hospital and the newborn was given to Dr. and Mrs. Thomas Middleton, a childless couple who I knew would adore the baby. Dr. Middleton was a colleague of mine, so I could occasionally inquire about the child's well-being without seeming to be intrusive."

"Did Irene Adler ever see the child?"

"She did on the day of the child's birth, and died before the night was out. But before drawing her last breath, she gave Sherlock Holmes the compromising photographs and letters that associated her with the King of Bohemia. She had withheld them all those years as protection, in the event the king ever threatened to cause her harm. So now Holmes possessed all the damning items."

"Which I assume he destroyed."

"To the contrary, he sold them."

"To whom?"

"To the King of Bohemia, of course," my father said with a sly grin. "Sherlock went to the king with the items and fabricated a story that he had purchased them from a master thief for the princely sum of five thousand pounds. The king was delighted and promptly reimbursed Sherlock, who placed the money in a trust fund, in case the newborn girl came on hard times. And Sherlock named me trustee of the fund, knowing I would watch over the child. I did this regularly until I learned that the daughter of Dr. and Mrs. Thomas Middleton was marrying into the family of Sir Henry Blalock. Thus, the future of Joanna Blalock who is the daughter of Sherlock Holmes appeared to be quite secure."

I could not help but applaud. "Bravo, Father! Bravo!"

"However," my father continued, "no one knows what the future may hold, and should Joanna Blalock ever face financial difficulties, the trust fund must be made available to her. Upon my death, I have stated in my will that you are to become trustee of the fund, which is the purpose of my telling you this story."

"I shall carry out your wishes faithfully, Father."

"As I knew you would," my father said, and then sighed to himself. "But the sadness here is that this most fascinating case involving Sherlock Holmes can never be written about. Here we have an adventure in which he and Irene Adler combined their wits to come up with a perfect answer to a seemingly unanswerable problem."

"What a story it would make," I remarked.

"Indeed, what a story," my father concurred. "But it is hidden from the public eye and it will remain there."

I carefully chose my next words before speaking them. "I do not wish to be unkind, but surely you must realize that it is possible that Joanna Blalock is not the true daughter of Sherlock Holmes."

My father shook his head firmly at the notion. "Only the genes of Sherlock Holmes could endow an offspring with such a magnificent brain and keen deductive skill."

"But did not Irene Adler herself have the wits to match Sherlock Holmes?" I pointed out. "Perhaps her genes were passed to the child who was fathered by someone else. This quick-witted woman eventually went to Sherlock Holmes when she had nowhere else to turn."

"I trusted Sherlock Holmes, and his instincts were always true in such matters."

"But still—"

"I was ninety-nine percent certain, and that was good enough."

"Yet there remains one percent of doubt which even you admit to," I persisted. "We must remember that a dying woman carrying an unborn child would be very desperate and turn to virtually anyone for help. Surely you agree."

"I do, and I must say there was the smallest possibility that your conclusion was the correct one. But that doubt was completely removed during our visit to the Blalock mansion."

"How so?"

My father rose from his chair and went to a stack of boxes that contained the cases and magazines involving Sherlock Holmes. He had to search for several minutes before finding the item he was looking for. It was a mystery magazine that featured a picture of a young Sherlock Holmes on its cover.

"Here," my father said and proffered the maga-zine. "Tell me what you see."

I stared at the photograph in utter and complete disbelief. "Oh, my God in heaven!"

My father smiled broadly. "Striking, isn't it?"

I still had difficulty believing the photograph. I quickly changed my position so that the light from the fire shone directly on the picture. But there could be no question about the face looking back at me. "Joanna Blalock's son is an exact replica of a young Sherlock Holmes. They are like twins."

"Which explains my shock when the lad first entered the Blalock library."

"Astonishing," I breathed as Sherlock's heavy-lidded eyes peered into mine.

"And there is more," my father said. "Do you recall the small, star-shaped birthmark on the Blalock lad's wrist?"

"Yes, of course," I replied. "It was so perfect, it resembled a tattoo."

"Sherlock Holmes had the same birthmark."

"And the lad has the quick observant mind that his mother possesses."

"And that his true grandfather had."

"The genetics involved here are fascinating," I mused. "The genes dictating the size and capacity of the brain were passed through from one generation to the next to the next. Yet the genes carrying Sherlock Holmes's physical features skipped a generation since Joanna Blalock has no resemblance to him."

My father nodded. "But the enchanting charm and beauty of Irene Adler was inherited by Joanna."

"I have noticed," I admitted.

"I have noticed you noticing."

"Am I that obvious?"

"As obvious as she is when stealing glances at you."

"I think you overstate."

"Oh?" my father asked warmly. "Have you not observed that when she looks at you she involuntarily reaches for her now unadorned ring finger and gently rubs at it?"

I sighed to myself and hoped that my father's observations were correct. "Her beauty and grace go far beyond enchanting, and her intellect knows no bounds."

"Her mind is much like that of Sherlock Holmes," my father said, nodding. "I would venture to say she would have no difficulty matching wits with him."

"That is high praise indeed."

"And when dealing with others, she will have an obvious advantage over Sherlock."

"How so?"

"People will underestimate her because she is a woman."

"They will do so at their peril."

"A most remarkable woman," my father concluded.

"In every possible way," I said, then brought my mind back to the heinous crime that we were investigating. "I wonder if Christopher Moran has any idea how formidable an opponent he is now up against."

"I suspect not," my father replied. "But I daresay he will soon find out."

6

St. Bartholomew's

We had no difficulty gaining entrance to the morgue at St. Bartholomew's Hospital because of my rank as assistant professor of pathology. I wore a long, white laboratory coat to signify my status while my father was dressed only in a fine tweed suit, but he was known by more than a few of the staff, as he had once been an attending physician at the famous hospital. I had asked Joanna Blalock to wear one of her well-starched nurse's uniforms so that her presence would not arouse any undue suspicion.

Before us on a marble slab lay the mangled body of Charles Harrelston, which was covered up to the shoulders with a white sheet. His head was badly disfigured and sharp ends of fractured bones could be seen sticking up beneath the covering.

"Will you be performing the autopsy?" my father asked.

I shook my head. "Dr. Willoughby insists on undertaking all the high-profile cases."

"Will you be allowed to assist?"

"That is unlikely."

"And very unfortunate, for your eyes and skills far exceed his."

Joanna moved in closer to the body and remarked, "I do not believe John's absence at the time of dissection will matter a great deal. For in this instance, it is the external examination of the body that will tell us the most."

"But the dissection could give us important information on his prior health," my father objected mildly. "These hidden findings might solve some of the mysteries in this case."

"Such as?"

"If he had severe disease of the larynx and could not utter loud sounds, it would explain why he did not cry out during his fall."

"He was dead before the fall," Joanna reminded him.

"Quite so," my father admitted. "But I was simply giving an illustration of why a thorough dissection could be vital."

"And a good illustration it was," Joanna said. "But here we are dealing with a sudden, yet pre-meditated murder. The perpetrator had to carry out his evil deed quickly and surely, and this almost always requires an external force, which may well be observed on examination of the outer body."

"An external force?" I pondered. "Are you referring to a gunshot wound to the disfigured head?"

"Not under the circumstances," Joanna replied. "A pistol shot would make far too much noise, something even passersby on the street could hear."

"A knife?" I ventured.

"Too much blood. And if the wound was not well placed, a struggle might ensue."

"Asphyxiation?"

Joanna pointed to the corpse's neck. "There are no marks or bruises present. In addition, his face does not show the terror of asphyxiation."

"Poison perhaps?"

"Too unpredictable."

"What, then?" I queried.

"That is what we must discover."

The door to the morgue flew open and Professor Peter Willoughby entered the well-lighted room. He glared at the three of us with an expression that told of his displeasure.

"What is the meaning of this?" he demanded of me.

"We are here to investigate the tragic death of Charles Harrelston," I answered.

"By whose authority?"

"At the request of the family."

"Which illustrates you are not here in an official capacity." Willoughby gave me a long, stern stare before saying, "Really, Watson, this is most irregular."

"I know it is, Professor," I said defensively.

"But the Harrelston family is much distressed and wishes us to look for any cause that might have precipitated his suicide."

"Humph," Willoughby grumbled, and walked over for a close look at the corpse. He made a few guttural sounds while performing the superficial examination, but made no mention of any findings.

I glanced at Joanna, who seemed to be intently studying Professor Willoughby. I did not see anything odd about the man. He was of short, wiry stature, with a large head and piercing dark eyes. The suit he wore fit poorly and had short sleeves that allowed most of his shirt cuffs to show. I had to admire his gold cuff links, but not the stained red tie he seemed to favor so often. There was little striking about the man's appearance, yet Joanna seemed to be greatly interested. I brought my attention back to the professor and now noticed he had the sort of color in his face common among men who work out of doors under a strong sun, but which would be quite rare in London this time of year.

"There is nothing here of note other than his traumatic injuries," Willoughby declared. "Obviously he suffered from a deep-seated mania and plunged to his death."

"I am convinced you are correct," I said. "But the family wishes me to briefly examine the corpse as well."

Willoughby nodded begrudgingly, growling to himself. "Who are your assistants?"

"I believe you know my father, Dr. John Watson, Sr.," I introduced. "The woman next to him is a nurse and the only witness to Harrelston's fall."

Willoughby eyed my father carefully. "Are you not the chronicler of the Sherlock Homes mysteries?"

"I am," my father said with pride.

Willoughby quickly turned back to me. "I must insist your father not include his visit here in any future stories involving the trumped-up detective."

"I can assure you he will not," I promised.

"And what of this woman?" Willoughby asked in a demeaning tone. "I don't see a reason for her presence and must ask that you escort her out immediately."

"He will do no such thing," Joanna said firmly. "He will perform the examination and I will observe."

Willoughby was thrown completely off balance. "I—I beg your pardon?"

"I stay," Joanna said. "I am here at the request of Lady Harrelston and I shall report directly to her and to those closest to her. Surely you will not deny her request."

"Of course not," Willoughby said, now suddenly servile. He fumbled uncomfortably with his stained tie before finding more words. "If there are other requirements, you must let me know."

"There is one other request," Joanna went on. "Lady Harrelston has asked that no one know of our visit here nor of her involvement. Will you see to that?"

"Most assuredly."

"And now, Professor, we should allow the Drs. Watson to begin their quick examinations. We will not detain you further, for I am certain you have many other pressing duties, particularly those which may be related to your recent conference in Italy."

Willoughby raised his brow. "You were aware of the pathology conference?"

"And the work you presented," Joanna said. "Was it well received?"

"Quite," Willoughby replied. "How did you learn of my presentation?"

"I have my sources," Joanna lied easily. "Did you enjoy the Amalfi coast as well?"

"Very much so," Willoughby answered. "Naples was a delight."

"It always is this time of year," Joanna concluded, and looked toward the door. "Well then, thank you for being so gracious to us."

Willoughby took the hint and, with a half bow, departed.

I stared at Joanna in amazement. "How in the

world did you know he had been to a pathology conference in Naples?"

"From the tone of his skin," Joanna said. "No one in England or France or Germany would be exposed to such a bright sun this time of year. That would only occur in the Mediterranean, and in particular the Amalfi coast of Italy, where the weather would be the warmest. Also the cuff links he wore were Italian. The interlocking Cs indicate they came from the jewelry house of Cassini. I suspect he purchased them while in Naples."

"But how did you deduce that he had been to a *pathology* conference?"

"Because our dear Professor Willoughby is a very frugal man who pinches every farthing," Joanna stated, as if she were reading from a book. "He makes a handsome income, yet he dresses in a cheap, ill-fitting suit and wears a tie so stained most men would throw it away. His shoes are scuffed and he will not buy polish or pay someone to polish them. Such a frugal man would never pay for a holiday to Italy; thus it is safe to assume someone else paid for it. So either the department or the hospital funded the trip and he would have been obliged to present his work in pathology while there."

"Extraordinary," I said.

"But one feature does not fit," my father rebutted. "The cuff links were made by Cassini, an exclusive and expensive Italian jeweler. Surely a frugal man would never buy them."

"If they were secondhand, he would," Joanna explained. "And they were. One of the links was badly damaged, with the bottom of a C broken off. He no doubt bought them in Italy, perhaps in a pawnshop, at a cut-rate price."

I had to smile at her stunning ability to gain so much information from a few simple observations. "Is there anything else we should know about Willoughby?"

"Hmm," Joanna hummed, apparently waiting for more thoughts to come to her. "There are several other things worth mentioning. His wife does not love him, he comes from a poor background in East London, and he is careless."

"Oh come now," I said, believing she was embellishing.

"Those characteristics are clearly obvious," Joanna went on without a moment of hesitation. "A loving wife would never allow her husband to appear in public that poorly dressed. His attire is so unseemly it caused me to wince. Even if his wife was also frugal, she would never permit that. No devoted wife would. Thus, she simply does not care, which means she has no affection for him whatsoever. His background is easily defined. Some of his language has a definite East London Cockney origin, particularly when he cuts the *t* off words like *what* and *don't*. His carelessness is demonstrated by his poor shave, in which some areas are quite clean while others show bristle. A careful man would shave carefully; a careless man would not."

She thought for a moment and asked, "Does the latter trait show up in his work?"

"I am afraid it does," I replied honestly.

"Which accounts for his meanness, which he uses to cover up his deficiencies."

"Remarkable," my father said admiringly. "And you had to quickly parry his threat to have you ousted. I liked the manner in which you caught him off guard, with your reference to Lady Harrelston. Are you truly a close friend and confidant?"

"I know the family," Joanna said evasively. "But my purpose was not to throw him off guard. I only wanted to show him his place. Even an oaf like Willoughby would be aware of Lady Harrelston's closeness to the royal family, and he is not foolish enough to venture into that territory. The use of Lady Harrelston's name will ensure that Willoughby keeps our visit here a secret."

"Others saw us, though," I said.

"Remember, it is Moran whom we are concerned about and who is also on staff here," Joanna said, unconcerned. "He might well approach Willoughby to learn of the autopsy findings and make certain his tracks remain concealed. But he will only ask Willoughby, not the lower staff members. And Willoughby would be tempted to talk of our visit, which would be to our disadvantage. So I dissuaded him from doing so."

"There is no need to let Moran know that we will soon be nipping at his heels," I concurred.

"Or at his throat." Joanna walked briskly to the corpse and pulled the sheet down to the body's navel. "Now, let us move to the chase."

I stepped in closer to begin my examination. The left side of Charles Harrelston's corpse appeared normal, whereas the right side was badly disfigured. His right arm was mangled with a compound fracture of both the ulnar and radius. The right side of his face was crushed in with an eyeball protruding.

"He obviously landed on his right," I observed, then went about examining the corpse's head. There was a blow-out fracture of the occipital bone, with macerated brain tissue exposed. On the crown of the skull was a rounded, depressed fracture. "He has two fractures of the skull that are separated from each other by normal bone. How do we explain that?"

"The occipital fracture was caused when the back of his head smashed into the granite curb," Joanna answered. "I witnessed that myself."

"But what of the rounded fracture located on the crown?" I asked. "How could a fall account for that?"

109

"It cannot," Joanna said, and came to my side for a better view. She examined the distorted skull, totally unmoved by its gruesome appearance. Then Joanna gave it a second look and focused in on the crown. After a long moment's thought, she reached for a rubber glove on a nearby tray and put it on, then stuck her finger into the rounded fracture. "It makes a rather neat circle, with rough edges."

"Perhaps when the body bounced, as your son described, the granite caused a second fracture," my father suggested.

"That would not produce such a rounded fracture," Joanna said at once. "This is the type of fracture that results when one is struck by a weapon that has a rounded end."

"I know of no weapon that fits that description," my father said.

"Oh, there are a number that would," Joanna informed him as she stripped off the bloodied glove and discarded it. "I would place a hammer at the top of the list."

"But when did this occur?" my father asked.

"Prior to his fall, obviously."

I reexamined the rounded, depressed fracture which measured an inch across. Beneath the wound was a large collection of clotted blood. "A single blow from a hammer could very well do this. And the excessive bleeding tells us the blow was delivered antemortem."

My father asked, "Why, Joanna, did you place a hammer as a weapon of choice at the top of your list?"

"Because they are easily gotten, easily used, and easily disposed of," Joanna answered. "A blow struck by a hammer carries an incredible amount of force and produces a fracture like the one we are seeing."

I thought nothing else about Joanna Blalock could surprise me, but I was wrong. Her knowledge on so many varied subjects seemed endless and was so readily at hand. It would not be an overstatement to say I was dazzled by her insight into head injuries inflicted by blunt force. I had encountered pathology residents who knew less on the subject. "Please tell us how you come to know so much about skull wounds and the weapons used to produce them."

"I read about them," she said simply.

"Come now," I said, shaking my head in disbelief.

"But it is true," Joanna went on. "Over the past several days my son, Johnnie, has asked me incessantly about various aspects of skull fractures, many of which I could not answer. In particular, Charles Harrelston's blow-out fracture of the occipital bone has fascinated him. Thus, I had no recourse other than to obtain Sir Michael Walton's monograph on criminally induced head wounds. It was brief, but quite informative.

According to Sir Michael, hammers are favored by the working class and iron stokers by those of higher rank."

"But an iron stoker would leave behind a long indentation, which we do not see here," my father commented.

"That leaves us with a hammer or hammerlike weapon," I said, and turned to Joanna Blalock. "Does it not?"

"So it would seem. But Sir Michael's monograph tells us that hammers are rarely used by the higher class. With that in mind, we should look for another weapon."

"Such as?"

"That is what we have to determine."

"Perhaps microscopic studies will provide us with the answer."

Joanna shook her head briskly. "Not with that idiot Willoughby leading the investigation. He believes this all can be explained by mania-induced suicide and nothing will dissuade him. We must conduct the search ourselves."

She reached for her magnifying glass and carefully examined the circular fracture. "I see nothing of particular interest, but here I am out of my depth. John, this is well within your purview, so we would be most grateful if you would apply your expertise to this matter."

I donned the rubber gloves and moved in beside Joanna to begin my examination. Our arms touched and, as she leaned forward for a closer view, a lock of her hair brushed upon my neck. A most pleasant warmth spread through my body, head to toe. It required all of my effort and concentration to focus on the mangled corpse before me. With deliberation I inspected the ragged edges of the skull wound, which showed only matted hair encased in shredded skin. The weapon had left no superficial traces behind. I gently pushed aside the clotted blood that covered the inner surface of the wound and peered in.

"Do you see anything noteworthy?" Joanna asked.

"Only splintered bone," I reported.

"Are there any foreign objects?"

"None so far," I said, and removed a thick blood clot with embedded hair. Seeing only macerated brain tissue with the naked eye, I reached for a nearby magnifying glass and moved it up and down over the open wound to increase its magnification. "Hello! What do we have here?"

"What?" Joanna asked eagerly.

I slowly raised and lowered the glass repeatedly to gain an even better look. "See if there are tweezers or forceps in the drawer to my left, would you, Joanna?"

Joanna hurried to the drawer and returned with slender tweezers. "Will this do?"

"Nicely," I said and, using both tweezers and magnifying glass, plucked a sliver of wood from the corpse's skull. I held it up to the light and reexamined it with the magnifier. "It is a splinter of highly polished wood, and atop it there is a bit of metal that has the appearance of silver."

"What do you make of it?"

"There are a number of possibilities," I replied. "But the one that keeps coming to mind is Dr. Christopher Moran's walking stick. As I recall, it was silver-headed and made of polished wood."

My father nodded. "A perfect weapon to bash in a person's skull."

"From behind," Joanna added. "That is how someone like Moran would strike."

"Hold on!" I said, raising my voice. "There is no real proof that a walking stick was the weapon involved here. In fact, we do not even know if a silver-headed stick could cause a circular skull fracture."

"True," Joanna said. "So let us prove it."

"How do you propose doing so?"

"By example," Joanna replied and gestured to my father. "Your walking stick, please, Watson."

She tested the firmness of the silver-headed walking stick and hurried over to a hanging skeleton in the corner of the morgue. The skeleton had been present for many, many years and was rumored to have once belonged to one of England's most celebrated poets. Joanna laid the skeleton on the floor, with its head up, and delivered a vicious blow, using the walking stick, to the crown of the skull. It made a loud, cracking sound. My father and I dashed over to see the result. At the crown of the skull was a depressed, circular fracture.

"There!" Joanna announced "And so we have our weapon."

My father stared at her, with his mouth agape. "How did you know to do that?"

Joanna shrugged. "It just came to me. And it proved my point, did it not?"

"Indeed it did," my father replied, and watched her return to the corpse of Charles Harrelston where she attempted to maneuver the head of the walking stick into the circular skull fracture. My father lowered his voice to a bare whisper and said to me, "I swear to you I once saw Sherlock Holmes perform the very same test many, many years ago. The only difference was the weapon. Back then it was a metal hook he used on the skull."

"Did you write about it?" I whispered.

"Not to my recollection."

"It is an excellent fit!" Joanna called out from the marble slab holding the corpse. "And what are you whispering so secretly about?"

I replied, "We were wondering if you had read about the illustration you just performed."

"No," she answered. "It was not mentioned in Sir Michael's monograph on the subject. Perhaps I should write him and suggest that he include the demonstration in his next edition."

"So you simply thought up the illustration?"

"I did not give it much thought," Joanna said, with complete honesty. "It was simply the most appropriate example to make my point."

"You are quite remarkable," my father said.

"It was elementary, Watson."

Not to the rest of us mortals, I wanted to add.

"Well," Joanna continued, "now that we have the weapon, let us connect the points. We have Dr. Christopher Moran striking Charles Harrelston and killing him. This event occurred in the secret room where the Chubb safe was located, for that is where we found the smears of blood that remained after the attempt to clean them away. So the key to our puzzle must center around the safe. Somehow, Moran lured Harrelston into that room to kill him. And the contents of that safe was the bait."

My father went right to the heart of the matter. "So how do we learn the contents of the safe? We certainly cannot approach Moran."

"Nor his secretary," I added. "For whatever we ask of him will surely get back to Moran."

"Can he be bought off?" my father suggested.

"Too risky," Joanna opposed. "The secretary may still be loyal to Moran."

"But he was gathering his papers and had given notice to Moran on the day we were there," my father said in a rush. "His loyalty may well have disappeared once he walked out the door."

"But some may remain," Joanna said. "And if Moran learns of our interest in the safe, all of its contents will suddenly vanish. Then the case will never be solved."

"So we find ourselves in a quandary." I summed up the matter. "What we need most to do, we cannot."

Joanna furrowed her brow and gave our dilemma considerable thought before saying, "We are going about this in the wrong fashion. In an effort to reach a satisfying outcome, we are omitting too many important steps. We surmise that Moran used his silver-headed walking stick to murder Charles Harrelston, but have not proved it. We have surmised that Moran's safe holds the key to the puzzle, but have little to support it. We require solid proofs to make our case. We need evidence that cannot be refuted."

"But surely the evidence at hand strongly points to Moran being the murderer and the safe holding the key to solving the case."

Joanna waved her hand dismissively. "They are no more than suppositions and circumstantial evidence that will never hold up before a hard-headed British jury."

"So how do we proceed?" I asked.

"We go after Moran and the secretary without them being aware of it."

"How do you propose we do that?"

"With guile," she said, and left it at that.

7

The Message

At noon the following day, as our carriage approached the Blalock mansion, my father instructed me to choose my words carefully should Sir Henry inquire about our request that Joanna join us.

"Only say that her familiarity with the Harrelston family could prove helpful in our investigation," my father said. "Make no mention of the message we received, for the fewer people who know of this matter, the better."

"But surely Sir Henry is not an idle gossiper," I remarked.

"Everyone is an idle gossiper if the gossip is interesting enough."

"What if Sir Henry persists in wanting an explanation?"

"Then persist in giving him none."

Stepping out into the mist, I hurried to the sturdy door of the mansion and found Joanna waiting in the anteroom, with Sir Henry at her side. His expression appeared both solemn and stern, making it difficult to read. I took it to be a bad sign that I was not being greeted in the grand library as on my earlier visit.

"Have there been further difficulties for the Harrelstons?" Sir Henry asked.

"We are unsure, Sir Henry," I replied. "But it appears they require our presence at the moment. My father thought that Joanna might be of some assistance, for she is familiar with the family and was a witness at his death."

"So tragic for this fine gentleman to meet such a terrible end," Sir Henry commented sadly.

"Indeed, sir," I said. "With that in mind, I think you can well understand why the family wishes to leave no stone unturned."

"Nor should you."

"Then we have your permission to include Joanna in our quest for the truth?"

"Of course," Sir Henry said, nodding his approval. "And if I myself can be of any service whatsoever, all you need do is ask."

"I shall pass along your kind offer to my father."

I opened my umbrella as we dashed out, for a heavy drizzle had begun and the darkening sky overhead foretold that there would be more to come.

"Why the urgency?" Joanna asked while being helped into our carriage.

"We have been summoned to the Harrelston house on a most compelling matter," my father replied.

"Did they state the nature of the matter?"

"Only that it dealt with their son's death."

"Let us hope it will provide us with some desperately needed clues," Joanna said, and pulled the blanket we afforded her up to her waist, for the day was both wet and cold. "I have the uncomfortable feeling that if this case is not solved quickly, it will not be solved at all. The tide is against us here and I am afraid it will remain so unless we act and force the issue."

"How should we proceed?" my father asked.

"I would like you to invite Dr. Moran to your rooms at 221b Baker Street for dinner and conversation," Joanna said. "He would be delighted for the two of you to share your experiences in the Second Afghan War."

"What do we hope to gain from such a visit?" my father inquired.

"Proof that Moran is the murderer," Joanna answered. "Of course we will require that you be totally at ease in his presence and show no sign that we believe him to be responsible for Charles Harrelston's death. If he detects strain or nervousness on your part, it will alert him and he will cover his trail even more completely."

"I did a bit of acting at university," my father said.

"It will be needed here," Joanna said. "And do not attempt to ply him with drink. That will never work with someone as clever as Moran."

The sky darkened even more and the rain came down heavily. It drummed down on the roof of our carriage and drowned out our voices momentarily. To be on the side of caution, our driver pulled on the reins and our horse slowed noticeably.

"The strong rain is most unfortunate," Joanna commented. "I had hoped to revisit the gardener and ask for a few more details, but he will surely not be at his work today."

"Perhaps tomorrow," I suggested.

"The passage of time is no good here," Joanna said. "It dulls and distorts the memory, particularly for the finer points."

"Which details were you interested in?"

"Moran's unseemly behavior, which the public will never be privy to," Joanna replied. "You see, the working class tend to form tight groups and tell indelicate stories about their upper-class employers. Our gardener would be on friendly terms with Moran's chambermaid, cook, chimney sweep, and so on. They would talk and share intimate information that we could never obtain otherwise. Such knowledge could be of great value in undoing the clever devil that Moran is."

"And he moves quickly with his cleverness," I informed. "He has already approached Willoughby and inquired about the autopsy findings on Charles Harrelston."

Joanna's eyes narrowed with concern. "What did Willoughby disclose?"

"Only the information I gave him, which was that all injuries and wounds were traumatic in nature."

"Did you omit the second fracture on the crown that was circular?"

"I could not, because Willoughby demanded to know why the hanging skeleton now had an obvious hole in the center of its skull."

Joanna drew a deep breath. "That must have presented a difficult problem for you."

"Only to a small degree," I said. "I explained the crown of Charles Harrelston's skull had a second, circular fracture, so we applied a blow to the skull of the hanging skeleton to prove that the smaller fracture was the result of trauma as well."

"And he was convinced of that?"

"Not only convinced, but delighted," I replied. "You see, he plans to include our experiment in his autopsy report. He will write that his carefully done studies in the department of pathology indicated that the smaller fracture was also caused by trauma."

"Well done," Joanna said. "But keep in mind that Willoughby is a fool and Moran is not. We must hope that Moran does not see through your deception."

We neared the Harrelston mansion, and Joanna

lowered her voice and gave it an even more serious tone. "Let me caution you not to be too revealing to Sir William. Do not in any way insinuate that Moran is involved in his son's death, for vengeance is a powerful force and could precipitate an unwanted action by the Harrelstons against Moran. Then all would be lost."

"Agreed," my father said. "But a carefully worded glimmer of hope would be most welcomed by Sir William."

"Please make certain it is not more than a glimmer."

Moments later we bounded out of our carriage and, under the shield of umbrellas, entered the Harrelston mansion. An elderly butler, who was very slow of gait, showed us into the library where Sir William Harrelston awaited. Despite his sadness, he seemed genuinely pleased to see us. My father and I were warmly greeted, but he appeared to have particular affection for Joanna.

"Thank you, Joanna, for agreeing to assist us in these most dreadful of times," Sir William said.

"It is my honor to be of service to you and your family," Joanna responded.

"Your father-in-law tells me you have keen insight into such matters."

"I possess some, but not nearly as much as Dr. Watson and his son," Joanna said generously.

"As would be expected with their years of

experience," Sir William said, and turned his attention to my father. "Do you have any hopeful news?"

"Only a hint or two to suggest that Charles's death may not be suicide," my father said.

Sir William brightened just a bit. "Perhaps he slipped while leaning out the window."

"We are investigating all possibilities and are of course interested in any evidence that might lead us away from suicide," my father said. "Could your urgent summons to us be helpful in that regard?"

"I believe it may." Sir William guided us over to chairs by a warming fire. As we sat, I noticed Sir William's somewhat bedraggled appearance. His gray hair was tangled and disheveled, his wide sideburns not well trimmed. The frock coat he was wearing was both worn and out of fashion. His son's death, together with the family's financial woes, had taken a heavy toll on the man, but his voice remained strong.

"Allow me to begin by saying I am not grasping at straws. What I am about to tell you are facts from which you can reach your own conclusions. If I may, permit me to give you some background."

"Please delineate every detail," Joanna implored. "Leave out nothing, no matter how painful."

"Very well then," Sir William began. "You are

no doubt aware that my late son was good friends with Christopher Moran, who was nearby when my son plunged to his death. Their friendship went back a very long way. You see, they were joined together in the Second Afghan War and remained close over the years. What you may not know is that there are two other officers who were also their comrades in arms. These four fine men—my son, Christopher Moran, Benjamin Levy, and Derek Cardogan—fought together and their friendship grew even tighter after the war. They were like a quartet, you might say."

Sir William offered cigarettes around before lighting one for himself. "I did not mention the other two members of the quartet to Scotland Yard because I did not consider it important. Then I read the newspaper this morning and realized I should not have withheld the information."

"What exactly did you read?" Joanna asked at once. "I want it word for word."

"That Benjamin Levy had died suddenly and unexpectedly yesterday evening."

Joanna quickly asked, "Was the cause of death given?"

Sir William shook his head. "None was mentioned."

"The pieces start to fall together," Joanna murmured softly, more to herself than to those seated around us.

Sir William did not catch the remark and cuffed

a hand to his ear. "My hearing is not what it once was. May I ask you to repeat your comment?"

"I was thinking how strange it was for two of the four to die so close to one another," Joanna said.

"My thoughts exactly," Sir William agreed.

"Did the newspaper article state where the death of Benjamin Levy took place?"

"At the Athenian Club."

"Was Moran a member as well?"

"Oh, yes. All four were long-term members."

"I see." Joanna strummed her fingers rapidly on the armrest, as if she was keeping time with her quick working mind. Gradually her fingers slowed, then stopped altogether. "But the death of Benjamin Levy alone did not merit an urgent summons."

"There is more that I believe will grab your attention and hold it." Sir Williams moved to his desk, where he lighted another cigarette from the one he was smoking, then continued. "On the morning of my son's death, he was busily writing a message when I entered the library. He was irritated that I had interrupted, but tried not to show it. Apparently my entrance had caused him to make some mistake, so he crumpled the message and threw it into the wastebasket. An hour later my son gave the butler a sealed message he wished delivered immediately. It was addressed to Dr. Christopher Moran."

Joanna was on her feet in an instant. "Do you have the message your son discarded?"

"I do," Sir William said. "I was curious about the message, so I retrieved it, but could make no sense of it. Then this morning while rummaging through my papers, I saw the message again and realized it might somehow be related to Charles's death."

"It may indeed," Joanna said eagerly. "Let us see it."

Sir William reached into a side drawer and placed the crushed note atop the desk. He carefully smoothed it out. "As you can see, it is the oddest of messages. It consists entirely of numerous lines that are slanted in varying ways, yet have no recognizable sequence."

The message read:

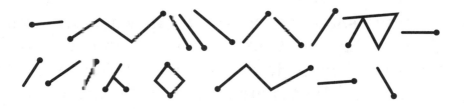

Joanna examined the note for some time, after which she turned it upside down and then on its sides, all the while studying each of its peculiar markings. If she detected a revealing clue, she made no mention of it.

"Could it be a foreign language of sorts?" Sir William asked. "Perhaps something they learned in Afghanistan or India during the war."

"That is a possibility," Joanna said. "And one that requires further study. May we use your library for this purpose?"

"Of course," Sir William said. "If you wish refreshments, simply ring for the butler."

"Thank you."

Joanna waited for Sir William to close the door behind him, then turned to my father and me. "This message is written in code."

"Are you sure?" my father asked.

"Beyond a doubt," Joanna replied. "What are the chances four Englishmen would learn to write and read the same foreign language while at war?"

"Four, you say?" my father inquired. "But there are only two involved here—the victim and Christopher Moran."

Joanna shook her head. "I will wager you ten guineas that Benjamin Levy's sudden death was no coincidence. He and Charles Harrelston and Christopher Moran are all part of this. And most likely, so is the fourth member of the quartet."

"Part of what?" I asked.

"Hopefully, the coded message will help with that."

Joanna studied the message at length before turning the sheet of paper over and holding it up to the light. Then she held it so it faced a mirror she had taken from her purse. The mirror image was indecipherable. "Nothing here," she reported.

My father sighed wearily. "We are in for a long morning."

"It will take much longer than that," Joanna predicted. "We simply do not have the skills required to break a tangled code."

"Perhaps Scotland Yard could be of service," I suggested.

"Most of those bunglers have difficulty even reading English," my father said.

"What then?" I asked.

"We should consult discreetly with an expert in these matters," Joanna said. She folded the message and tucked it away in her purse. "But for now our time is better spent at the Athenian Club."

"What should we tell Sir William?" I asked.

"That there are clues here that need to be followed, and that is the truth."

My father rubbed his chin pensively. "I do not think Sir William will be satisfied with that statement. He will be very eager to know the meaning of his son's message."

"As will we," Joanna said. "For if my assumptions are correct, the deciphered message will tell us why Charles Harrelston was murdered."

8

The Athenian Club

It was nearly noon when we arrived at the Athenian Club on Regent's Circle and were promptly refused entry by a rather pompous manager named Jonathan Cole. Like most men who overrate their importance, he spoke in a clipped, condescending fashion.

"The club is closed to all visitors today," he announced. "There are no exceptions."

"May I ask why?" my father asked.

"It is a private matter."

"Such as the untimely death of a member?"

Cole was taken aback for a moment, but quickly recovered. "Are you a friend of Mr. Levy?"

"No," my father said, and noticed a junior detective from Scotland Yard hurrying by. "I see that Scotland Yard is involved."

Cole made no reply.

"Which indicates that Inspector Lestrade is here." My father reached for his personal card and handed it to the manager. "Please give this to Lestrade and tell him I wish to see him."

Jonathan Cole read the card at a glance before rapidly disappearing down a long, poorly lighted corridor. When he was out of earshot, my father turned to me and said, "Something is amiss here, otherwise Lestrade would not be present."

"There must be evidence of a crime," I surmised.

"Either that, or the simple fact that Benjamin Levy was the son of a longstanding London councilman," Joanna said. "I read of this relationship in the morning *Standard*, but paid it little consideration, since at the time I was unaware of the deceased's connection to Charles Harrelston."

"Your point is well taken," my father agreed. "The sudden death of a public figure or one of his family always catches the attention of the police."

"Lestrade will wish to know why we are here," I thought aloud.

"I will deal with that," my father said.

"What if Moran is here?" I asked.

"There is no chance of that occurring," Joanna answered with confidence. "He will now distance himself from the death of another comrade in arms, other than to show fake grief and sadness."

"But he did not exhibit a great deal of sorrow when we questioned him about Charles Harrelston's death," I recalled.

"He is too clever to overplay his hand," Joanna said.

The manager of the club returned, and gestured for us to follow him down a very long corridor. Off to the right was a large reading room, appointed with leather-upholstered chairs and fine, polished furniture. Next we passed an enclosed area that held a well-stocked bar, and beyond that was an expansive gaming room, which contained numerous green-felt-topped card tables, as well as several roulette wheels. Finally we reached a spacious, comfortable lounge area. Contained within it were cushioned chairs and a couch upholstered with a thick, canvaslike material. Behind the furniture was the opened door to a tiled washroom, and next to that was a hall that led to a row of small bedrooms.

"It seems our paths cross again, Dr. Watson," Lestrade cried as he stepped out of the bedroom closest to the lounge.

"It is always a pleasure to see you," my father said.

"What brings the famous Dr. Watson to the scene of this misfortune, might I ask?"

"An interested family, who wishes to remain anonymous, asked us to look in briefly," my father replied.

"Then I shall tell you everything we know and you may draw your own conclusions. If you wish, I can give you a summary of the events that took place last evening."

"Please."

Mr. Cole cleared his throat audibly and said, "Inspector, I must inform you that women are never allowed in the Athenian Club. It is against all regulations and they must be strictly adhered to. With this in mind, I trust you will allow me to escort the lady out to a suitable waiting area near the front staircase."

"The lady stays," Lestrade said bluntly. "And you will assist her and her colleagues in any way they wish. Is that understood?"

Mr. Cole managed a nod, to go along with his reddening face.

"Now, as to my summary." Lestrade returned his attention to us. "Mr. Benjamin Levy arrived at the Athenian Club just before ten o'clock last night in the company of his friend Dr. Christopher Moran. They gambled heavily and won, I should add. Perhaps it was their good luck that encouraged them to drink to excess. By all accounts they were a happy pair. Unfortunately, the consumed alcohol brought a sickness to Mr. Levy's stomach. He was accompanied to this lounge area by Dr. Moran. After several bouts of vomiting, Mr. Levy rested on the couch here to gather himself. Dr. Moran, in his professional opinion, thought it best for Mr. Levy to rest further, and left him to do so. According to Dr. Moran, Levy was comfortable and dozing off when the doctor left him to return to the gaming room. Mr. Levy was seen to be sleeping on the couch by a number of club members as they passed through on their way to the washroom.

Early this morning Mr. Levy was found dead by a steward who had come to arouse him from his sleep. There was absolutely no evidence of foul play."

Joanna asked, "Was a well-respected physician such as Dr. Moran able to discern the cause of death?"

"He could not be certain, but believed that excessive drink led to a very sound sleep," Lestrade replied. "And while deeply asleep, Mr. Levy may have again lost the contents of his stomach and sucked these same contents into his lungs, which brought on sudden asphyxiation."

"Was there evidence that Mr. Levy had vomited again?" Joanna inquired.

"Indeed there was," Lestrade answered, and pointed to the cashmere scarf on an arm of the couch. "Mr. Levy's scarf was soaked with vomit when it was found around his neck this morning."

Joanna looked to my father. "I take it, Watson, that vomit-induced asphyxiation is a well-known phenomenon."

"Oh, yes," my father said promptly. "I myself have witnessed it on several occasions."

"And there you have it," Lestrade concluded. "I am afraid, Dr. Watson, that you have wasted your time on this one."

"So it would seem," my father agreed.

"Of course the coroner will have the final say on this matter," Lestrade said, and straightened his derby in preparation to leave. "But I feel confident he will side with Dr. Moran's well-thought-out medical opinion."

"I have just a few more questions," Joanna said, her gaze going from the washroom to the couch, then over to the adjoining bedrooms.

"Of course," Lestrade said without hesitation, but his eyes narrowed suspiciously.

"It seems odd that Mr. Levy would choose to spend the night on a most uncomfortable couch when a bedroom is so nearby, does it not?" Joanna asked.

"I thought so, too, madam," Lestrade responded. "But when one has imbibed far too much, any resting spot will do. And perhaps he wished to be close to the washroom in the event his nausea returned."

"Well put," Joanna said. "But the bedroom is also close by and would be far more comfortable. By the way, how tall would you estimate Mr. Levy to be?"

"He was slightly under six feet, I would say."

"Which would cause him to be quite crowded on that relatively small couch."

"I would have certainly chosen the bedroom," Lestrade concurred. "But that seems to be a minor matter here."

"There may be yet another reason why Mr. Levy elected to remain on the couch," Cole interjected. "In order to reserve a bedroom, a member must sign in at the front desk. Perhaps Mr. Levy did not feel well enough to do so."

"There you have it," Lestrade said with finality. "Rather than stumble his way to the front, Mr. Levy chose to remain at rest on the couch."

"I see," Joanna said, as if the issue was settled. "There is one more minor matter here that I am certain can be easily answered. Was Mr. Levy's scarf, laden with vomit, found where it now lies?"

"No, madam," Cole replied. "The scarf was securely around Mr. Levy's neck when he was discovered motionless on the couch. It was removed by a member-physician to search for a carotid pulse. None was detected."

"Thank you for clarifying that point," Joanna said, then turned to my father. "I think I see the picture more clearly now, Watson. Are there other questions I should have asked?"

"Only one relatively small consequence," my father responded. "Were there signs of vomit on the victim's lips and in his mouth?"

Lestrade and Cole exchanged puzzled looks, with neither being able to give the answer. My father's question was not of small consequence, but one of great significance. Had Benjamin Levy truly choked on his own vomit, there would be evidence of it in and about his oral cavity.

"I cannot be certain," Lestrade said finally. "But I shall pass on your inquiry to the doctor who attended Mr. Levy."

"All well and good, then," my father said. "And now Inspector, I know that you are busy with other duties that you must attend to. Would it be too much for me to ask to remain behind and retrace Mr. Levy's steps from last night? It would satisfy my curiosity and make certain nothing is left unanswered."

"I see no reason why not," Lestrade said. "The manager here will assist you and show you how and where Mr. Levy moved prior to his death. If anything unusual is discovered, I trust you will notify me."

"Promptly," my father promised.

"Excellent," Lestrade said and, after tipping his derby, gestured to the manager. "And now Mr. Cole will be good enough to accompany me to the front desk where we will prepare a detailed statement for his signature."

I waited for the pair to depart, then said, "Lestrade seems very accommodating to us these days."

"That is because he knows which side his bread is buttered on," my father remarked. "He realizes that if we solve the case he will be given most of the credit, just as in the times of his father and Sherlock Holmes. But I must admit I find his lack of depth astounding."

Joanna nodded. "You are referring to asphyxiation being the cause of death."

"Precisely," my father said. "How in the world

could he accept such a superficial notion? Mr. Levy was not in a state of drunken stupor during which he would have retched up contents from his stomach and sucked them deep into his lungs. He had already relieved himself and was seated on the couch, alert and talking to Moran. Mr. Levy then lay down to rest and dozed off. Had he vomited again and sucked the nasty fluid into his lungs, he would have awakened and jumped up, coughing and wheezing and racing about seeking help. That he would have simply lain there and died is nonsense."

"Your medical expertise is most helpful here, Watson," Joanna said. "But you must give Moran credit. He planted the seed beautifully and Lestrade could not wait to swallow it. And that he happily accepted the notion that a tall Benjamin Levy would choose to sleep on a cramped couch rather than a soft, comfortable mattress is equally incredulous. Even a large, senseless animal would much prefer the bed."

"Why are you so concerned where Benjamin Levy slept?" I asked.

"I am concerned because obviously Christopher Moran was," Joanna replied. "He went to great lengths in his story to keep Mr. Levy's presence away from the bedroom. Moran continued to say that everything occurred while Levy was on the couch, always on the couch. Never once does he mention the bedroom."

"Which meant?"

"Moran wishes to keep all eyes away from the bedroom," Joanna said. "Something happened in there that he does not want us to know. And I see one simple answer. That is where Moran caused the death of Benjamin Levy." She paused to glance at the couch and studied it at length, then nodded to herself. "Moran could not chance killing Levy on the couch. It was too exposed, with people coming and going to the washroom. He had to perform his evil deed in the bedroom."

"Allow me to play the devil's advocate," I requested.

"Please do."

"Suppose Mr. Levy wished to occupy the bedroom, but was too heavy with drink to navigate his way to the front desk where he had to register in order to reserve a room. Then he would have been obliged to spend the night on the couch."

"Pshaw" Joanna said, quickly dismissing the idea. "That could have been easily remedied. Moran could have acted in Benjamin Levy's behalf and gone to the front and reserved the bedroom, saying that he was Levy's doctor and Levy was feeling poorly and needed the room."

"And had Moran done that, it would have connected him and Levy to the ill-fated bedroom," my father added. "That is the very last thing Moran would have wanted."

"It all points in one direction, does it not?"

Joanna said. "Moran is cleverly covering up the deed he committed in that bedroom."

"But which bedroom?" my father asked. "There are six of them, and by now all of them have been cleaned and sanitized. And to make matters even more difficult, we do not know which of the six to search."

"Hmm," Joanna uttered, which was the sound she made when her brain shifted into highest gear. She glanced over to the washroom, then the bedroom, and then to the couch where she focused on Benjamin Levy's soiled cashmere scarf. Moving in closer, she sniffed the air and said, "Even from this distance, I can detect the unpleasant odor of vomit."

"Of what significance is that?" my father asked.

"That is how we shall determine which bedroom Benjamin Levy occupied briefly," she said and hurried over to my father. "Tell me, Watson, is Toby still with us?"

"I am not sure," my father replied. "She was some years ago, but now she would be very old."

"You must see if she remains alive," Joanna said, with some urgency. "We need a hound that can sniff out the faintest of scents."

"Toby would do very well here."

"Then you must fetch her for us."

As my father and I headed for the corridor, he looked over his shoulder and asked, "How did you know of Toby?"

"I read about her in one of your Sherlock Holmes adventures," Joanna replied.

My father nodded slowly, thinking back. "Oh, yes. I believe she was mentioned in *The Sign of Four*."

"And a fine tale it was," Joanna commented. "Now please hurry. Time is of the essence, for the scent will quickly fade."

"I shall have to stop by Baker Street and consult my files for the address where Toby is housed."

"No need," Joanna said, her eyes blinking rapidly while she searched deep into her memory bank. The blinking ceased when the answer was retrieved. "The dog resides at number 3 Pinchin Lane in lower Lambeth, assuming the address you mentioned in *The Sign of Four* still holds."

"Extraordinary," my father murmured, moving quickly down the corridor. "Absolutely extraordinary."

As I hurried to catch up, I could not help but remember Sir Henry Blalock's description of Joanna's brain. It was like a steel trap. Once a fact entered, it never escaped.

"Did Sherlock Holmes have the same remarkable memory?" I asked my father in a whisper.

"Both Sherlock and his brother Mycroft were similarly endowed," my father whispered back.

"It must be a family trait, then," I concluded.

"Beyond any question," he agreed. "It runs in

those amazing genes that Joanna inherited from her father."

"And perhaps from her mother, Irene Adler, who was the only woman ever to outwit Sherlock Holmes."

"Are you suggesting that Joanna received a double dose of this memory gene?"

"I am."

As we approached the front lobby, my father lowered his voice even more. "Are you further suggesting that her uncanny memory might be a cut above Sherlock's?"

"That, my dear father, would not surprise me in the least."

9

Toby Two

On our journey to fetch Toby my father regaled me with the exploits of the remarkable dog. A half-spaniel mix, she could track a scent under the most severe of conditions. Once, after two days of heavy rain, she was able to follow the faint odor of creosote across half the city. Despite Toby's successes, she never received so much as a pat on the head from Sherlock Holmes. There was no affection between them, yet a special bond connected the two. Both lived and breathed for the sole purpose of utilizing their skills, and together they had foiled some of London's craftiest criminals. I wondered if the hound would work as well for Joanna as it had for Joanna's father.

Nearing the neighborhood where Toby resided, my father cautioned, "Prepare yourself for a strange sight."

"Are you referring to the dog, or its kennel?"

"Both."

Pinchin Lane was a row of shabby, two-storied brick houses, all of which faced the street. My father had to rap repeatedly on the door to number 3 before a blind on the second floor parted and a face looked out.

"Go away!" a voice cried down. "Whatever you are selling, I do not want any."

"I must speak with you," my father called up, only to watch the blind close. Again he knocked loudly and added, "It is of utmost importance."

"Begone or I will call the police on you, I will," the voice threatened.

My father yelled, "I wish to talk to you for the purpose of hiring a dog."

"None are available."

"It is Toby I am interested in."

"Then you must go to dog heaven, for that is where she now resides. Old Toby passed on nearly five years ago."

A sense of dejection crossed my father's face, but it quickly faded. "I require a dog with a keen sense of smell," he requested. "Like the one that served Sherlock Holmes so well."

"And who are you to mention Mr. Holmes's revered name?"

"Dr. John Watson, his close associate."

"Dr. Watson! Why did you not say so from the start?"

Moments later the door to number 3 was unbarred and opened. Before us appeared an odd-looking man. He was lanky and lean and very old, with a heavily lined face, stooped shoulders, and a humped back. His arms seemed too long for his body.

"Ah, Dr. Watson!" Mr. Sherman said warmly, squinting through blue-tinted glasses. "It has been many a year, has it not?"

"Too many," my father replied.

"And sorry I was to hear of Mr. Holmes's passing."

"It was a sad day."

"Indeed it was. But I will wager that some of London's nastiest criminals danced at the news." Sherman flicked a wrist, as if waving away the memory and got down to the business at hand. "So, you require a real sniffer, do you?"

"The best you have," my father requested. "I need one whose skills rival those of Toby."

"Well then, you might just be in luck. For in her later years, Toby took a real fancy to a bloodhound and they mated to produce a litter, all of which I have sold, save for one. I have named her Toby Two. Would you care to see her?"

"I most certainly would."

"Then step in, sir," Sherman welcomed. "But keep clear of the Scottish wildcat. He appears tame enough, but every now and then he pounces at moving targets. That is bred into him, I would guess."

We gave the wildcat a wide berth. Larger than a house cat, it had a bushy tail and long legs, and it uttered a foreboding hiss as we walked by.

Sherman showed us the way past a line of cages that contained a variety of animals, including cats and dogs and a mean-looking badger that clawed at its wire enclosure. Even the rafters held partially hidden fowl that silently glared down at us, as if they were sizing up intruders. The heavy, unsanitary smell of unwashed animals filled the air.

"Toby Two lives at number 15 on the left here," Sherman said, and pointed to the cage at the very end.

Suddenly from on high, a gray owl with large wings swooped down and by us, and a moment later flew back clutching a rat in its talons. The rat squealed briefly before becoming a tasty meal. My father and I watched with fascination, while the kennel keeper paid it no attention at all.

"Hey, old Toby Two," Sherman said affectionately, as we came to her cage.

Toby Two proved to be a most peculiar-appearing animal. She had many features of a long-haired spaniel, but the drooping, floppy ears as well as the snout were those of a bloodhound. Upon reaching the floor, the dog immediately sniffed our shoes but, finding little of interest, sat on its haunches and stared up at us. Mr. Sherman handed my father a lump of sugar, which Toby Two accepted after the briefest of hesitations. The alliance between the dog and my father was sealed, and Toby Two eagerly followed us out and into our waiting carriage.

The return trip was uneventful except for Toby Two who, for the entire journey, stuck her head out the window to sample the air and savor the aromas contained in it. Every so often she would yelp pleasantly, giving the impression of having detected something familiar. My father told me that Sherlock Holmes had once commented that dogs had a sense of smell a thousandfold greater than that of man, and could easily discriminate between a hundred different scents at the same time. If true, I thought to myself, a dog that was half Toby and half bloodhound could follow the steps of Benjamin Levy as if they were lighted with torches.

On reaching the Athenian Club we found our way blocked by a very indignant Jonathan Cole.

"Dogs are never allowed in the club under any circumstances," he rebuked. "The animal will wait outside on a leash and well away from the front entrance."

"The hound comes with us," my father said firmly. "She is an important part of the investigation and you will not interfere. If you choose to do so, there may be consequences that you will find very unpleasant."

"But we have rules here, sir!"

"And you also have a very dead body."

Lestrade appeared at the entrance and said,

"Here, now! What seems to be the problem?"

"They wish to enter with this dog, which I cannot allow," Cole argued. "The laws of the club are very strict on this matter and the members will undoubtedly stand with me."

"What say you, Dr. Watson?" Lestrade asked.

"I say Mrs. Blalock wishes to employ the dog to retrace the steps taken by Mr. Levy last night," my father said, even-tempered, although the look in his eyes told of the little regard he held for the club manager. "This will prove beyond any question the accuracy of Mr. Levy's movements just prior to his death. Thus, any qualms on what might have occurred will be put to rest."

Lestrade gave our request only a moment's thought before saying, "That seems reasonable to me. The dog will be allowed in."

"Most irregular," Cole protested, determined to have the last word.

"The dog, or the death?" I asked bluntly.

Mr. Cole wisely chose not to answer.

"This way then," Lestrade said, and accompanied us down the long corridor. When we were well out of Cole's earshot, he asked, "Has Mrs. Blalock found something noteworthy?"

"So far not," my father replied. "But a few things bother her a bit."

"Such as, may I ask?"

"Such as why Mr. Levy slept on an uncomfortable couch rather than a nearby comfortable bed."

Lestrade shrugged. "I suspect Mrs. Blalock has not had much experience with those who are tipsy. Men under the strong influence of alcohol are known to sometimes sleep on sidewalks in winter."

"Even when a warm bed is close at hand?"

Lestrade cocked his head, obviously not impressed with my father's argument. "But surely, Dr. Watson, that is not a major point in the investigation."

"It may not be important, but it seems out of place, at least to her," my father said. "And good detectives never leave the *out of place* unexplained."

"That sounds like something Mr. Sherlock Holmes would say."

"She is under the influence of Sherlock Holmes."

Lestrade stopped in his tracks and stared at my father. "Pray tell how so?"

"First, I must have your oath that what I am about to tell you will go no further," my father said solemnly.

"You have it," Lestrade said at once.

I could not believe my ears. After demanding my secrecy, would my father now divulge Joanna Blalock's hidden and incredible lineage to a person who, despite his promise, was certain to speak of it? I was very tempted to interrupt.

"Not a word of this story is to be repeated

either to Mrs. Blalock or anyone else," my father insisted. "Are we absolutely clear on this?"

"Indeed," Lestrade said, his ears pricked so as not to miss a syllable.

"Some years ago when Joanna Blalock was in her late teens, a case Sherlock Holmes was investigating brought him in contact with the young woman," my father said as he began a fabrication. "Holmes was impressed by Mrs. Blalock's mind and insight into crime, and took her under his wing, he the teacher, she a willing student."

Lestrade raised his brow. "Her family allowed this?"

My father nodded. "Under the guise that she was being trained to be a novelist, which accounted for my presence at the teaching sessions. You see, her family trusted me absolutely. I was their physician. In any event, this went on for several years, until Holmes's retirement. He taught her a great deal of what she now knows."

"Was all the teaching done orally?"

"Oh, by no means. At her disposal was a soon-to-be-published text entitled *The Whole Art of Deduction*, which was written by Holmes himself. Joanna Blalock read and digested every line, for she has a most remarkable memory. The end result is that we may well be looking at a young Sherlock Holmes. So, it would be to our advantage for you to allow her the most latitude possible."

"And so I shall," Lestrade vowed.

"I will hold you to your word as a gentleman not to utter a word of Mrs. Blalock's connection to Sherlock Holmes," my father said.

"You have that as well."

"Such a connection might prove awkward to the Blalock family."

"The story you have told is already forgotten."

It now became clear why my father had fabricated the tale of Joanna Blalock's training under Sherlock Holmes, whom Lestrade held in such high regard. Joanna would immediately be given freedom to do whatever she wished during the course of the investigation. She would be treated as if she were, in fact, Sherlock Holmes.

Straining at her leash, Toby Two leaped ahead and ran directly into the lounge where Joanna was waiting. The dog hurried over to her and sniffed her shoes at length, then wagged her tail briefly and sat on her haunches. She stared up at Joanna Blalock as if instinctively anticipating her commands.

"Her name is Toby Two," my father said and quickly summed up the dog's background. "Thus, she is the mix of Toby and an amorous bloodhound, the end result of which should be well suited for our purposes."

"Excellent," Joanna said, and showed no particular affection for the dog, much as Sherlock

Holmes would have done. After all, they were both about to go to work.

Joanna walked over to the soiled cashmere scarf on the couch, then came back for Toby's leash. They strolled down the corridor to the empty gaming room where Joanna rubbed the scarf under the dog's nose and gave it ample time to detect the various scents. The dog raised her head and licked her lips, savoring the aroma as though it was a favorite dish. Joanna next threw the scarf into the gaming room, then closed the door and pulled Toby Two back down the corridor. At the entrance to the lounge she released the leash and commanded Toby, "Go, girl! Go!"

The dog raced into the lounge nose down and went directly to the couch, sniffing it voraciously from end to end. She seemed to favor an armrest where I surmised Benjamin Levy had laid his head. Nose to the floor, Toby Two moved quickly into the washroom and chose the stall nearest the entrance. Joanna quickly shut the door and stepped back. "Shortly, we shall see the exact route Mr. Levy took."

In under a minute Toby Two began scratching at the door. Joanna motioned everyone aside, then opened the door. The dog raced out and again went directly to the couch where she busied herself with one of the cushions.

"Wait," Joanna said patiently.

Toby Two soon grew tired of the couch and its

various scents, and once more placed her nose to the floor. The dog was clearly in no hurry, for now she moved much more slowly and took a circuitous route back to the entrance to the lounge. Then abruptly Toby Two stopped and made a gradual reversal, and broke into a half run for the nearest bedroom.

"Tallyho!" Joanna cried out, and led us into a small, windowless bedroom.

The dog tried desperately to leap up onto the bed, but its legs were too short. Joanna hurried over and gave Toby Two a lift, before stepping back to observe. The dog sniffed the entire mattress, but seemed most interested in the pillow. With her snout she moved it aside and smelled at the sheet for a full minute. Seemingly satisfied, the dog jumped off the bed and onto a sturdy chair nearby. She tried her best to push the seat cushion away, but it stayed firmly in place. Out of desperation, the dog let out a pitiful bark for help.

Again Joanna came to the rescue and lifted the cushion up. Toby Two stuck her snout deeply in and yelped happily at some newly discovered object.

"Hello!" Joanna said, and reached down for a narrow strip of flexible rubber tubing that was two feet in length. "What do we have here?"

Lestrade stepped in for a closer look. "Perhaps it is some lining in the chair that became dislodged."

"There is no rubber lining remaining behind on either the cushion or chair," Joanna observed. "So it must have another source."

"Could the chambermaid have left it?" Lestrade asked.

"For what purpose would a chambermaid use rubber tubing?"

"None that I can think of, madam," Lestrade had to admit. "What do you make of it?"

"I have no answer," Joanna replied as she studied the narrow tubing more carefully. "But there is something familiar about it, yet I cannot place my mind on what."

"Well, it is of little matter," Lestrade said. "At least we have solved the puzzle of why Mr. Levy did not rest in the bedroom, for in fact he did."

"Yes, he did," Joanna said, and deliberated over the matter further. "But how did he end up on the couch?"

Lestrade considered the question at length before nodding to himself. "I would say he was asleep in here and awoke to use the washroom. On his way back, because of illness or drowsiness, he chose to rest on the couch."

"That is a possibility," Joanna said, but the tone of her voice indicated she was not convinced.

"Do you have another explanation?"

"None that I could prove."

Lestrade eyed Joanna suspiciously. "Madam,

I have the distinct feeling that you are holding back information."

Joanna gestured with her hands. "Inspector, I saw only what you saw, nothing more, nothing less."

"I trust you will make me aware of any new developments you might come across."

"I shall," Joanna said, but as Lestrade was walking to the door, she called after him, "Inspector, since both of us are a bit uneasy over the man's sudden death, it might be wise to leave yourself a little latitude on cause."

"How so?"

"You and the coroner will list the cause of Mr. Levy's death as being asphyxiation. Correct?"

"That is correct. Even Dr. Watson states that may well be the diagnosis."

"But we have no solid proof," Joanna told him. "So I suggest you place the word *suspected* in front of *asphyxiation,* just in the event new evidence comes to the surface."

"I shall give that my consideration."

"Excellent," Joanna said. "And thank you again for allowing me to participate in your investigation."

Lestrade tipped his derby and departed.

Joanna waited until the inspector was out of hearing range, then wrinkled her face in total disbelief. "You place the evidence directly under his nose, and he ignores it. Good old Toby Two informed us that Benjamin Levy spent considerable time in the bedroom, which contradicts Moran's story, yet Lestrade makes nothing of it."

"But it only tells us that Moran was lying," I said. "Nothing more."

"You miss the point, John," Joanna said. "When a fact contradicts a long train of deductions, you must find another line of reasoning to fit the fact. The bedroom is the contradiction here. By dismissing it, Lestrade has ignored the place where the crime occurred."

"And if the crime did take place in the bedroom," I said, following her train of thought, "then the scene on the couch in the lounge was a setup by Moran."

"Of course it was," Joanna concurred. "He could not dispatch Levy in the lounge. It is wide open, with a fair amount of foot traffic coming and leaving the washroom. The chance of being seen was too great. He could not risk it."

My father joined in as he envisioned the murderer's every move. "So Moran plied Benjamin Levy with drink. Levy suffers the gastrointestinal consequences of too much alcohol. His stomach sickness requires a visit to the washroom, and it was a simple task for Moran to lure Levy into the bedroom for a rest. And there the evil deed was done."

Joanna nodded her agreement. "And that, John, is how the train of deductions now fits the facts."

"A physician!" my father spat out. "A distinguished doctor with aristocratic bearing, and he commits blatant murder."

"Looks and social standing never stood in the way of crime," Joanna said.

"So true," my father concurred. "Sherlock Holmes once told me that one of the most winning woman he ever saw was hanged for poisoning three little children for their insurance money."

"All well and good," I said. "But proving that Moran killed Benjamin Levy requires solid evidence, and we have none. We do not even have a notion of how the deed was committed."

"It cannot be blunt force," my father opined. "That would be too easily noticed."

"And a knife or gunshot wound is out of the question, for obvious reasons," Joanna deduced. "The noise and blood would be certain giveaways."

"Then how?" I asked.

My father began to pace back and forth across the lounge, lost in thought. But he soon stopped in his tracks and exclaimed, "Poison! That would be the weapon of choice for a learned physician."

"But how would it be administered?" Joanna challenged. "The poison surely could not be placed in Levy's drink. It would be far too difficult to accurately calibrate the dose and the time it would require to take effect. Remember, it was important to Moran that Levy's death appear to be natural or accidental."

My father went back to pacing as he searched for yet another answer. His silent lips appeared to be moving with his brain when he came to an abrupt halt and turned to us. "An injection! A doctor would know of poisons and how to inject them. Then there would be no doubt as to dose and the time for it to take effect."

"Capital, Watson! Absolutely capital!" Joanna cried out. "An injection it was. And I know when, where, and how it was done."

"Based on what?" I asked.

"The narrow strip of rubber tubing," Joanna replied. "Come, and I will demonstrate for you."

We followed her back into the bedroom and over to the cushioned chair where the rubber strip had been discovered by Toby Two. Joanna reached for the strip and held it up to the light. "At first I could not place it, but now I can." She moved to my father and wrapped the rubber strip around his upper arm, then pulled it tight. "Well, Watson, what comes to mind?"

"A tourniquet!" my father burst out. "I myself used a similar tourniquet years ago, when I was in practice and drawing blood from my patients."

"Precisely!" Joanna said. "And the good Dr. Moran used this tourniquet on Benjamin Levy's arm to allow a vein to reveal itself so that the poison could be injected. The rubber strip must have slipped beneath the cushion where Moran could not find it."

"Which may be yet another reason why Moran wished to keep the investigation away from the bedroom," I conjectured. "Moran must have been greatly concerned by the loss of the tourniquet, but apparently he did not have much time to search for it after he had given the injection."

"The clue was sitting right before my eyes," Joanna admonished herself. "But I did not make the connection at first and should have, for I too witnessed the use of rubber tourniquets while a nurse at St. Bartholomew's. I may have been thrown off by its use here to administer a deadly poison."

"I wonder what poison Moran chose," I pondered.

"Perhaps an autopsy would help in that regard," my father suggested. "The poison might even be extracted from Levy's tissue by an experienced pathologist, such as yourself."

I held up a hand to dampen their enthusiasm. "With the evidence we now have, which is all circumstantial, I seriously doubt an autopsy would be permitted."

"Why not?" my father demanded.

"Because the evidence is not strong and Levy's Jewish faith does not allow autopsies," I said. "They believe the body must be returned to the Maker in the same condition it was given."

"Do they make exceptions?" Joanna asked at once.

"Rarely," I replied. "And only when it is ordered by the court, which is not likely to occur here."

Joanna grumbled audibly. "We have to at least examine the body."

"That too presents a problem," I said. "For the Jewish religion requires that the body be buried within twenty-four hours of death."

"So he is not yet buried."

"But he will be shortly."

"Then we must hurry."

"For what purpose?"

"To examine the body of Benjamin Levy before it starts out on its final journey."

10

Greenbaum's Funeral Home

The preparation room at Greenbaum's Funeral Home was as quiet, I daresay, as a cemetery in winter. The air was so still a speck of dust would hang in suspension. On the table before us lay the body of Benjamin Levy, neatly wrapped in a white shroud.

We had been allowed to view the corpse only because the owner of the funeral parlor, Mr. Aaron Greenbaum, felt a deep debt to Sherlock Holmes and my father. Years earlier they had assisted Mr. Greenbaum in the mystery entitled *The Missing Coffins*, which remained in the files at 221b Baker Street, but had not yet been published. Mr. Greenbaum had approached Holmes to solve a riddle in which someone or a group was stealing newly purchased coffins from his funeral parlor. The police were of little help and believed the most likely candidates were other funeral homes or thieves who sold the coffins on the black market. It was neither. It was the coffin maker who had sold the coffins to Mr. Greenbaum. The thief would quickly alter them with different finishings and change of upholstery, then sell them back to Greenbaum's Funeral Home. To Sherlock Holmes the case was so trivial he insisted my father not bring it to publication. To Mr. Greenbaum the solution saved him from bankruptcy, for which he was eternally grateful. He was now more than willing to stand by our side in case we required more from him.

As we gazed down at the shrouded corpse, my father inquired, "Why the shroud?"

"It is part of our Jewish burial ritual," Mr. Greenbaum replied. "You will note that the shroud has no pockets. That is to signify that we brought nothing into this world and will carry nothing out."

"As was done for Lord Jesus Christ," I commented.

"And for the same reason."

Joanna said, "I trust the shroud can be temporarily removed."

"Down to the waist would be appropriate, if that would suffice," Mr. Greenbaum proposed.

"Quite," Joanna agreed.

Mr. Greenbaum lowered the white shroud and, while departing, said, "You must hurry for the rabbi will soon arrive to assist in the final preparation."

He stepped over to the door and closed it silently behind him.

We quickly moved in for a closer inspection of

the corpse. Benjamin Levy had been a tall, lean man, fair complected and in his middle years, with carefully trimmed hair, beard, and mustache, the latter of which was free of dried vomit. His expression seemed placid.

"What do you make of his final expression?" Joanna asked me.

"I would say with some certainty that Mr. Levy did not accidentally choke to death," I replied.

Joanna nodded. "Had that occurred he would have been terrified in his last moments."

I nodded back, again struck by the woman's insight into criminal death. "Might I ask how you came to know this?"

"It was noted in the monograph I read on suicide," Joanna explained. "If Mr. Levy had in fact choked on aspirated vomit, his face would show horror at his impending death."

"Correct," I said, and hurried to the corpse's head where I opened one of its eyes and pulled down on the lower lid to expose its inner surface. "He did not strangle for I see no petechiae."

Joanna asked, "What are petechiae?"

"They are tiny hemorrhages on the conjunctiva caused by a great increase in the pressure within the small vessels," I elucidated. "When one is attempting to cough up an object completely blocking the airway, it markedly increases the venous pressure and this causes tiny blood vessels in the eye to burst. The absence of these petechiae is strong evidence that the cause of death was not sudden asphyxiation."

"Your expertise in matters of pathology will be most helpful here, John," Joanna said. "What else can you tell us?"

Carefully I looked about his face for evidence of trauma, but found none. But that was not the case when I examined his posterior neck. There was a definite bruise mark just below the left ear. "I fear Mr. Levy was struck on the cervical spine prior to his death."

"Could it be the result of a fall?" my father suggested, viewing the bruise. "Remember, Mr. Levy did imbibe heavily and may have been unsteady on his feet."

"That is unlikely, Father," I answered. "The position of the mark, high up beneath the earlobe, would be difficult to reconcile with a fall backward."

Joanna leaned in to study the finding close-up. She appeared to be taking a very long time to observe a simple bruise that had been recently inflicted. "What do you believe caused it?" she finally asked.

"At first I thought it might have been made by a blunt weapon, such as a club," I replied. "But such an instrument would have resulted in far greater subcutaneous bleeding than we see here."

"What if the blow was delivered by Moran from behind?"

"It is too narrow to be caused by a clenched fist," I said.

"But what if the hand were extended and held sideways, such as in an open-handed blow?"

"Yes," I agreed. "That would account for it."

"And you will observe the blow is on the left side of Levy's neck," Joanna noted. "This indicates that the blow was delivered by a left-handed person."

"So?"

"Christopher Moran is left-handed."

"He is indeed. I recall he carried his walking stick in his left hand."

"And when he reached for his gold watch for the time, he did so with his left hand."

My father inquired, "But why did Moran have to deliver such a blow? Mr. Levy was already quite drunk, according to witnesses."

"Perhaps he was not so inebriated that he would hold still for a needle stick," Joanna ventured. "But let us continue with our inspection of the corpse, for the time allotted to us is running short."

Quickly she turned her attention to the corpse's face. "Please note how precisely trimmed his beard, hair, and mustache were. There is not a hair out of place. And see how carefully manicured his fingernails appear," Joanna said, and pointed to the corpse's hands folded onto his chest. "Here was a very neat man, almost obsessively neat. Yet we are asked to believe he would wrap a vomit-doused scarf around his neck, for public display no less."

"Moran must have placed it on him," my father said.

"Of course he did," Joanna went on. "It was all part of a setup to show that Benjamin Levy had thrown up his gastric contents and accidentally aspirated the foul liquid into his lungs. And I suspect Moran knew that no autopsy would be performed here, so his diagnosis of death by accidental asphyxiation would stand since there would be no further scrutiny."

"So clever," my father murmured.

"Indeed, but perhaps not clever enough," Joanna said. "Let us put the icing on this cake by finding the site of injection."

I stepped forward and was able to unbend the corpse's arms without force since their rigor mortis was already subsiding. As Joanna and I pressed in for a better view, our arms and shoulders touched and remained together. Her closeness and warmth caused a passionate impulse to surge through every part of my body, and I lost all concentration. I could not help but steal a glance at her loveliness before suppressing the impulse and returning to the task at hand.

"Is something amiss?" Joanna asked.

"Just arranging my thoughts," I murmured. "We should begin with the antecubital fossa."

It was the inner surface of the elbows that we were most interested in, for that is where the veins are quite prominent and easy to inject. But the areas were clear and free of any puncture marks.

"Anything yet?" Joanna asked.

"Nothing," I pronounced. "Both the antecubital fossa and the back of the hands are unblemished."

"Unexpected," Joanna said, then she too carefully examined the corpse's arms, and came to the same conclusion.

"What now?" I asked.

"We have not excluded injection," Joanna told us. "We simply have not yet discovered the injection site. And now we must depend on your father's medical expertise. In your clinical experience, Watson, if you could not find an arm vein to inject, where would you go next? Let us assume it was an emergency and you had to either inject a medication or draw blood for a laboratory test. Where would the next most reliable site be?"

"To the femoral artery or vein," my father replied at once. "It is in the groin area and easily accessible."

Joanna shook her head. "It would be too risky there. Levy would have to be undressed and redressed, and that would be burdensome and time-consuming. And again there would always be the chance of being discovered."

"And one would not require a tourniquet for the femoral artery," I added.

"Then that leaves us with the next-best site, which would be the carotid artery," my father said. "But that also would not require a tourniquet to reach."

"Let us see." Joanna immediately turned her attention to the corpse's neck where she found a slender gold chain upon which rested a six-pointed star. "What does this represent?"

"It is called the Star of David," I said. "Those of the Jewish faith wear it to remind themselves of their great king-warrior David."

"Does it have supposed mystical powers?"

"Of that I am not sure."

"I shall have to read on that subject," Joanna said, and focused on the slender, linked gold chain. Quickly she reached for her magnifying glass and studied the links again. "Does the chain usually come with encrusted blood?"

"Never to my knowledge."

Joanna used the magnifying glass to inspect the skin beneath the chain, but found nothing. Then she moved up to the edge of Levy's short beard and carefully spread the outer whiskers apart. "Eureka! Here it is!"

My father and I took turns examining the puncture mark with Joanna's magnifying glass. There was a small punctate lesion crusted over with clotted blood just inside the beard. It was the size of a pinhead.

"Thank goodness he was wearing his Star of David necklace," I commented.

"Perhaps it does have mystical powers, after all," my father mused.

"Whatever the reason, the necklace directed us to it," Joanna said. "And the puncture site in Levy's neck ties together the final two clues we were presented with. First, it tells us why Levy had a vomit-doused scarf around his neck at the time his body was found. It may have been placed there to convince the investigators that Levy's death was caused by accidental asphyxiation. But I suspect Moran also put it there to prevent anyone from removing it and possibly noticing a puncture wound. After all, who would touch a vomit-laden scarf, much less remove it, except for the doctor who searched for a carotid pulse? And I can assure you the doctor did not carefully inspect Levy's neck."

"What was the second clue you mentioned?" I asked.

"The length of the rubber tourniquet," Joanna answered. "At two feet, it was far too long to be used on the upper arm."

"But it had to be that length for Moran to use it on Benjamin Levy's neck," I suggested.

"Exactly," Joanna said. "But that also presents us with another unanswered question. Namely,

Moran would not need a tourniquet to inject a pulsating carotid artery. So what was the purpose of the tourniquet?"

Her question was met with silence.

There was a brief knock on the door and Mr. Greenbaum stuck his head in the preparation room. "The rabbi is here," he said urgently. "You must conclude."

"We require a few more minutes," Joanna requested. "Please inform the rabbi we are here representing the pathology department at St. Bartholomew's. Since an autopsy is not permissible, we have been asked to inspect the body to ensure that no evidence of foul play is present."

"Asked by whom? The police?"

"Say Scotland Yard and use Inspector Lestrade's name."

"Very well," Greenbaum said, stepping away. "But please hurry."

As the door closed, my father commented, "I do not believe Lestrade would appreciate your using his name and office, should he learn of it."

"Oh, his ruffled feathers would be smoothed once we solve the case for him," Joanna said, unconcerned, and then turned to me. "Now, John, we require your expertise in pathology here. In anatomical terms, which blood vessels would pop up or protrude if a tourniquet were tied around the neck?"

"Only the jugular vein would be visible," I replied promptly.

"Could it be injected?"

"Easily," I said. "And there would be several advantages to injecting the jugular vein rather than the carotid artery. First, the pressure in the carotid artery is very strong so a simple puncture wound could bleed excessively and leave a large ecchymosis or blood bruise on the neck's surface, which would be obvious to even a casual observer. By contrast, the pressure in the jugular vein is quite low and, as we have seen, would not bleed at all or very little if punctured by a needle."

"Would Moran be aware of this?" Joanna asked.

"Any physician would."

Joanna took in the new information, and then asked, "You mentioned there were several advantages to injecting the jugular over the carotid. What is the second?"

"Time," I said. "If one injects a poison into the carotid artery, it arrives in the brain in an instant and can cause an immediate, catastrophic event. Whereas injected into the jugular vein, the poison must travel down to the right atrium of the heart, then into the right ventricle before being propelled through the pulmonary artery into the lungs where it must circulate and be oxygenated. Only then will it be returned to the left ventricle of the heart via the pulmonary vein, and finally then will be expelled to reach all the body's tissues where it will begin to act. Thus, injecting the poison into the jugular vein could give Moran minutes more to move Levy from the bedroom to the couch in the lounge."

"Excellent! Very excellent, John!" Joanna said, clearly delighted. "Your expertise has proved to be invaluable. So now we have all the ends tied up, save for one."

"Which is?"

"What poison did Moran use?"

"I hope you will permit me." My father reached into his medical kit that he sometimes carried with him, even in retirement, and retrieved a long cardiac needle that was attached to a syringe. He palpated the space between the fourth and fifth ribs on the left side of the thorax, where he knew the left ventricle of the heart would be located, then jabbed the needle deep into the chest of Benjamin Levy. He was able to extract 10 ccs of unclotted blood. "Perhaps the answer lies here."

"How shall we test it?" Joanna asked eagerly.

After a moment's thought, I replied, "I will hand a sample of the blood to one of our very fine chemists at St. Bartholomew's and see if he can detect any foreign substances that should not be present."

"That may prove difficult and time-consuming," my father said.

"I know, Father. That is why I shall extract the

serum from this blood sample and inject it into laboratory mice. If the animals become sick and die, we shall be certain a very toxic substance was circulating in Benjamin Levy's blood."

"Well thought out," my father said with pride. "That would be a much shorter route to take."

"I know an even quicker test," Joanna said. "And it is waiting outside for us."

We hurried through the waiting room and past Mr. Greenbaum and the rabbi, pausing only long enough for Joanna to assure them briefly, "All is in order."

Approaching the carriage that held Toby Two, Joanna made a most peculiar request. "Watson, I will require you to prick my finger and draw blood."

"For what purpose?" my father asked.

"You will see shortly," she said, and extended her hand, palm up. "I trust you also carry glass slides in your medical kit."

"I do."

"Then proceed with the pricking."

My father expertly pierced her fingertip with a needle, then gave her a glass slide upon which Joanna smeared her blood. "Now, John, I would like you to remove a drop of Mr. Levy's blood and spread it thinly across a fresh glass slide that your father will hand you."

Once the task was done, Joanna placed the slides on the sidewalk and separated them by twenty feet. Somehow Toby Two anticipated what was coming and already had her head out of the carriage window to sample the newly arrived scents.

"What are we about to do?" I asked.

"A test," Joanna said, and rubbed her hands together expectantly. "And we shall use one of the most sensitive instruments in all of nature, which is the nose of a hound. According to a monograph written by a group of German scientists, a dog's sense of smell is a hundred thousand times superior to that of humans. If a trace of a given aromatic chemical is diluted a billionfold in water, the dog could still identify it."

"Can they detect poisons as well?" I asked.

"Oh, yes. They can sniff out a remarkable number of toxins and poisons."

"But will not the various scents present in decaying blood interfere?"

"Not in the least. Dogs can easily discriminate between a hundred different odors at the same time, according to the scientists at Munich University."

"But how are we to know that Toby Two has detected a poison?"

"She will tell us," Joanna said. "If a scent is agreeable, the dog will dwell on it, perhaps to store the information in its memory. If it is a toxin or poison, they quickly bring their heads up and back away. This trait is believed to be inbred in them to prevent the animal from consuming tainted or poisoned food."

"Perhaps the dog will find the smell of death in Levy's blood disagreeable," my father suggested.

"Not at all," Joanna rebutted. "The German monograph specifically states that hounds find the scent of cadavers interesting and they tend to hover over it. So death presents no problem."

With that explanation, Joanna led Toby Two over to the glass slide that was smeared with her blood. The dog sniffed the blood at length, displaying moderate interest but no excitement or displeasure. Then the pair moved to the slide containing Benjamin Levy's blood. Toby Two lowered her snout to the slide and in an instant raised her head and backed away. Joanna gently pulled on the leash in an attempt to bring Toby Two back to Levy's blood, but the dog sat on her haunches and resisted.

"There is a toxin in Benjamin Levy's blood that no doubt was injected into him by Moran," Joanna announced.

"But the evidence to show Moran as the culprit is circumstantial at best," my father argued. "It would never stand up in a British court of law. In all likelihood, a jury would never hear it."

"Then we shall have to dig deeper."

"And what shall we specifically look for?"

"A way to entice Moran to put the noose around his own neck."

11
Moran's Secretary

Mr. Martin Morris, the former secretary for Christopher Moran, had rooms in a pleasant, middle-class neighborhood located at the north section of Edgware Road. He greeted us at the door with warmth and no suspicion whatsoever.

"Oh, I recall you," he said cordially. "You were with the inspectors at Dr. Moran's house."

"You have a good memory," Joanna told him. "We were with Inspector Lestrade, who requires a bit more information to bring the investigation to a close."

"Of course," Morris said with no hesitation, and stepped back. "Please come in."

We entered a large parlor that appeared to be in total disarray. Boxes, some packed, others not, were everywhere. Furniture was covered with white sheets, while fixtures and vases were securely wrapped in paper. Books were strewn about and stacked in a haphazard manner. We had to step over an opened map on the floor to reach a cleared area. It was obvious Morris was in the process of moving.

"You will have to excuse the untidiness, but

the movers are due here tomorrow and I must be prepared for them."

"Where do you move to?" Joanna asked.

"A house on the east coast of Spain that I was fortunate enough to inherit from a very kind uncle," Morris answered.

"Was there something that precipitated your departure?" Joanna asked innocently.

"My asthma," Morris replied. "The polluted air of London is worsening my condition, so the fine air of Spain will be most welcome."

"A wise move," Joanna said. "But surely Dr. Moran was not overjoyed at losing such a good secretary on such short notice."

"To the contrary," said the very talkative Morris. "He seemed genuinely pleased, and encouraged my move to Spain. He was even generous enough to pay for my moving costs as a parting gift."

"Most generous," Joanna agreed. "It must have been very comforting to have such a kind and considerate employer."

Morris hesitated before speaking again. "I should not be so candid about my experiences with Dr. Moran, but all was not well in that household." He hesitated once more, this time longer. "I should say no more."

"We understand your reticence, but please understand this is an official investigation," Joanna lied. "Thus, all facts related to this case must be revealed openly and honestly. I can assure you that everything and anything said in this room will be held in the utmost confidence."

"Very well then," Morris went on, but only after taking a deep breath, as if readying himself. "Dr. Moran could be quite kind and warm on one hand, then in an instant become mean-tempered and angry enough to frighten those around him. And it does not take much to set him off. I can give you two examples, if you would like."

"Please."

"The first occurred when I walked into his parlor unannounced to deliver an important message. I found Dr. Moran in the side room where he was in the process of opening his safe. For no apparent reason, he flew into a rage and yelled obscenities at me that I surely did not deserve."

"Were you able to see what was in the safe?"

"No, madam. I was not," Morris replied. "Dr. Moran asked me the very same question, and I shall give you the same answer I gave him. The safe was only partially open and was for the most part blocked by Dr. Moran's body."

"Did he apologize for his unseemly outburst?"

Morris nodded. "He claimed that I had startled him and that caused an involuntary alarm that he blamed on his experiences in the Second Afghan War."

"Did you accept his apology?"

"In words I did, but in my heart I did not, for

I could think of nothing that could excuse such outrageous conduct."

"What was the second example of his ill-tempered behavior?"

"A magician, who was a friend of Dr. Moran's, came to visit one afternoon. They retired to the parlor where the magician entertained Dr. Moran with a variety of card tricks. I of course remained at my desk, but the door to the parlor was cracked open and I could not help but overhear their conversation. The most amazing trick was the magician showing the doctor how to deal any cards he wished using a special deck. Apparently there was some secret method of performing this trick that I did not understand. In any event I rose to close the door so I could continue my work in silence. Dr. Moran noticed me doing so and became infuriated. His face grew bright red and for a moment I thought he would strike me."

"What was your response?"

"I ran."

"But you returned."

"The very next day," Morris said. "I was certain to be let go, but again he apologized and explained his rage on the belief I was attempting to overhear a very private conversation between close friends. I assured him I was only closing the door to provide them more privacy and had no interest whatsoever in their conversation."

"So all was forgiven."

Morris nodded slowly. "And all was remembered as well."

"I am surprised you stayed on."

"My salary was generous and I wished to place as much income as possible in my retirement fund, so I thought it in my best interest to remain. In addition, Dr. Moran had long ago promised me a sizable bonus on my eventual departure."

"Did this occur?"

Morris nodded again. "On the day I walked out of his office. I had to insist he live up to his promise, however."

"Good for you," Joanna approved. "I am glad things worked out to your benefit."

"Thank you, madam," Morris said, obviously moved by Joanna's apparent concern. He suddenly became aware that our conversation had occurred with everyone standing. "Oh, where are my manners? I should have offered you seats. Please rest yourselves on my covered chairs while I make some freshly brewed tea."

"There is no need," Joanna declined politely.

"Oh, but there is, for you will no doubt have further questions."

Joanna waited for the secretary to disappear, then turned to us in a low voice. "What do you make of him?"

My father and I shrugged, for Martin Morris seemed altogether quite ordinary.

"There must be something that catches your eye," Joanna prompted.

"He is very loquacious," I commented.

"There is much more to him than that," Joanna said. "Martin Morris is a bachelor and rarely has visitors. When younger he attended university, but did not complete his studies. He is frugal, yet has money and excellent taste. Traveling is not in his blood as he is moving to a country he has never seen. And he has become a great deal more security-minded since the recent attempted break-in at his rooms."

"On what do you base these features?" I asked.

"Simple observations," Joanna said, still glancing around the generously sized parlor. "Did I mention he speaks fluent French?"

I shook my head and smiled. "You investigated Mr. Morris before we came."

"I did not have to," Joanna said. "All you need to do is look about and you will see where my information is derived."

Martin Morris returned with a bounce to his step. "The tea is now brewing. May I offer you cream?"

The three of us nodded at once.

Joanna pointed to the door and asked, "I see that you have had two double locks recently installed. Was there an attempted break-in?"

"Indeed there was. Fortunately the door held while the neighbors notified the police," Morris replied, then inquired, "How did you know that the break-in was attempted and not successful?"

"I observed the antique clock and delicate figurines on your mantel," Joanna said. "Had the break-in succeeded, surely the thieves would have taken those exquisite items."

"Which were quite dear, I might add."

"I was wondering about that," Joanna probed gently. "The expense must have strained the income of a secretary."

"On a secretary's salary!" Morris forced a laugh. "That money came from the sale of a parcel of the Scottish real estate my family owned."

"Is that where you attended university?"

Morris squinted an eye suspiciously. "How may I ask did you know I went to university?"

"You have books on your shelf by Shakespeare and Voltaire. Those are works read by the educated."

"I did indeed attend a fine university, but I foolishly dropped out after my second year to try my hand at business, at which I failed miserably."

"Well, perhaps your new life in Spain will bring you better fortune. Yet I am surprised that a man who reads and speaks French so well chose the coast of Spain rather than the Mediterranean region of southern France."

"I do not recall telling you that I am fluent in French."

Joanna gestured to a stack of books on a nearby

182

table. "Those novels are by French authors, and one can readily see that the titles are written in French. If one can read a novel in French, one obviously must be fluent in that language."

Morris shook his head in wonderment. "Are all the detectives at Scotland Yard this clever?"

"Some are."

"Then I must be careful to give the facts as I know them."

"That would be most helpful."

I had to admire the manner in which Joanna had used her marvelous skills to ensure that Morris would be straightforward and honest. He would not dare to mislead someone as sharp-minded as Joanna. She had befriended him with her earlier chatter and now she had him mesmerized.

"I shall fetch our tea," Morris said, and gave Joanna a long, admiring look before leaving.

I leaned in closer to Joanna and whispered, "At times, you are beyond belief. You make so much of so little."

"Simple observations," Joanna said again. "Surely you can see how I determined he was a bachelor and rarely had visitors to these rooms."

Pausing to gather my thoughts, I answered, "It is quite clear that he is a bachelor with no female companion. There is no ring on his finger and nothing in this room shows even a hint of a feminine touch. And his loquaciousness tells us he is alone much of the time and is eager to share his stories with a rare visitor. But how did you predict he had never been to Spain?"

Joanna gestured to the opened map on the floor. "You will note that the map is new and that Mr. Morris has drawn a thick line from London to Southampton, then over to the Atlantic coast of France and southward to Spain. In even broader ink he has traced his route across Spain to Barcelona. This is only done by a man unaccustomed to traveling to Spain."

"It is so obvious," I muttered to myself.

"At times the most obvious is the most easily overlooked," Joanna remarked. "The lesson here, according to Sherlock Holmes's text on the art of deduction, is to watch for out-of-place objects, such as a map on the floor, that do not belong there. Do not dismiss it out of hand without examination."

"Finally, what observations told you that he had not completed university?"

"Again, the books he read indicated a higher education, which should have afforded him a better station in life than that of a secretary. Thus, it is safe to assume that his university days were numbered and so were his work opportunities."

I sighed heavily. "I must learn to truly observe."

"The text I just mentioned will be a most helpful guide in this regard," Joanna Blalock said, keeping her voice low. "Now, the two of you tell me what you make of Moran's outbursts. Let us begin with his behavior at the partially opened safe."

"Obviously there is something in that safe of great value," I surmised.

"Obviously. But what?" Joanna asked.

"Money?"

"Unlikely. Large amounts of money would be placed in banks, where it could draw interest."

"What if the money were illegally obtained?"

"A clever man could easily spread the money into multiple accounts in Great Britain and on the Continent without arousing suspicion."

"Stocks and bonds?"

"One must be careful here. Those may be numbered and, if stolen, could be decertified."

"Gold, then."

"Moran's safe is not nearly large enough to hold a fortune in gold."

I pondered the matter for a moment. "What else could it possibly be?"

"Something so valuable that Moran was more than willing to kill two men over it," Joanna replied.

"Two, you say?" my father questioned at once. "But we can only connect one death, that of Charles Harrelston, to the contents of the safe. I see no evidence to involve the death of Benjamin Levy to the hidden fortune."

"One can by inference, Watson," Joanna

explained. "Think of this entire matter as a chain that has Moran at one end and the treasure in the safe at the other. Between the ends are the murders of two of Moran's close friends, which occurred within days of each other. Now, are you seriously willing to include the death of Charles Harrelston, yet exclude the carefully planned murder of Benjamin Levy? I do not believe so. This pair of murders is tied together as closely as Siamese twins. They were killed by different methods, but for the same reason."

"The reason being greed over the contents of the safe," my father agreed.

"Indeed," Joanna said. "Greed is a strange transformer of the human character. Which also explains Moran's outburst when the secretary appeared at the door while Moran was conversing with his magician friend. The magician was showing Moran how to use a trick deck of cards, which the doctor wished to keep secret so he could utilize the cards later while gambling with Charles Harrelston. Moran knew he would win from the outset and that too was part of the plan."

"A cheat!" my father roared.

"Which was a mere sideline to a murderer like Moran."

Morris returned carrying a tray laden with a tea service. As he poured the tea he said, "I am sorry for the delay, but I had to locate, then remove the cups and saucers from their wrappings. The tea is Earl Grey, which I trust you will find to your liking."

"It is my favorite," Joanna said, sipping tea and looking over the cup at Morris. "And perfectly brewed."

"Thank you, madam."

"There are a few more questions I wish to ask, but you will have to remember back to the dreadful day of Mr. Harrelston's death," Joanna said, smoothly resuming the interrogation. "Will that present a problem?"

"Not at all."

"Excellent. Let us return to Mr. Harrelston's arrival. Were you at your desk when he first arrived?"

"Oh, yes."

"Was he in good spirits?"

"So it had seemed."

"Did Dr. Moran and Mr. Harrelston begin gambling shortly thereafter?"

Morris thought back briefly. "I cannot be certain because I left immediately upon Mr. Harrelston's arrival. Dr. Moran had instructed me to take a prolonged lunch for my presence would not be required."

"How long did he instruct you to stay away?" Joanna asked pointedly.

"For an hour and a half, which was most

unusual. On most occasions, Dr. Moran was very strict that I be absent from my desk for only an hour to partake of lunch."

Joanna and I exchanged knowing glances. Moran wanted the secretary well away from his desk. He also wanted the extra time that might be needed to murder Charles Harrelston.

"Every now and then, however, my lunch hour was extended to attend to various errands."

"Such as?"

"To pick up office supplies or to purchase rats for Punch to train with."

"Ah, yes. Punch was the terrier that had the makings of a good ratter."

"Not the makings, madam," Morris corrected. "He was already a champion that had won several important contests."

"Yet he was bitten and poisoned by a rat, you say."

"That is exactly so."

"Is it not somewhat unusual for a champion ratter to be bitten by a rat?"

"Very," Morris concurred. "But I believe old Punch may not have been well. Some sort of illness may have been upon him."

"Was he listless and lying about?" I asked. "Or perhaps showing a lack of interest in food?"

Joanna nodded at my deduction, clearly pleased with my question. I was raising the possibility that Moran was testing small doses of a toxin on

188

the dog, like the one used to kill Benjamin Levy.

"No, nothing at all like that," Morris replied. "It was his strange behavior. Some weeks ago, while Dr. Moran was visiting relatives in the Midlands, the house was broken into. A window was smashed for entry and the office searched. Desks and file cabinets were opened, with their contents strewn about the floor. Even the chairs and couch were overturned and searched. All of this occurred while I slept in a room on the second floor, which I consent to do when Dr. Moran is away. Yet the dog did not bark or raise a ruckus as he always does when a stranger enters the house at night. I could only conclude that poor old Punch was ill, or perhaps that his senses were diminished for some reason."

"He made no sound at all?" Joanna asked.

"Not a sound that I heard, and I am not a deep sleeper."

"Curious," Joanna uttered to herself, then asked in a louder voice, "Was anything missing?"

"Nothing. I did a complete inventory, and could not discover anything absent."

"I suspect Dr. Moran was very upset about this break-in," Joanna queried.

"Not to any great extent," Morris replied. "And that surprised me, for I expected a major outburst similar to the ones I described earlier."

"Perhaps he was relieved that nothing of value had been stolen," Joanna said.

"He could not have known that, for I had not yet completed my inventory."

"Then he may have been pleased to learn that neither you nor Punch had been injured."

"That is a possibility."

"With our final question answered, we must be on our way," Joanna concluded, and rose to her feet. "Thank you for your time and assistance."

Heading for the door, I almost stepped on the open map that Joanna had paid so much attention to. "I hope you have safe travels to Barcelona, Mr. Morris."

"How were you aware that my destination is Barcelona?"

I gestured to the map beneath me. "You have your route carefully lined in black ink."

"I am not well traveled, sir," Morris said. "As a matter of fact, I have never been to the Continent. Thus I thought it best to clearly delineate my route of travel."

Joanna smiled at me ever so sweetly and I again reminded myself that I must learn to observe more carefully. She gave Moran's secretary a final wave, but I had the distinct impression that he had not seen the last of us.

Outside the air was foul, with a thick, yellow fog that covered everything like wet snow. The sun was hopelessly trying to break through the thick mist that held the smell of burned sulfur. I thought the chances of Martin Morris leaving

London without experiencing another asthmatic attack were poor.

In our waiting carriage, Joanna remarked, "More and more of the pieces come together, do they not, Watson?"

"They show Moran to be a very methodical killer," my father replied. "He lured Charles Harrelston in to gamble, and knew full well he would win, for the cards could be dealt secretly in his favor. He of course made certain his secretary would be away for an extended lunch, so he could take his time with the killing."

"And he allowed Harrelston to gaze upon the fortune in his safe," Joanna added.

"How did you reach that conclusion?" I asked.

"From two observations. First, there was blood on the floor in front of the safe. Secondly, the blow to the crown of Harrelston's skull was struck from behind. Since Harrelston was nearly as tall as Moran, this could not be accomplished with Harrelston in a standing position."

"He had to be kneeling down," I envisioned.

"And deeply distracted," Joanna said. "What better way to do this than to open the safe for Charles Harrelston and allow him to kneel down and gaze hungrily at the fortune?"

"And the story of a rat biting the dog is absolute nonsense," Joanna went on. "The terrier was a champion ratter that on his good days could kill fifteen rats in under a minute. You can go to any ratting contest and see this for yourselves. Let me assure you that there has never been a rat that could outlast a champion terrier."

"Do you believe the dog was injected with some sort of poison?"

"I have trouble with that notion. If you wished to inject a dog, you would not stick the paw where the dog is most sensitive, but rather on its backside where it would put up little protest. And I very much doubt Moran would test a toxin on a champion ratter since they're difficult to come by. More likely, he would try it on one of the rats Morris purchased for him."

"If the dog were ill, perhaps it would not resist having its paw injected," I argued.

"The dog was not ill," Joanna said firmly. "In the earlier interview, Morris told us that Punch was playful and his usual self before dashing into the parlor where the supposed bite occurred. In addition, Punch showed no illness at the time of the break-in."

"So why did the dog not bark at the intruder?"

"Because the intruder was not a stranger," Joanna deduced. "Terriers are among the most territorial of dogs and will bark or growl at any stranger who ventures into their home. Thus, the dog must have known the intruder from previous visits."

"Charles Harrelston!" I exclaimed.

"Almost certainly," Joanna said. "He would

have known that Moran was out of the city, and this would have given him the opportunity to break in and search for the fortune that he was somehow involved with. This also explains why Moran was not overly upset at the break-in. He had a good idea who the intruder was and the purpose of his visit. He also knew that his hidden fortune was still secure."

"Charles Harrelston was driven by desperation," my father thought aloud. "His family was in such dire need."

"And his desperation hastened his demise," Joanna said. "Moran could not risk Harrelston being pushed to even more desperate acts."

I sighed heavily. "This Christopher Moran is very clever and always seems to be several steps ahead of us."

"That is because he had a head start."

"Is there a way to close the gap?"

"Of course," Joanna said confidently. "We shall now focus on Derek Cardogan."

"The fourth and last member of the quartet from the Second Afghan War," I recalled.

"And the final piece to the puzzle."

12

The Visit

We were making haste to prepare for the arrival of Christopher Moran. Miss Hudson was in the kitchen downstairs, putting the finishing touches on roasted pheasant, while my father selected a fine Bordeaux. The fire was burning nicely, with fresh logs having been recently placed.

"I must say it was no simple matter making this dinner arrangement," my father grumbled.

"Oh?" Joanna asked. "Was Moran hesitant?"

"He was more evasive than hesitant," my father said. "He always seemed to have some last-moment excuse to cancel or delay."

"Your exchange of notes appears to have had a cat-and-mouse element to them."

"I thought that as well," my father agreed. "So I decided to press Moran a bit and told him I would soon leave for Italy where I planned to spend an extended visit with friends. Under those circumstances, I continued, it might be best for us to consider dining together in the somewhat distant future. I made certain there was no tone of anger in my note, but simply that of a man losing interest."

"Nicely played, Watson!" Joanna congratulated.

"You applied a gentle but well-directed push and got the desired effect."

"But why the evasions?" I pondered. "Was he trying to avoid the possibility of disclosing incriminating information?"

"There is another, more plausible explanation for his change of mind," Joanna said. "A clever man such as Moran would never be concerned with giving himself away. More likely, something has occurred that has emboldened him. He now wishes to know what we know, and he will attempt to glean that knowledge tonight. Thus, Watson, you must play him very carefully. Moran will be probing for details, and most interested in learning the progress of our investigation."

"I shall give him a tidbit here and there, but nothing more," my father said.

"Please keep in mind he is very much aware that we are on his trail and that he is a prime suspect. Do not attempt to mislead him. Only color a few truths."

I suggested, "He may not believe he is such a strong suspect since he has covered his tracks so well. Recall that he has encountered us a single time during this investigation, and that was in the presence of Scotland Yard. That does not indicate great interest on our part."

"But he has now received a definite signal that we are on the hunt and may be closing in," Joanna said.

"From our visit to his former secretary?" I asked.

"I would doubt that was his source," Joanna replied. "There is no affection lost between those two. Moran, in all likelihood, already has Mr. Morris and his goods on a ship bound for Spain. A stronger possibility is Mr. Cole at the Athenian Club. I can assure you he will share every detail of our visit with Dr. Moran. And Moran is far smarter than Lestrade. He will grasp the significance of Toby Two tracking the exact path he took with the inebriated Benjamin Levy."

"I shall be doubly careful when our conversation turns to the Athenian Club," my father said.

"You should make every attempt to avoid it," Joanna advised. "Try your very best to guide the talk to the Second Afghan War, in which you both participated, for that will be most helpful in solving this puzzle. The quartet were close comrades during that campaign and some event occurred in that far-off land that is the basis for all we have witnessed thus far."

"What so convinces you of that?" I asked.

"It is the one common denominator that bound them and kept them together," Joanna replied. "And whatever that event was, it necessitated their constructing a secret code to conceal it."

"It all appears to center around the contents of Moran's safe," my father opined.

"Which you must not mention," Joanna cautioned. "That would surely raise his guard and we will learn nothing."

There was a gentle rap on the door.

"Good Lord!" my father groaned. "He is early by twenty minutes. Everything is ruined."

We remained perfectly still and tried our best to delay the inevitable, but we had neither the time nor wit to do so. There was yet another knock.

"You must answer," Joanna whispered.

"But then we will not be able to carry out the script you devised," my father whispered back quickly.

"We shall have to play it by ear. Now answer."

"Yes?" my father had no choice but to call out.

The door opened partly and Miss Hudson, the housekeeper, looked in. "Dr. Watson, the pheasant is nicely done. Should I keep it warm for the present?"

"If you would be so kind," my father replied.

With the closing of the door, Joanna breathed an audible sigh of relief. "Had that been Moran, the evening would have been a total waste. Now we must hurry and not get caught short. Watson, do you have that special solution Sherlock Holmes devised to detect the presence of human blood?"

My father walked briskly over to a long laboratory table against the far wall. It held scattered papers and textbooks off to one side, but most of the table was occupied by a microscope and

Bunsen burner, as well as by various chemicals and reagents. My father reached for a small vial that contained a clear solution. "I dissolved the white crystals in water exactly as Holmes did many years ago. It is now active and will remain so for forty-eight hours."

"Excellent," Joanna said, and placed the vial in her purse. "Now I require some dust. Pray tell, Watson, where in your rooms am I most likely to find dust?"

"Atop the mantel," my father replied. "For some reason, it is the only area Miss Hudson often neglects to run a cloth."

Joanna rushed to the mantel and used a tissue to wipe up plentiful dust, then raced over to the door to Sherlock Holmes's former bedroom. She applied the dust liberally to the doorknob and said, "Now the room will appear to be unused and unoccupied by anyone recently."

"For what purpose is this necessary?" my father asked.

"As a sign to Moran, should he inspect," Joanna replied. "John and I will presently retire to Sherlock Holmes's bedroom. Under no circumstances should Moran be allowed to enter the room. It would be wise for you to leave the key in the lock to indicate the bedroom is empty. It will also inform Moran that no one is peeping out through the keyhole. These are important steps, Watson, so please follow my instructions."

"Done!"

"Then light your pipe, sit by the fire, and appear totally at ease."

"I have practiced that often enough since Sherlock's passing."

"Well then, let us resurrect a bit of Sherlock Holmes."

I gave my father a firm clap on the shoulder and said, "Make Sherlock proud, Father."

"With pleasure," he said, and a happy twinkle came to his eyes.

Joanna took my arm as we hastened to the bedroom. As we reached the doorway our bodies pressed together, so we turned to make room for each to enter. Now we were very close, face-to-face, our eyes fixed on each other. It was such an enchanting moment that I believe we both wished for time to stretch out and allow us to enjoy it even longer. But time was something we had precious little of. I placed my hand on the small of her back to guide her into the bedroom and received the warmest of smiles in return. It required all of my effort to take my hand away.

Sherlock's bedroom was simply furnished, with a bed, dresser, and small night table. According to my father, Sherlock Holmes spent more nights sleeping on the couch in the parlor than in his bedroom. This was because he awakened so often with a new thought or question and had to apply himself to it immediately. The answer could be gotten at his laboratory bench or library, which were located in the parlor and not in his bedroom. Waste of time when concentrating, even minutes, was a cardinal offense to Sherlock Holmes.

"Thinking of Sherlock, are you?" Joanna asked.

"Do not tell me you are also a mind reader."

"In a way," she said. "I noticed your expression was that of a man who had entered a place of worship. Since we are not in church and the only deity whose presence you so obviously feel is our Sherlock Holmes, the answer is simple. You are thinking of Sherlock Holmes."

"I was also wondering how Holmes would deal with Christopher Moran," I added.

"He would do it very carefully," Joanna said. "Moran is not only a clever killer who knows how to cover his tracks; he also has a very vicious side that is easily set off."

"I do not believe my father is at great risk from physical harm this evening."

"I do not either, but keep in mind that Moran has a vile temper that at times he must strain to control."

"You raise a good point," I said, and walked over to the night table where I retrieved a well-used pistol. "This is my father's old service revolver, which we have kept in sound working order."

"Are you a good shot?"

"Quite." I checked the revolver to make certain it was fully loaded, but allowed the hammer to remain uncocked. "I take my father target shooting every two weeks, for he enjoys it so and it is one of the few pleasures left to him. He is a marksman from his military days, and insisted that I become one as well."

"Have you ever shot at a human being?"

"No. But I would not hesitate if I believed Moran posed a terrible threat to my father. I might even look forward to it."

"Well and good, but do not forget to aim low."

"The better target area is up high."

"I know, but we want this prey alive."

A sudden worry came to my mind. "But the key is in the door to the room, and Moran could easily lock it."

"No matter. One well-placed kick and it will come off its hinges." Joanna hurried over to close the blinds while I went to lower the light emitted by a small lamp.

"A slight glow should not be noticed from the parlor," I said.

"But it might streak by the edges of the blind and be seen from the street below," she warned as she moved to my side. "If, on alighting from his carriage, Moran saw the faintest glow, he would know the room was occupied."

At that moment we were both peering into a mirror on the wall above the lamp. We had pleasant smiles on our faces and our eyes appeared to be on each other.

"It is impossible for me not to stare at your reflection," I breathed.

"Tell me what you see, John," Joanna said softly.

"The essence of loveliness, which captured my heart from the very start," I replied. "When I am not with you, all I dwell upon is when I will see you next. Do you feel the same?"

Joanna nodded slowly, her sweet gaze never leaving me. "It is at night, when I am all alone, that your face always comes to me. And it is at that moment that I so look forward to being with you again."

"I must tell you that at times you absolutely take my breath away."

"And you, me."

I kept my eyes on the lovely face reflected back to me from the mirror. Every part seemed flawless. "I was unaware."

She then gave me a wonderful smile that was only for me and no one else in the universe. "Perhaps my signals are too subtle."

"I must learn to observe more carefully."

We both laughed. Then Joanna's gaze sharpened as she turned away from the mirror to study me directly. "You have your father's strong jawline and thick, brown hair, and your face would be most attractive were it not for your nose, which is a bit misshapen because it was once broken. May I ask how that happened?"

"Joanna Blalock, the detective," I said, amused.

"I am surprised you cannot solve the puzzle of the broken nose."

She quickly increased the lamp's light, and moved in to examine every feature of my face. She seemed interested in my brows and cheeks. "You were a boxer, probably at university, because your career in the ring was relatively brief. You were very good defensively, and you won more matches than you lost."

"I should have known better," I said, and shook my head at the woman's marvelous deductive skills. "Please do not tell me you gathered all this information after one, quick observation."

"But it is true, dear John, and again it is that which is out of place that is so important. A physician with your background is very unlikely to participate in street fights, and thus we must find another solution for your broken nose and for the formation of some excess scar tissue under your eyebrows. Those are the features one discovers in boxers. The most plausible place for you to box would be at university. Correct?"

I nodded with a grin. "The Oxford Boxing Club."

"And your boxing career there was brief because your nose was only broken once and the scar tissue is not very evident about your brows. This, together with your hands, which are not gnarled, vouches for a brief career. The absence of more facial damage indicates you won more matches than you lost, and that you knew how to defend yourself." Once again she gave me a special smile and added, "I might be able to tell more in a brighter light."

"From where did you acquire all this information?"

"Books. I read a lot," she replied. "And your next question should be—why would I choose to read about the sport of boxing? The answer is straightforward. When I was a nurse at St. Bart's, a patient I cared for was a professional boxer who was in a coma from striking his head on the floor during a match. I noticed all the peculiar features that boxers have and decided to study their causes."

"Remarkable."

"Not really. It is cause and effect, with all the changes readily apparent."

I shook my head. "I was referring to the manner in which you continually sweep me off my feet. I never tire of gazing at your beauty or waiting for your next smile and touch. It is as if some spell has been cast upon me. Are you aware you do this?"

Again came the perfect smile. "Of course. It is my way of saying I am fond of you and your rugged good looks that contrast so wonderfully with your stately manner. You are a genuine paradox, dear John, and I happen to delight in genuine paradoxes."

"So I might conclude, for reasons beyond me, that you are attracted to this battered boxer?"

"Why else would I allow your arm to rest on mine for such an extended period?"

I glanced down and saw our hands against each other, but made no attempt to separate them. My heart raced as I said, "I am out of words."

Joanna reached up and touched my face. "At this moment, none are required."

I was about to draw her to me when we both heard the sound of a carriage approaching outside. We doused the light completely and went to the window, where we carefully peeked around the edge of the blind. I was directly behind Joanna and was so close I could hear her breathing and enjoy her delicate perfume.

"I forgot to tell you something important," I whispered.

"What?"

"That you are beautiful."

She rested her head back against my chest and replied, "And you are handsome. But now we must focus on Christopher Moran, and everything he says and does."

The carriage below had come to a complete stop with its door open, yet no one could be seen alighting. At length Christopher Moran stepped out and looked directly up to the second floor of 221 Baker Street. He pointed up to our window with his walking stick before turning to speak with someone who remained in the carriage.

"Do you believe Moran saw us?" I asked in a low voice.

"No," Joanna replied at once. "He was pointing to the upper floor before he reached the side-walk. I think he is giving someone instruc-tions."

"To what end?"

"I have no idea."

We watched Moran adjust his cape and top hat, then discard the cigar he was smoking. Once more he glanced up to the second floor, but only briefly.

"Ah!" Joanna said. "The cunning devil comes. Please alert your father."

I hurried to the door and knocked. "Father, Moran is here! Prepare yourself."

"You have my service revolver at hand?"

"And ready to be used."

"Good fellow."

We could easily hear the sound of footsteps coming up the stairs. At near two hundred pounds, Moran's weight caused the wooden steps to creak, and the louder the creak, the nearer he was. Joanna held a finger to her lips to reinforce the need for absolute silence, then led the way in the dim light to the door of Sherlock Holmes's bedroom. Then we waited. The creaking stopped, but there was no rap on the front door.

"He is delaying," I worried aloud.

"He is removing his cape and hat and adjusting his tie," Joanna said. "He plans on making a grand entrance."

A moment later we heard a very loud knock on the front door, and after another moment Moran's booming voice.

"Ah, Watson! How kind of you to invite me for what certainly will be an enjoyable evening."

"It was gracious of you to accept on such short notice," my father said. "Please give me your hat and cape."

Joanna and I quickly positioned ourselves against the door to overhear every word spoken. Unfortunately, the key was in the door lock so we could not peer out through the keyhole.

"Do you have your revolver in hand?" Joanna asked in a barely audible whisper.

"At the ready," I whispered back.

"If possible, remember to aim low, for the kneecap. I have read that a gunshot to that area is intensely painful and immediately incapacitating."

"And crippling."

"An added benefit."

The conversation between Moran and my father continued in earnest after Miss Hudson served up the roasted pheasant. They spoke in an amiable fashion about the unrelenting, thick London fog and the recent election of Prime Minister Asquith. Both seemed most interested in the problems involving the colonies, particularly the unrest in South Africa.

After dinner my father suggested they retire by the fireplace to enjoy cognac and cigars. Because of the noise made by the crackling logs and the rain outside, we had to press our ears to the door to clearly hear their words.

"I must congratulate you, Watson," Moran was saying, "on the excellent cuisine."

"The credit must go to our housekeeper," my father replied. "Miss Hudson does wonders with pheasant."

"We never saw this kind of food in India, eh, Watson?"

"Hardly," my father guffawed. "The food was barely edible, but I must say it kept me trim."

The men shared a laugh, then went silent for a long moment.

"Strange that we should not have met or heard of each other during the war," Moran said. "After all, we were both assigned to the Fusiliers."

"As I previously mentioned, I arrived in Bombay after the corps had advanced through the passes," my father explained. "And this accounts for us missing each other. When I finally reached Kandahar, you were no longer with the regiment."

"By then we were taken prisoners by the Ghazis," Moran said. "And so we remained for two months under the harshest of conditions."

"I am surprised the rebels allowed you to survive."

"That was only because they discovered I had medical training and needed my skills," Moran said. "And I might add, this saved the lives of some of my fellow officers whom I passed off as being my assistants."

"Good show!"

"And this is how Charles Harrelston and I became such good friends," Moran went on. "He was one of the officers I saved."

"How many others were there?" my father pried gently.

"Several," Moran said evasively. "In any event, the rebels who were our captors decided to attack a passing caravan that was loaded with goods and other valuables. Unbeknownst to the rebels, the caravan was heavily guarded and a fierce battle broke out, during which we managed to escape."

"Luck was with you once more," my father said.

"In more ways than I can say," Moran went on. "To avoid being captured again, we hid during the day and traveled at night with only the stars to guide us. Eventually we spotted another caravan and joined it, and thus found a route back to safety in Peshawar near the Afghan border."

"And then home, eh?"

Moran hesitated. "We had to stay longer because of the enteric fever we contracted. Our departure was further delayed by a rather long recuperation at the base hospital near Peshawar. But this was not too unpleasant, for we were allowed freedom to see the nearby countryside. Altogether, it was the most fascinating journey of my life."

"Fascinating indeed," my father said. "It is unfortunate that my son is not here. He is particularly intrigued by India, and is well versed on the subject."

"Is he traveling?" Moran asked in an innocent voice.

"Yes, but only a short distance," my father replied. "He had business in the Edgware Road district."

"Oh? The Edgware Road district seems a strange place for a pathologist to be late at night."

"One of his colleagues is ill and requires assistance filing a final report." My father paused to stoke the fire, for we heard the logs suddenly cracked loudly. "He did not go into detail, except to say he would be away for the evening."

"Perhaps I will have the opportunity to see him when we dine next."

"I will mention that to him."

"Please do." Moran swallowed audibly and made a soft groaning sound. "May I use your loo?"

"Of course," my father said. "It is the second door on the right."

"I shall only be a moment."

We heard his heavy footsteps coming toward us, for the loo was next to Sherlock Holmes's bedroom. Then, to our surprise, the doorknob to Holmes's room began to turn. I brought my revolver into firing position in the event Moran became violent on discovering our deception. Joanna placed her hand on my weapon and gently pushed it down.

"Not that door!" my father cried out. "It is the next one down."

"You will have to forgive my curiosity," Moran said. "When I saw the key in the lock I wondered if this was in fact the former bedroom of Sherlock Holmes."

"It is," my father replied sharply. "And that room is off limits and will remain so."

"How sentimental," Moran said. "I see you have left all of his papers and examining devices in place as well."

"And there they will stay," my father said in a firm voice.

"But some of the papers and notes appear quite recent. Have you yourself been doing some investigating?"

"I am only reviewing old cases that Holmes and I were involved with."

"Too bad Sherlock Holmes is not here for the current spree that pervades all of London."

"Most unfortunate."

We heard the door to the washroom close loudly. A moment later Joanna darted out of the bedroom and over to the coat rack. She picked up Moran's walking stick and quickly examined its silver head and the polished wood adjacent to it. With a hurried glance toward the washroom, she removed the vial of liquid from her purse and wet the handkerchief. It required only seconds for her to rub the handkerchief over the silver cap and the wood next to it. After replacing the cane in its original position, she dashed back into our room.

"What was the purpose of that?" I inquired.

"Evidence," she said, and brought a finger up to her lips.

The door to the washroom opened and Moran stepped out. The direction of his footsteps indicated he was walking to the coat rack. "Allow me to thank you for your generous hospitality, Watson."

"Must you leave so soon?"

"I am afraid so," Moran answered. "I have a very early start tomorrow morning."

"As do I."

"Thank you again," Moran said. "I will see myself out."

We tiptoed silently to the window and waited until we saw Moran enter his carriage and drive away. We waited another full minute in the event Moran decided to double back.

Joanna led the way into the living room,

with a smile. "Well done, Watson! Well done!"

"Masterful!" I complimented him.

"Well, I did a bit of acting at Cambridge," my father remarked.

"It paid off for you handsomely," Joanna said.

My father went for his cherrywood pipe and carefully lighted it. "And Dr. Moran played it exactly as we thought he would."

"But he left so abruptly," I said. "I was worried he saw through our deception."

Joanna waved away my concern. "He departed because he got what he came for. He learned John was in the Edgware Road district where Martin Morris lives, which indicated we were on his trail."

"But why let him know that we have picked up his scent?" I asked.

"To force his hand," Joanna replied. "Now he knows he must move quickly."

My father nodded slowly. "So he is aware that John is not there to assist an ill colleague."

"Pshaw! A sick colleague is a lame excuse, and Moran is a very clever fellow. He may well believe John is in the Edgware Road district. It is the reason you gave that he does not swallow."

My father looked at Joanna slowly. "Then he knows I lied?"

Joanna shook her head. "He believes you were misinformed to prevent you from unwittingly telling him what John was really up to."

My father's face hardened. "He does not think much of me."

"He has underestimated you, Watson," Joanna said. "And in the end, it will cost him dearly. Now, let us examine the handkerchief that I rubbed on Moran's walking stick."

Joanna produced the handkerchief and held it up for us to see. "There is only a very faint brown spot on the linen where I rubbed the wood. It is no doubt polish from the cane."

"But the spot next to it is a dark, mahogany brown," I observed.

"Which indicates that Sherlock Holmes's test to detect human hemoglobin is correct. This rich, mahogany color proves that there is human blood on the silver cap of Moran's walking stick."

"From Charles Harrelston's head," I added.

"No doubt."

"But we cannot prove the blood belonged to Harrelston," my father argued. "And unless we do, there is nothing more than circumstantial evidence."

Joanna smiled thinly. "Circumstantial evidence can at times be very convincing, Watson. Such as—to quote Thoreau—when one finds a trout swimming in milk."

"But I am amazed that a clever doctor like Moran would not know how to remove all traces of blood from the walking stick," I said.

"And how would he accomplish that?" Joanna asked.

"As we do with surgical instruments," I replied. "Boiling water or diluted acid would do the job nicely."

"But he would not do that," Joanna said at once. "Because boiling water or acid could ruin the wood of a very expensive cane. And besides, even in his wildest imagination, he could not conceive of someone connecting his cane to the murder of Charles Harrelston."

"So he is not so clever after all," my father said.

"Do not underestimate him," Joanna warned. "He is a cold-blooded killer with a brilliant mind. This combination makes for the best of criminals."

Joanna began to pace the room, hands clasped behind her. Back and forth she went, mumbling to herself, off in some world that others were not privy to. Finally she stopped and said, "Watson, your question asking Moran to name the other members of the quartet was brilliant."

"But he refused to," my father noted.

"That is precisely the point. We already have him associated with the deaths of Charles Harrelston and Benjamin Levy, and he is aware of that."

"So why not mention all the names?" I asked.

"To avoid giving us the identity of the fourth member of the quartet. Had he named Benjamin Levy, he would have been obliged to speak of

Derek Cardogan and this may have led to more questions."

"But surely Moran realizes that we will eventually uncover the fourth member, if we have not done so already," I countered.

"It is not the name of Derek Cardogan that Moran wishes to conceal, but the information it carries," Joanna said. "There is something in Derek Cardogan's past—weakness or an addiction—that Moran will use. This of course is an assumption, but a worthwhile one. Remember, Moran is a physician and utilized his knowledge of medicine to cover his first two murders. In all likelihood, he will do so again, and do it very soon."

"Then we must act immediately," my father implored.

"That will not be possible without gathering in-depth information on Derek Cardogan. For then and only then can we play our cards correctly."

"What if such information is unattainable?"

"In that event, I am afraid that Derek Cardogan will die on our watch."

"And Christopher Moran will come into sole possession of a great fortune," my father said.

"While he gets away with cold-blooded murder," I added.

"That too, John," Joanna noted. "For these two conclusions are joined, as surely as night follows day."

13

The Stroll

With the permission of her father-in-law, I arranged to take Joanna, along with her young son, Johnnie, on a Sunday stroll through Hyde Park. The day was mild and glorious, with a bright sun and a crisp breeze. Yet despite the fine weather and pleasure of each other's company, we could not divorce our minds from the complexities surrounding the death of Charles Harrelston.

"You seem so confident of Christopher Moran's involvement," I remarked. "But he has an eye-witness who for all intents clears him. And unlike the gardener, she was very near when the event occurred."

"You are of course referring to his housekeeper, Mrs. Lambert," Joanna said.

"I am indeed," I replied.

"And you are convinced that her account is in all ways accurate?"

"Why should she not be truthful?"

"I do not doubt her honesty," Joanna said. "It is her observations that have to be tested."

"Are you saying that her observations and

her statement may not be one and the same?"

"I am saying that is what we must determine, for as you just mentioned the housekeeper provides the only truly solid alibi that can dismiss Christopher Moran as the prime suspect."

"I doubt that she will change her words."

"I do not expect her to."

"Then why re-question her?"

"Because I wish to hear her words with my ears and not with Lestrade's," Joanna replied. "It is also important that we speak with her in Moran's absence."

"Do you believe Moran has prompted her?" I asked.

"That thought crossed my mind," Joanna said. "But I am more concerned that so much time has passed and we are still not allowed to interview the housekeeper."

"Which is Christopher Moran's doing," I explained. "According to my father, the good Dr. Moran insists that Mrs. Lambert remains much distressed from viewing the event and should not be questioned further until she recovers."

"The delay of course works to his benefit," Joanna continued. "You see, the more time that passes, the more her memory will dim and be open to suggestion."

"But surely she will remember the major points."

"It is the small details I am interested in, for those are the ones that are often the most telling."

Joanna gazed up at the sky, as if waiting for some new thought to come. Her eyes twinkled for a moment before she asked, "Did your father actually contact Mrs. Lambert in person?"

"He has spoken to the housekeeper at her home on several occasions and on each visit she stated that Moran had prescribed complete rest until the shock passes," I recounted. "But my father believed her composure to be quite calm and collected, and he wondered if her continued so-called distress might have been conjured by Moran."

"Then let us put an end to this pretense," Joanna said firmly. "Please instruct your father to again call on Mrs. Lambert and advise her of the urgency of our interview. If she resists, he should suggest it might be best for the questioning to take place at Scotland Yard where she can officially repeat her account to us and to Inspector Lestrade."

"That should light a bit of fire under her."

"And under Christopher Moran as well."

We strolled on, enjoying the quiet beauty of London's most famous park. Up ahead of us, young Johnnie had stopped and was intently studying a brown and white collie that was lying quietly in the grass while its owner was giving it food. I saw nothing unusual, but there was obviously something about the scene that interested the lad.

Johnnie turned to us and called out, "Look, Mummy! The dog is ill."

"What brings you to that conclusion?" Joanna asked.

"He is refusing the food and his tail is not wagging when the food is being offered," Johnnie said.

"Perhaps he has just eaten and has no appetite," Joanna suggested.

"I think not, Mummy," Johnnie said earnestly. "Dogs will happily eat anything placed in front of them, regardless of how recently they have been fed. I have noticed this on numerous occasions with our golden retriever, Oliver."

"You make an excellent point," Joanna praised. "Why do you believe they behave so?"

Johnnie considered the question carefully before shrugging. "I have no idea, Mummy."

"It is inbred in them," Joanna explained. "Dogs are descended from wolves who never knew when their next meals would appear. Thus, when food was available, they would fill their stomachs over and over again, gorging themselves, as a precaution in the event no food would be obtainable for days on end."

Johnnie grasped the explanation immediately. "So it is a survival habit from long ago."

"Precisely."

"That is most interesting, Mummy."

I could not help but be impressed with the

young lad's keen sense of observation and deduction. Yet I should not have been surprised by his skill, considering his lineage. He not only looked like a junior Sherlock Holmes, he also behaved like one. In a quiet voice I asked Joanna, "Has he always shown this deductive talent?"

Joanna smiled adoringly at the lad as he raced ahead. "He comes by it naturally, but I must admit I encourage him as much as possible."

"How so?"

"With a game we play," Joanna replied. "Would you care to see an example?"

"I would indeed."

Joanna surveyed the expanse of green lawn until her eyes came to rest on a couple, with a young toddler, near the Serpentine Lake. The child was frolicking by the water's edge and shrieking with joy as she chased a group of pigeons. "What do you make of that family by the lake?"

I studied the couple at length and sought out any peculiarities, but none were to be found. The man and woman were appropriately dressed and behaving in a most cordial fashion. I was attracted briefly to the gentleman's silk top hat, which was finely made, but saw nothing worthy of mention. With a shrug, I commented, "I see parents and a happy child."

"You are half correct," Joanna said, then motioned her son over and asked the very same question she had asked of me. "Johnnie, what do you make of that family by the lake?"

The lad carefully viewed the setting, with his gaze moving back and forth between the couple and the child. He appeared most intent when the toddler let out a cry of happiness, then he lost all interest and said, "I think, Mummy, that the woman is the girl's mother, but the man is not her father."

"Why so?" Joanna asked.

"Because the woman watches the child's every move, while the man shows no concern."

"Perhaps she is being overly protective, while the father leaves the chore of watching the child to the mother."

The lad shook his head. "He is unconcerned, even when the little girl is near the water and cries out. Thus, he is not attached to her as a father should be."

As if on cue, the gentleman tipped his top hat to the woman and walked away. There was no embrace or touch of farewell. He ignored the child altogether. Remarkable, I thought, how truly remarkable. The lad saw what I saw, but in fact saw so much more.

"Well done, Johnnie," Joanna said.

The lad nodded, pleased but not impressed with his performance, then dashed on, no doubt seeking something else to observe.

I lowered my voice and said to Joanna, "You

do realize that the woman could be the child's governess."

Joanna waved away the notion. "I believe otherwise. Her dress is much too fine for the salary afforded a governess." And as we drew closer to the woman, Joanna added, "You will also note the presence of a wedding band on her hand, which excludes the possibility she is a governess."

"It does indeed," I agreed, for governesses were always unmarried young women who lived in the house of their employer and were responsible in every way for the child they looked after. The ring was a simple observation that I had neglected, yet told so much. "I see where I must be careful around the two of you or I shall continue to be outdone."

"But to a lesser extent with Johnnie," Joanna said forthrightly. "For at this stage, he requires more knowledge and life experiences to connect all of his observations, such as in this instance, the cost of a fine dress and the salary of a governess. But he reads voraciously and his mind captures and keeps everything it comes across, and thus his storehouse of knowledge increases at an amazing rate. The day will come when his deductive skills are truly spellbinding."

"Will he eventually be your equal?"

"And beyond."

We sauntered on and passed the Serpentine

Lake, then approached the portion of the park that bordered central Knightsbridge. In what seemed an instant, the sky darkened and the weather changed. The cool breeze picked up abruptly and brought with it a definite chill. Joanna and I drew closer together against the sudden cold, and I could now feel the exciting warmth of her body flowing through me. Our shoulders and hips touched and rubbed gently with each step, and whatever chill was in the air disappeared completely.

"I am glad we did not wear our heavy coats," I said, taking her arm into mine.

Joanna smiled sweetly and asked, "Are you enjoying the unexpected drop in temperature?"

"At the moment, yes," I replied.

"And do you find it stimulating?" Joanna inquired, moving in even closer.

"In many ways."

Joanna's smile widened as she said, "Well, we do seem to be making some progress, are we not, John?"

"So it would appear," I said. "But I would not mind if the pace were to pick up a bit."

"Then I believe it appropriate for me to tell you that this is by far the most pleasant stroll I have ever taken."

"For me as well."

"I hope this will not be our last."

"I can assure you that will not be the case."

Once more I became aware of how close we were and how much closer I desired to be with this most enchanting woman. The more I was in her presence, the more I became attracted to her, and despite my best efforts I found myself staring at her trim figure. Unlike most in her class, Joanna was tall and slender, with a remarkably narrow waist. I could envision my hands easily encircling her lower abdomen, which would not measure more than twenty-two inches.

"Without being too bold, may I ask what so draws your attention to my midsection?" Joanna asked, without even a hint of a blush.

"I—I was studying the fine fabric of your dress," I stammered.

"I think not," Joanna said. "If you were curious about my dress, your eyes would have scanned from the collar to the hemline. But you concentrated only on the midsection."

"It was your waist," I confessed. "I was wondering how in the world it became so narrow. Is it the result of a tight corset? Or perhaps some other device I am unaware of?"

"Neither of those," Joanna replied. "It is simply the way it is and always has been."

"I probably should not have inquired."

"Why not? It is one of my better features."

I sighed resignedly. "I must learn to be more honest with you."

Her son must have overheard the latter part of

our conversation, for he turned to us and said, "Or learn how to shade the truth."

Joanna and I chuckled softly, but the lad remained straight-faced, for his remark was not meant to be amusing but only good advice.

"Where did you learn of this shading the truth?" Joanna asked, trying to suppress a grin.

"From Grandfather," Johnnie answered. "He told me that there may be different views of the truth depending on what is being seen and by whom."

"And this often occurs when all the facts and clues are not carefully considered," Joanna informed.

"Like with the family by the lake," the lad noted.

"Like with the family by the lake," Joanna agreed.

I watched Johnnie run ahead, then turned to Joanna and added, "As in the case of the gardener who supposedly witnessed Charles Harrelston's fall to his death."

"As in the case of any eyewitness," Joanna said with a firm nod. "That is why it is so imperative that we interview Mrs. Lambert and determine whether she has shaded the truth."

"I shall have my father attend to—" I stopped in mid-sentence and quickly reached for my timepiece. "Good heavens! I am afraid I have lost track of time. We must take Johnnie home immediately and hurry to the British Museum where my father awaits us."

"What lies in store for us at the museum?" Joanna asked.

"A unique opportunity to unlock the mysterious code."

14

The Knighted Curator

An hour later we entered the British Museum and found my father intently studying the Rosetta Stone while listening to a rather odd-looking fellow who was introduced as Sir David Shaw, a curator in charge of ancient Mesopotamian script and languages. Sir David was tall and stoop-shouldered, with reddish-gray hair and a hawklike nose upon which rested the thickest spectacles I have ever seen. We were later to learn that behind those heavy lenses was a brilliant mind, the owner of which had been knighted by Queen Victoria for his wartime skills in deciphering top secret, coded messages, some of which were so sensitive they would never be allowed to see the light of day.

"Sir David and I served together in the Second Afghan War," my father informed us. "And I have intruded on our friendship to ask for his assistance."

"Not at all, Watson," Sir David said. "It is my pleasure to do so. But would you care to hear the end of the Rosetta Stone story before we move on to more pressing matters?"

"I very much would," my father replied. "Please be good enough to give my son and Mrs. Blalock the particulars on this remarkable tale."

In captivating detail Sir David described the history surrounding what might justifiably be called the most informative rock ever found. The Rosetta Stone was discovered in Egypt by soldiers in Napoleon's army while they were digging near the town of Rashid, which translates as *rosetta*. Carved into the stone were three distinct scripts. The upper text was Egyptian hieroglyphs, the middle written in demotic Egyptian, and the lower in ancient Greek. Because all three of the scripts read essentially the same, the stone provided the key to unlocking the mystery of the Egyptian hieroglyphs.

"Fascinating," I commented. "But tell me, Sir David, if the Rosetta Stone was discovered by Napoleon's army, how did it end up in the British Museum?"

"We defeated Napoleon in the Egyptian desert and the stone became the property of the British under the terms of the Treaty of Alexandria. It has been on display here since 1802."

Joanna said, "I am surprised the French did not insist on its return."

"The French insist on many things," Sir David replied, with a shrug that dismissed the idea the stone would ever leave British soil. He gazed admiringly once more at the Rosetta Stone and seemed to nod at it. "How remarkable is it that a rock that measures only four-by-two feet in total has provided such a flood of information?"

"Let us hope that our problem does not require a Rosetta Stone for solution," my father said.

"We shall see," Sir David said, and led the way to the quiet and nearly deserted upper floor of the museum. The few people in the corridor spoke in hushed tones, as if they were in some holy place. A stale, somewhat musty odor filled the air.

My father and Sir David walked ahead, deep in conversation, while Joanna and I stayed several steps behind. Our hands and arms touched when we rounded a sharp corner and, moving even closer, I allowed my cheek to brush against her hair. We exchanged secret smiles as Sir David stopped and reached for a closed door.

We entered Sir David's undistinguished office, which was small and crowded with no room to spare. Every inch of the walls was taken up by books, ancient artifacts, and framed photographs from archaeological expeditions. Even his desk was cluttered with papers and notes held down by a clay tablet with an unrecognizable script written upon it.

Sir David waited for us to take our seats, then walked over to a small blackboard behind his desk and said, "Now I hear you have a code that is proving somewhat troublesome."

"We can make neither heads nor tails of it,"

my father told him. "The code appears to consist entirely of lines drawn in a most peculiar fashion."

"Are the lines straight and uninterrupted?"

"Yes, but all are slanted at varying angles."

"Do they contain adornments?"

"Only very small beads placed at one end or the other of each line."

Sir David nodded slowly. "Then they are surely symbols, which in itself is a most helpful clue. To conceal a message individuals often create symbols that by themselves demonstrate little or no significance. However, once it's recognized that these symbols stand for letters, one can apply the rules that can guide us through all secret readings. As you may be aware, the letter *e* is the most commonly used letter in the English language and it predominates to such a marked extent that in any message you will see it used over and over. So you must pick out the symbol that appears most often, for that invariably represents the letter *e*."

My father reached in his coat for a copy of the message and, studying it, counted silently to himself. "There is one symbol that is slightly slanted and appears four times. Thus, it must signify the letter *e*."

Sir David's eyes narrowed noticeably. "How many symbols are contained in the entire message?"

My father counted again. "Eighteen in all."

"Your message is quite short."

"So it would seem."

"And that, my dear Watson, presents us with a great problem, for in short messages the usual rules for deciphering may not apply. As a matter of fact, the briefest messages may be among the most difficult to unravel."

"I would think the opposite."

"That is a mistake the uninitiated often make, for they see only a line of simple symbols and expect the answer to jump out at them," Sir David explained. "And it rarely does."

"So we have learned," my father said. "We were hoping you could break the code for us during our visit."

"I am afraid you will in all likelihood be disappointed," Sir David said frankly. "For the most part, codes employing symbols cannot be quickly solved, regardless of their apparent simplicity. It is not usually a matter of days, but weeks before one can uncover the hidden meaning of a cleverly constructed code."

"Even with your expertise?"

"Even so," Sir David replied. "But I shall give you guidelines that might shorten your search. You may wish to write them down."

My father and I reached for pen and paper, but Joanna did not. Instead, she kept her eyes fixed on Sir David and watched as he picked up a small stick of chalk and jotted down the numeral 1 on the blackboard.

"First," Sir David began, "do not concern yourself with immediately breaking the code, but rather how to deconstruct it. You must look for the frequency and pattern in which the symbols are written. The symbols most often used are likely to represent the letters *e, t, a,* and *o,* usually in that order, but not always when dealing with a short code. Nevertheless, search for the symbols most frequently seen in the message, for they will signify the letters I just mentioned. Then you must move the letters about and determine what pattern they fit into best."

"But surely patterns are difficult to see when the message consists of only eighteen letters," Joanna said.

"Exactly right, madam. And that is yet another reason why brief codes are at times the most difficult to decipher," Sir David said, and wrote the numeral 2 on the blackboard. "Next, keep in mind that short messages require that only a limited number of words be included. For example, the word *importance* would seldom be used because it takes up too much space. Remember, as a rule, a symbol represents a single letter. Thus, if you have a total of eighteen symbols, the message must be restricted to eighteen letters. So you can readily see letters here will be at a premium and used most sparingly."

"We should therefore search for the shortest possible words," Joanna surmised.

"Correct again, madam," Sir David said, nodding his agreement. "In a message of eighteen letters, there will be a number of quite short words, such as *I, a,* and *at.*"

"Of course these are generalities," Joanna said impatiently. "Do you have any absolutes to offer?"

"Several," Sir David replied. "One of the surest keys to uncovering certain letters is the presence of an apostrophe. Are any included in the message?"

"None."

"That is unfortunate because apostrophes are always followed by the letters *s, t, d, m, ll,* or *re,*" Sir David went on, then wrote the symbol # on the blackboard. "What about numbers? Do any of the symbols have the configuration of a number, such as 1 or 7?"

"None that appear so."

"Oh, my!" Sir David said gravely. "This could turn out to be quite difficult. You see, numbers can often tell a lot. As an example, the number 1 could represent an *a,* the first letter in the alphabet, the number 2 a *b,* and so on."

"Are we to deduce that the creator of the code is most clever?" Joanna asked.

"Ah!" Sir David smiled. "Now you are beginning to understand the art of code-breaking. Look for every clue the code may offer. As a rule, it requires considerable intellect to say a lot in a few words. So with that in mind, let us talk of a bright chap who knows a sophisticated method to hide his message in a code. Have any of you heard of the Caesar shift?"

The three of us shook our heads collectively.

"It was supposedly invented by Julius Caesar," Sir David continued on. "It is simple to use, but very difficult to crack. In this code you shift the alphabet a certain number of spaces in one direction. Allow me to give you an example. A shift of three spaces to the right would tell the reader to replace the letter *a* with *d,* or *b* with *e,* and so on. Using a Caesar shift of three to the left, the nonsense word *krz* would translate into *how.*"

"But how could this Caesar shift apply in any way to our symbols?" Joanna inquired.

"It could if the individual who constructed the code is a very clever fellow. For example, if the symbols represented numbers, with each number assigned a letter in the alphabet, the words spelled out might appear nonsensical. But if you applied the Caesar shift, the true meaning would come into view."

Joanna quickly asked, "Would not the message include a number to indicate how many spaces to shift?"

"Not necessarily," Sir David replied. "The

number and direction could be agreed upon beforehand between the sender and the recipient."

"We seem to be reaching one dead end after another," my father said unhappily.

"Perhaps if I examined the message I might be able to give more assistance," Sir David offered.

"Of course," my father said before adding a caveat. "But I must insist that the message and its code go no further than the confines of this room. We are involved in a criminal matter at the highest level and any disclosure to the public could adversely affect bringing the case to a successful conclusion. Thus, I must have your word that you will neither show nor discuss it with anyone."

Sir David's eyes sparkled briefly. "Like in the case of *The Adventure of the Dancing Men* that you and Mr. Holmes were so kind to bring to my attention."

"Similar, but the circumstances are different."

"Then I shall give the coded message careful study and all will be held in the strictest confidence."

My father handed him a copy of the message and watched Sir David scrutinize it at length. The curator's lips moved silently as his eyes scanned the code over and over. He seemed to be counting off numbers to himself and this went on for a while, but his expression told us he was having little success.

Finally Sir David shook his head and said, "As I thought, it is proving to be quite difficult to decipher. I am afraid it will take considerable time to solve this riddle."

"How long?" my father asked.

"It is impossible to say," Sir David replied.

"We desperately need this code broken," my father urged. "And unfortunately we have so little time."

"I shall give it my best."

"But you are not optimistic."

"I have learned over the years, Watson, not to make promises I cannot keep."

We thanked Sir David for his time and left his cramped office, no closer to an answer than when we entered.

Outside the sky was gray and gloomy, which matched our moods after such an unproductive visit. We strolled away from the museum and down Great Russell Street, which was crowded with tourists. Keeping our voices low, we discussed our problem that had no apparent solution.

"Perhaps Sir David was simply being modest and downplaying his code-breaking skills," I suggested.

"I believe otherwise," my father said. "I think he was being realistic and telling us not to raise our hopes too high."

"But he was quite helpful in assisting you and Sherlock Holmes decipher the devilishly clever code in *The Adventure of the Dancing Men.*"

"It was not he who solved the code, but Holmes himself," my father said. "When Sherlock received the first of the dancing men messages, he could make little of it, so he consulted with Sir David because he wondered if the figures were hieroglyphs. But even with intensive study, David could not come up with a suitable answer. Over time, more pieces of a message containing the dancing men appeared and Holmes, with his usual brilliance, solved the code on his own. Indeed, it was then that he informed me he had written a monograph on secret writings, in which he analyzed 160 different ciphers. Yet the dancing men ciphers were new to him. Thus, it required days of deep study for Holmes to finally break the code."

Joanna quickly asked, "Do you have a copy of his monograph on secret writings?"

"I have looked everywhere, with the assistance of Miss Hudson, but it was not to be found."

"Then we are entirely on our own," Joanna said.

"Perhaps Sir David will shortly come up with the answer," I hoped.

Joanna shook her head. "To him, it is another interesting puzzle. To us, it is murder. If the code is to be deciphered shortly, it will be up to the three of us to do it."

"And sadly, even if the code is broken, it

may be to no avail," my father said, with a heavy sigh. "For the message itself may not solve our mystery."

"I am certain it will," Joanna said assuredly. "It is the key to everything."

"Why so?"

"Because it will reveal the crime the quartet committed while in Afghanistan," Joanna replied. "The deaths of both Charles Harrelston and Benjamin Levy revolve around that singular event."

15

The Housekeeper

Another day passed before we were allowed to interview Mrs. Lambert. But this was only permitted after Christopher Moran had visited her and given his approval, which afforded him yet another opportunity to rehearse the woman. Joanna was not deterred by this possibility, although she did caution us.

"Remember, she is an employee of Moran's," Joanna warned. "She will say nothing to refute his account, so we must pry gently."

"But then her words will be his," I said.

"We shall see," Joanna said as our carriage slowed and stopped at the front door of the housekeeper's home.

Mrs. Emma Lambert lived in a small house with a thatched roof near the Surrey Docks in Brixton. Her home was modest by any standard, but seemed grand when compared to the seedy slum only blocks away. As we seated ourselves in a shuttered parlor, I watched Joanna take a rapid inventory of its well-worn furnishings before turning her attention to the housekeeper, whom she studied at length. I saw nothing unusual about

Mrs. Lambert, other than her poor hearing, which necessitated her repeatedly bringing a cupped hand to her ear, so as to catch all of my father's words. He raised his voice to make certain he was being clearly understood.

My father's kind bedside manner, from his many years as a practicing physician, quickly put the housekeeper at ease. "I am delighted to see you are recovering from your ordeal," he was saying.

"It has been slow, but I have been coming round." Mrs. Lambert was a plump woman, in her mid-fifties, with totally gray hair that was held back in a tight bun. She showed no signs of distress, although the dark circles under her eyes indicated a lack of sleep. "It cannot be rushed, you know."

"Indeed," my father agreed. "And I know you must be most grateful for Dr. Moran's concern."

"He came to see me regular, he did," Mrs. Lambert said in a pronounced Cockney accent. "Like a proper doctor would."

"Such kindness," my father remarked. "It sounds as if he stopped by on a daily basis."

"That he did."

"Were any medicines prescribed?"

"Not a one," Mrs. Lambert replied. "He just took the time to assure me that Mr. Harrelston's fall was the result of a brain sickness and that I should try to erase the terrible memory from my mind."

"Not an easy thing to do," my father commented. "It is particularly difficult if one knows the poor man who fell to his death. I of course assume you knew Mr. Harrelston."

"Oh, yes," Mrs. Lambert replied. "I had seen him a good many times and he always seemed so cheerful, but not on that awful day. I could see his unhappiness the moment I opened the door."

"Unhappiness, you say?"

"Clear as day, it was," Mrs. Lambert said. "And Dr. Moran noticed it as well."

"He made mention of this to you?" my father asked.

"Oh, yes. Dr. Moran told me it was no doubt part of the brain sickness," Mrs. Lambert said. "This of course led to the man's terrible ending."

"It all seems to fit," my father said sympathetically, then motioned to Joanna. "Mrs. Blalock here, who also represents the Harrelston family, will wish to know some particulars about the poor man prior to his fall. Please be good enough to oblige her."

"Of course, sir."

"I take it you alone greeted Mr. Harrelston when he arrived," Joanna said, entering the conversation and speaking loudly for the housekeeper's benefit.

"Yes, madam," Mrs. Lambert answered. "As I do for all visitors, be they patients or friends of the doctor. I show them both in and out."

"Was Mr. Harrelston by himself when you opened the front door?" Joanna asked.

Mrs. Lambert thought for a moment, then replied, "All by himself, except for the hansom that brought him."

"Do you recall the hansom?"

"An expensive one, it was. You could tell from the shiny carriage and well-groomed horse."

Joanna nodded at the description. "You have a very good memory, Mrs. Lambert."

"I pride myself on it."

"Excellent," Joanna said, lowering her voice to a normal level. "I am certain your recall of events will be most helpful."

"What was that you just spoke?" Mrs. Lambert asked, and cupped a hand to her ear. "I didn't quite get your words, for my hearing is a bit off."

Joanna repeated the comment with a louder delivery, then continued on. "Please take us back to the very moment he arrived."

"Well, I opened the front door and there he was, dressed as finely as usual," Mrs. Lambert said. "But unlike his normal self, he was in a hurry and dashed up the stairs, with me a step behind."

"Did he offer you any greetings?"

"Only a brief 'good day' or something similar," Mrs. Lambert replied, then added, "And, oh yes, there was one other thing. He did inquire about the dog and was somewhat saddened to hear of

Punch's death. You see, Punch and Mr. Harrelston got along quite well together."

"So I take it the dog never barked at Mr. Harrelston?"

"Oh, no, madam. Punch looked forward to Mr. Harrelston's visits because the gentleman would often bring along a treat for old Punch to chew on."

Joanna gave my father and me a subtle smile, for Mrs. Lambert's words told us why the dog had remained so quiet the night Charles Harrelston broke into Moran's home. Harrelston had fed the dog a treat, guaranteeing its silence. "You are being most helpful, Mrs. Lambert. Now please describe the events once you and Mr. Harrelston reached the third floor."

"Nothing happened," Mrs. Lambert said with a shrug. "The doctor greeted Mr. Harrelston and they went into the parlor, closing the door behind them. I then hurried back to my duties down-stairs."

"When passing the second floor, did you notice Mr. Morris at his desk?"

"As usual, he was busily working away."

"According to Inspector Lestrade, you returned to the third floor some hour and a half later, which would have made it approximately one o'clock," Joanna recalled. "Is the time correct?"

"It was just after one," Mrs. Lambert said. "I came upstairs to see if the gentlemen required any refreshments. The door was closed, so I knocked and announced it was me." The housekeeper's face suddenly lost color and she hesitated to gather herself. "That was the start of the awful happening."

"Here we need details," Joanna urged. "Please do your best to remember them."

Mrs. Lambert took a deep breath before continuing with the unpleasant memory. "Dr. Moran opened the door and said Mr. Harrelston was not feeling well. He asked that I go downstairs with him to obtain a glass of water for Mr. Harrelston while he fetched his medical kit. And so we did. I then—"

"Before you moved toward the stairs," Joanna interrupted, "tell us if you recall any conversation between Dr. Moran and Mr. Harrelston through the open door."

"I remember Dr. Moran's exact words, plain as can be," Mrs. Lambert said. "He told Mr. Harrelston to remain on the couch until he and I returned."

"Did you hear him mention your name in particular?"

"I did indeed," Mrs. Lambert said at once. "The good doctor called out that I was going for water and he for his medical kit, and for Mr. Harrelston to rest on the couch."

"Did Mr. Harrelston respond?"

"Oh, yes." Mrs. Lambert said. "In his high-pitched voice, he assured us he would be all right."

"High-pitched, you say?"

Mrs. Lambert nodded. "That was his usual tone, which I easily recognized."

"Was his voice strong?"

"It sounded like that of a sick man."

"Did you actually see the frail condition Mr. Harrelston was in?" Joanna asked.

Mrs. Lambert nodded again. "The poor man was lying on the couch. I could clearly see his feet sticking out, for Mr. Harrelston was quite tall, as I'm certain you know."

"So you saw only his feet," Joanna said.

"And heard his voice as well," Mrs. Lambert said. "No doubt it was him."

"So it would appear," Joanna said agreeably, then thought for a moment before asking, "Are you certain no one else was in the house at the time?"

"No one, for Mr. Morris had taken his lunch leave and the front door was locked."

"Is there not a tradesman's entrance?"

"There is at the rear of the house, but it too stays locked at all times and only Dr. Moran and I have keys to it."

"A wise precaution."

Mrs. Lambert nodded a third time. "You never know what characters might be lurking about, even in as fine a neighborhood as Curzon Street."

"One never knows," Joanna agreed with a hint of sarcasm, then gestured to me. "Do you have any questions for Mrs. Lambert?"

"Only a few," I said. "Tell me, Mrs. Lambert, how long did it require for you and Dr. Moran to race downstairs and return to the parlor?"

"No more than a minute or two," Mrs. Lambert replied. "Dr. Moran urged me to hurry, you see."

"And what was his response when the two of you entered the deserted parlor?"

"The doctor was quite puzzled. He checked the loo and found it empty, then came back worried. It was then he noticed the open window and—and." Mrs. Lambert paused to swallow hard at the memory before continuing in a weak voice. "And all became clear."

My father patted Mrs. Lambert's hand in a consoling fashion and said, "You are being quite helpful and we know how difficult this must be for you, but there are still several matters we feel you might be able to shed some light upon. Do you feel up to it?"

"I will try," Mrs. Lambert said, collecting herself.

"The tradesman's entrance you mentioned is of concern to us," my father told her. "Is it possible you inadvertently left the door unlocked?"

"Oh, no, sir," Mrs. Lambert responded. "There were no goods being delivered that day, so I had no reason to open the tradesman's entrance."

"Good," my father said approvingly. "So no one could have entered that way."

"Not without me seeing them, sir."

Joanna's head went up and stayed up, for something just spoken had aroused her interest. "Were there any other visitors to the house that morning?"

"There were no visitors other than Mr. Harrelston, and only two patients who were in real need of seeing the doctor," said Mrs. Lambert.

"Did you know these patients?" Joanna asked casually.

"Quite well, for the doctor had attended to them over the years. Mr. Michaels has terrible lung disease and poor Mrs. Hunter suffers from awful rheumatism."

"And you showed them both in and out?"

"I did."

Joanna rose and walked over to a narrow fireplace no more than ten feet away and rubbed her hands together over a few smoldering logs. "You must excuse me while I ward off a slight chill I have."

"What's that?" Mrs. Lambert cried out, bringing a cupped hand to her ear.

Joanna raised her voice to a shout and called back, "I have a slight chill and wished to warm myself."

"Aye, this weather will do that to you, all right."

We thanked Mrs. Lambert for being so cooperative and walked out into a gray, fog-shrouded day. There were more than a few people on the street, all of whom seemed interested in both our fine clothes and our faces.

"Clever," Joanna remarked. "This Christopher Moran is one cunning devil who is surely guilty of murder."

"Do you doubt Mrs. Lambert's observations?" I asked.

"It is her conclusions I doubt," Joanna said. "She neither saw Charles Harrelston on that couch nor heard his voice."

"But she described his feet," I argued.

"She saw a pair of feet, which may or may not have belonged to Charles Harrelston."

"But she distinctly heard his voice," I countered.

"Rubbish!" Joanna said firmly. "The poor woman is so hard of hearing she can barely carry on a conversation unless she cups her ear and you raise your voice. So please tell me how she could possibly recognize a voice ten feet away?"

"That is a supposition that cannot be proven," my father said.

"It is not a supposition, but a fact, and I did prove it," Joanna said. "That is why at the end of our interview I walked over to the fireplace, which was ten feet away from her, and spoke to the housekeeper in a normal voice. She could not make out a word I uttered. The ten feet is important here, for that is the approximate distance between the door to Moran's parlor and the couch that lay within. Now, are you seriously contending that this hard-of-hearing woman could stand at the door and hear the distressed voice of Charles Harrelston ten feet away? Under no circumstance could this occur. So, with this in mind, there can only be one explanation for Mrs. Lambert's statement to Inspector Lestrade. She did not clearly hear the voice of Charles Harrelston, but was only repeating what Moran told her the voice had said."

"What a cunning scoundrel!" I roared. "It was all rapidly rehearsed down to the very letter. And now that I think of it, why did Moran bother to mention Mrs. Lambert's presence and assistance before dashing downstairs? If I were the attending physician and Charles Harrelston was truly ill, I would not have wasted a moment on conversation and simply rushed downstairs for water and whatever instruments I required."

"Well put, John," Joanna said, clearly pleased with my deduction. "That very thought crossed my mind as well. The reason Moran mentioned Mrs. Lambert's name was to alert the person on the couch that the housekeeper was close at hand. Moran was no doubt blocking her view into the parlor, and this gave the accomplice time to set up the charade."

"An accomplice!" my father hissed under his breath.

"But who?" I wondered aloud. "And where would Moran find such a villain?"

"On the dark streets of London where such a man is easily found and bought," Joanna replied.

"And who will now slink back into the shadows and never be discovered," my father predicted.

"Do not be so certain of that," Joanna said.

"Is there some clue to his identity?" I asked hurriedly.

The indecipherable Mona Lisa smile came to Joanna's face and she asked, "Tell me, John, aside from Charles Harrelston, how many visitors entered Moran's house that fateful morning?"

"Only two longtime patients, both of whom were shown in and out by Mrs. Lambert," I replied.

"That is the clue that should draw your attention," Joanna said.

I looked at her oddly. "But all it does is to exclude the two patients as suspects."

"Precisely," Joanna said and, with her parasol, signaled a passing carriage.

16

The Code

The three of us were again summoned to the Harrelston mansion by a message that promised new information on the coded note. This was most welcome news, for despite our best efforts the code remained a mystery. We had worked individually and together as a group in an effort to decipher the note, but could not come up with even an inkling of success. Joanna had consulted two texts on code-breaking while my father had spoken with yet another language expert at the Imperial College, all to no avail. Thus, a major clue in the murders of Charles Harrelston and Benjamin Levy continued to elude us.

As our carriage approached the Harrelston home, we were startled to see Christopher Moran departing on foot. He appeared to be in a great hurry.

"I fear the worst," my father said dejectedly. "Whatever evidence there was is now in the hand or mind of Christopher Moran."

"How did he learn of the information so quickly?" I asked.

"It must have been an informant." my father surmised.

"It was not an informant, but us," Joanna said. "During Moran's visit, I suspect he glanced down and studied the contents of Sherlock Holmes's workbench while on his way to the loo."

"He did," my father recalled. "And something there caught his interest."

"It was no doubt a text on code-breaking and our notes and attempts to decipher the message," Joanna said.

"But the dinner was days ago," I queried. "Why did Moran wait until now to see the Harrelstons?"

"I would wager this is not his first visit, but one of several," Joanna replied.

I nodded at Joanna's suggestion. "It would be just like him to come fishing around the bereaved."

"Fishing, indeed," Joanna agreed. "And he has caught a big one, for now he has the information that was meant for our eyes only."

"A foolish mistake on our part," I grumbled. "We should have removed everything from sight."

"Yes, we should have. But that is now water under the bridge," Joanna said. "Let us hope that Moran has not distorted or somehow destroyed the new information."

As we alighted from our carriage, the door to the mansion opened and we were shown directly into the library where Sir William awaited us. The room was cold and no fresh logs had been added to the dead ashes in the fireplace. I wondered if this was another indication of the Harrelstons' financial woes.

"You have just missed a good friend of Charles's," Sir William told us. "Christopher Moran stopped by to pay his respects. He is a most pleasant chap."

"So I have heard," Joanna said, without so much as a hint of a blush. "May I ask if he was of any assistance in decoding Charles's last message to him?"

Sir William smiled briefly through his quite evident sadness. "Your father-in-law told me of your deductive skills and how easily you display them. And the answer to your question is that he was of little help. The message was a complete riddle to him."

What a liar! I thought. The man lied almost as well as he killed.

Joanna asked, "Did you show him the new information you summoned us to examine?"

"Oh, yes," Sir William replied. "But he explained it as a game he and my son and the others played. It is called anagrams, in which lines are laid out in a random fashion, then assembled to construct letters. The line of letters make no sense and have to be rearranged to form recognizable words. They invented the game to amuse themselves while recuperating in Afghanistan."

Joanna and I exchanged quick, sharp glances, both of us surprised by Christopher Moran's revelation. Was this the clue to solving the code? Was it truly an anagram or was the cleverly dishonest Moran fabricating a story to throw us off track?

"In Afghanistan, you say?" Joanna asked.

"Yes. From many years ago."

Joanna squinted an eye, which was her habit when encountering an important fact. "Pray describe in detail the new information you have come upon."

"Better yet, I shall show it to you," Sir William said, and reached for a letter on his desk. "Here is the message Christopher Moran wrote to my son. I do not know if it was a reply to my son's last note to Moran, for it is not dated. In any event I happened on it last night while going through my son's remaining effects."

He held it up for us to view, for it was a very short note written on Christopher Moran's high-quality stationery. It read:

SOME OF YOUR ALIGNMENTS
ARE AGAIN OFF THE MARK

"A puzzle within a puzzle," I commented.

"But there is a helpful clue here," Joanna noted,

still carefully studying the letter. "It is the word *alignment,* for it reinforces my belief that it is the angle of the lines that dictates the message."

"How will you proceed?" Sir William asked.

"By consulting an expert," Joanna said evasively.

We had not heard Mary Harrelston enter the library nor noticed her standing in the background. She approached us with virtually silent footsteps and spoke to Sir William. "Father, I have heard parts of your conversation with Dr. Watson and his associates, and wonder if I might make a comment or two."

"Of course, my child."

"First, there are a number of contradictions that I feel I must address. You should know that dear Charles and Dr. Christopher Moran were not such close friends. Their relationship was civil, but not much beyond that, for they often quarreled. So if there was any real friendship between them, it was strained."

"Was that also true of your late brother's ties to Benjamin Levy and Derek Cardogan?" Joanna asked.

"Oh, no. Quite to the contrary," Mary Harrelston replied. "Charles and Benjamin Levy were particularly close. When Mr. Levy learned of his death, he wept."

"Was your brother's relationship to Derek Cardogan equally close?" Joanna inquired.

"Nearly so," Mary Harrelston answered. "But we have seen little of Derek Cardogan recently, for he is quite ill from his repeated bouts of malaria."

"Has he not been treated?" I asked.

"On many occasions," Mary Harrelston said. "But, according to my brother, poor Cardogan's disease has become resistant to all remedies. He has consulted with the very finest specialists in London, but to no avail."

"I suspect he could throw some light on these coded messages," Joanna suggested.

"As do I," Mary Harrelston agreed. "But he was so ill with jaundice when we saw him last. I have doubts he could think clearly."

"It is worth asking," Joanna said. "Would you happen to know where he resides?"

Mary Harrelston shrugged. "He has a home in Knightsbridge, but I am not certain he will be there. The last we heard, he was on his way to Paris for some new form of therapy."

"When was this?"

"Close to a month ago."

Joanna squinted an eye. Something said by Mary Harrelston was of importance. "You mentioned there were several contradictions in our earlier conversation. Might I be made aware of the others?"

"It was the anagram game. I can assure you that game would be of no interest to my brother who was a poor speller of words. He had struggled with this flaw his entire life. Thus, it is fair to say he would have avoided a game of complex anagrams as if it was the plague."

Joanna and I again exchanged knowing glances, both of us realizing that something was obviously off-key here. Why would the message be in the form of an anagram if Charles Harrelston was so poor at the game? At this point I had the distinct feeling that Christopher Moran was toying with us and deliberately leading us astray.

"That is most helpful," Joanna said, then thought for a long moment before asking, "Where there ever any financial dealings among the four men?"

"Not that I am aware of," Mary Harrelston replied. "My brother had suffered some recent financial reverses, which would have made his participation impossible."

"What about in the past?"

Mary Harrelston was in the process of shaking her head when she abruptly stopped the motion and said, "Some time ago I overheard my brother and Mr. Levy discussing a future business venture. But it was only to occur after they had cashed in. I do not know what they were referring to."

The contents of the safe! I immediately thought to myself.

Joanna's expression remained unchanged but I was certain she had reached the same conclusion. "Do you recall the nature of this business venture?"

"I believe it was of the import-export type."

"Did they happen to mention what merchandise would be involved?"

"I do not think that was mentioned."

"Thank you for being so helpful," Joanna said. "Now we must be on our way, for your last note, Sir William, will require a great deal of study. I believe there is a clue within the new message that will greatly assist us in solving this riddle. If you do not mind, I would like to take the note with us."

"Of course."

"Then we shall wish you good day."

Sir William accompanied us to the door, promising to search further through his son's belongings for any additional messages.

As we approached our carriage, my father remarked, "A most peculiar game, I must say."

"Pshaw!" Joanna said at once. "This is no game, my dear Watson, but a deliberate attempt by two individuals to hide a message, the content of which led to the death of one of the participants."

"But what could be so sinister or valuable as to require such concealment?"

"What, indeed, for therein lies the key to our mystery."

"Yet if secrecy was so important, why did not Moran send his last message in code as well?"

"A very good question, Watson, and one that crossed my mind earlier. There are a number of possibilities, of which two seem the most likely. Either the coded message contained new symbols that could have provided guidance in unraveling the code, or Moran was concerned Charles Harrelston, who was a poor speller, would have difficulty assembling the word *alignment*. I favor the former, but both are guesses, neither of which advance our cause."

We rode in silence during the first half of our journey back to Baker Street. For the very first time, I observed Joanna scribbling notes to herself. She had taken a mechanical pencil and small writing pad from her purse and was jotting down either ideas or thoughts, and giving each an underlined number. I stole a glance at the top item on the list. It read "*(1)* Malaria."

"Give me another moment," Joanna requested. "The Harrelstons have provided us with some most instructive information and I do not wish to lose even a fraction of it."

I concentrated on the conversation we'd had with the Harrelstons and searched for the informative portions Joanna was referring to. The only obvious one was the comment that Charles Harrelston and Benjamin Levy had planned to cash in for funds to begin their new business venture. Surely they were speaking of the hidden treasure in Moran's safe.

"Ah, yes!" Joanna announced. "Now I have the chain of events that links all together. Let us begin with malaria, which I would wager Watson is quite familiar with."

"Indeed I am," my father said. "During my service in India and Afghanistan, I saw more cases of that dreaded disease than I care to count. It can be a most awful disorder, which, in its most vicious form, may cause death."

"From Mary Harrelston's description, do you believe Derek Cardogan has the vicious form?"

"I doubt it, for if he had that type of malaria he would be dead," my father explained. "He most likely has the chronic form of the disease, which can become quite nasty when it resists treatment."

"But it is fair to say that he acquired the disease while serving in the Second Afghan War, is it not?"

"Most certainly."

"And according to Moran, this must be one of the fevers the quartet suffered while recuperating in Peshawar."

"Agreed."

"Good." Joanna checked off the first item on her list. "Next, you will note that the secret code was invented by the quartet while recuperating in Afghanistan. What does that tell us?"

My father and I shrugged and gave each other perplexed looks.

"Come, come now!" Joanna urged. "You must reason backward here, for that is how most crimes are solved. With that in mind, ask yourselves *why* the group would invent a secret code."

"To hide the meaning of their messages," I answered promptly.

"Why hide the meaning?"

"To prevent others from learning their contents."

"And what is this content that so desperately needs to remain hidden?"

"The treasure in the safe!" I exclaimed.

"Precisely so," Joanna said, and checked off the second item on her list. "We now know that their treasure was illegally obtained in Afghanistan and had to remain hidden for a prolonged period. We can also reason that this treasure is not money."

"Because it had to be cashed in," I deduced.

"Very good, John. So we can conclude this treasure is not money, was illegally obtained in Afghanistan and thus cannot be sold immediately on the open market, and must fit inside a modest-sized Chubb safe. What meets all of these criteria?"

After long deliberation, my father raised his hand and spoke out. "I think I know."

"Pray tell," Joanna beseeched.

"It is an ancient, priceless work of art that a museum or collector would pay dearly for," my father replied.

"And it would have to be relatively small, such as a rolled-up painting or statuette, which they could bring back to England without it being seen or arousing suspicion," I added. "I believe that covers all the necessary criteria."

"Your answer has some merit," Joanna said, yet her tone indicated she was not convinced. "But there are problems with your selection. They fought in the barren mountains and deserts of Afghanistan where priceless works of art rarely exist. Moreover, how would these four young men know how to recognize and appraise some obscure Afghan work of art?"

"Perhaps it was bejeweled," I suggested.

Joanna shook her head briefly. "They would not know if the gems were real or, if they were, what value to place on them. Still, your last guess is within the realm of possibility and one we should not exclude altogether." She glanced down at her list once again and said, "There is another important clue in Moran's last message to Charles Harrelston, that being the admonishment 'some of your alignments are again off the mark.' In regard to her brother's ability to solve the anagram, Mary Harrelston was less than correct. The admonishment I just mentioned tells us that the coded message is not a mind-bending anagram, but a simple one that only requires attention to the alignment of a limited number of lines. It is one that a poor speller like Charles Harrelston could still master."

"You are of course assuming that Christopher Moran was being truthful with his explanation that the message was in the form of an anagram," I argued mildly.

"It is an assumption we have to make, for it is the only clue at our disposal and we have no choice but to follow it."

"If this is the case, the expert you mentioned will certainly be able to decipher the code," I hoped.

"It is we who will decipher the code, John. The expert I was referring to is a chapter dealing with ciphers and anagrams. This chapter is in a recently translated Russian monograph that I have yet to read."

"Where is this monograph?"

"On Sherlock Holmes's workbench at 221b Baker Street."

Joanna Blalock was wrong in her conjecture that the code would be a simple anagram that we could finally unravel with the help of a monograph on that very subject. We worked diligently through the entire afternoon and, despite our best efforts, remained baffled by the coded message, which read:

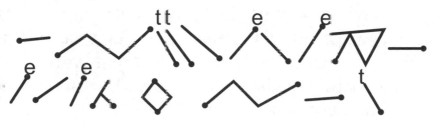

The strange symbols made no sense, regardless of the order we placed them in. There were no letters or numbers to guide us, nor any apostrophes, which would have been most helpful since, according to our notes, they were always followed by the letters *s, t, d, m, ll* or *re*. We forged on for yet another hour, but made no progress in unraveling the mysterious code. Evening was falling, and so was our mood, but we persevered and again applied Sir David's rules to decipher the message.

His first instruction was to determine which of the symbols appeared most frequently, for the three most commonly used letters in the English language were *e, t,* and *a,* in that order, with *e* predominating by far. We found one symbol that presented itself four times and another one three times, and thus believed them to represent the letters *e* and *t:*

But we could advance it no further, for there were three symbols that appeared twice. Even if we arbitrarily chose one of these symbols to signify the letter *a,* it would leave us with *e, t,* and *a,* which could only form a number of small words, such as *a, at, eat, ate,* and *tea,* none of which served our purposes. And to confuse matters even more, the words when lined up together may have been part of an anagram. We soon realized it would have been an endless task to try each combination until a meaning was arrived at.

"Perhaps it is not merely an anagram," I suggested. "There must be twists and turns we are neglecting."

"It cannot be complex," Joanna insisted. "A simple anagram is the only code that four young men could devise under the circumstances. They were at war and they were sick, so they had to construct a code they could all easily remember."

"But if it is that easy, why are we having so much difficulty?"

"Because we are going about solving it in the wrong manner," Joanna said, nodding to herself. "We are searching for a hidden anagram in the code, while we should be concentrating on just the code itself. Our most important task is to find the key that will unlock the first word. That mechanism can then be employed to unlock all the other words in the code."

"But how do we determine the key?" I asked.

"By guessing," Joanna replied. "It is the only avenue open to us."

"That is what we have been doing for hours," I said wearily. "But the solution continues to elude us."

My father reached for his timepiece and glanced at it briefly. "Perhaps we should adjourn for dinner and refresh ourselves. I am afraid we are facing a very late night."

Joanna stared at my father for a long moment, then quickly returned to the coded message and began counting silently to herself over and over. She performed this task at least three times before tilting her head to the side and counting yet again, finally stopping at the number 12. As her eyes came back to us, a Mona Lisa smile crossed her face. "There is no need for refreshment, for I have deciphered the code," she announced.

"How?" my father cried out. "Pray tell how?"

"Why, you told me, my dear Watson."

"But I said nothing, other than to suggest an early dinner."

"It was not your words, but your actions."

"Which were?"

"Gazing at your timepiece," Joanna explained. "For that was the clue that deciphered the code."

My father gave her a most quizzical look. "I must say this is far beyond me."

"Please view your timepiece, Watson, and tell me the time."

"It is 5:25."

"How do you know this?"

"Because the timepiece so informs me."

"No, no! You are missing the point. I wish you to describe exactly what you see when you study your timepiece."

"Both hands are clearly directed to the 5."

"The number 5 indeed, which represents the fifth letter in the alphabet and thus signifies the letter *e*."

My father's eyes suddenly widened as the deciphering mechanism came to him. "How clever! The lines in the code symbolize the short hand on a timepiece that points to a given number, with the number corresponding to a letter in the alphabet. And the little bead at the end of each line informs us of its direction."

"Spot on, Watson! Thus, if the line is directed at one o'clock on the timepiece, it translates to the letter *a,* which is the first letter in the alphabet. If it says two o'clock, it represents the letter *b,* the second letter in the alphabet, and so on."

"But I see a problem," I interrupted at once. "There are twenty-six letters in the alphabet, and only twelve on the face of a timepiece. How does one account for the letters farther down the alphabet?"

"I too was aware of this discrepancy and it

took a moment to see how they circumvent it," Joanna elucidated. "Again, it was done simply. Any letters that come after the number 12 were drawn in a difficult-to-recognize form. Allow me to return to the message and demonstrate. For reference, I will pencil in two timepieces next to the message, which should help orient you."

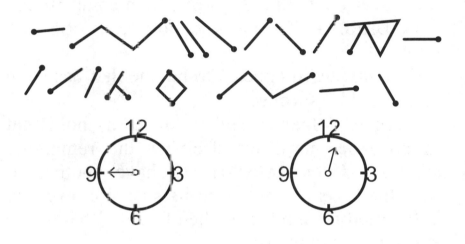

"You will note that in the first timepiece the hand points to one o'clock, which is the number 1 or the letter *a*. Of more importance is the second timepiece in which the hand is directed at the 9, which corresponds to the ninth letter in the alphabet or *i*. This could represent either the small letter *i* or the capital *I*. In this instance I assumed it was the capital *I* and was correct. Therefore, in our message the initial symbol represents *I*, which is the first word in the code. Now please follow my finger as we proceed down the line of symbols that come after the *I*. Next we have three interconnected, slanted lines that are a stretched-out version of the letter *N*. Then we have two lines pointed at five o'clock or the letters *EE,* and finally a line directed at four o'clock which is *D*. Thus we have the words I NEED. Next is a line to one o'clock which is *A,* followed by another *D*, another *A,* and a peculiarly shaped *R,* and then the letters *C, A,* and *H,* all of which comprise the word DARCAH. The message now reads I NEED A DARCAH."

"The last word appears to be one that has been concocted," I surmised.

"Perhaps," Joanna said. "But let us hold that in abeyance until we decipher the remaining symbols. After DARCAH, we have another *A,* then the letter *T* slanted on its side, followed by a distorted *O,* another *N,* then *C* and *E*. Thus, the entire message reads:"

I NEED A DARCAH AT ONCE.

"By Jove, Joanna! You have truly outdone yourself," my father lauded warmly. "I doubt that even Sir David has reached a solution."

"Oh, he eventually will," Joanna said, waving off the compliment. "But how ingenious was Moran to employ a timepiece in constructing the code. It was simple to use, easy to conceal, and always at their disposal, even during the war. And more ingenious yet was his plan to hide the key word deeper within the deciphered code. For if we do not understand the term DARCAH, the decoded message has no meaning and we are once again in the dark."

The three of us stared down at the strange word and shook our heads in bewilderment. We were now faced with yet another riddle within a riddle.

"There is no such word in the English language," I stated.

"Nor does it appear to be German," Joanna said, but she consulted the German-English dictionary to be certain. "It does not exist."

"Nor is it French," said my father who was fluent in that language.

"Perhaps it is the anagram Moran spoke of," I ventured.

"I think not," Joanna said. "The word we are searching for is a noun, and few nouns can be made from *darcah*. *Arc, cad, car,* and *card* come to mind, but none fit here."

"Nor does *rad,* which is a measure of radiation," my father added.

"I still favor an anagram," I persisted.

"Most unlikely," Joanna said. "Charles Harrelston was a poor speller and even simple anagrams would be beyond him."

"But he could have employed the Caesar shift that Sir David mentioned," my father proposed.

"Let us see," Joanna said and, using pen and paper, went about shifting individual letters a given number of spaces in the alphabet. "We will begin by moving the letters one space over, and so *d* becomes *e, a* becomes *b,* and so on. Thus, *darcah* is transformed into *ebsdbi,* which makes no sense at all."

Joanna strived on, going through each possible combination without success. It was a most time-consuming ordeal and time was something we had little of. Two lives had already been lost and a third was now at stake. We waited anxiously, hoping against hope that Joanna could provide an answer to our dilemma.

After an hour of diligent effort, Joanna stood and stretched her back, then announced, "It is all gibberish. The Caesar shift was not used."

"Could the word *darcah* be an abbreviation of some sort?" I suggested.

"It is certainly not one that I have ever encountered," Joanna said, and thought for a moment before asking, "Watson, might *darcah* be a military term they acquired during their stay in Afghanistan?"

"It is most assuredly not a term I heard while serving in the Second Afghan War," my father replied.

"But it might be an Afghan word," Joanna said quickly. "Do you recall how many languages are spoken there?"

"Two primarily," my father answered. "Pashto and Dari."

"Which of the two is the most commonly used in the area of Peshawar, where the quartet spent a long period of recuperation?"

"Pashto, by far."

"Does Sir David speak Pashto?"

"Fluently," my father replied. "He was frequently used as a translator during the Afghan War."

"Please call him, Watson, for he may be our last, best hope."

My father looked up Sir David's phone number and had the language expert on the line without delay. "David, sorry to intrude on you at this late hour, but we have come across a word that may be Afghan in nature. Might we ask for your assistance? . . . Thank you, my friend. The word we are interested in is *darcah,* which is spelled D-A-R-C-A-H."

I kept my eyes on my father's expression, but it remained impassive. Seconds seemed to drag by.

"No such word, eh?" my father said without inflection. "Neither Pashto nor Dari? . . . Would you check and determine if it belongs to any nearby languages? . . . I see. Not Persian either?" . . . My father pressed the phone to his ear. "You say there is a similar Persian word, but with one letter of difference . . . Please spell and translate it . . . D-A-R-G-A-H, which denotes the tomb of a Muslim saint. That does not seem—" Joanna stepped in closer and whispered,

"Charles Harrelston may have misspelled the word we are after. Ask Sir David if objects of great value are ever buried with the holy man." My father repeated the question, then waited a moment before shaking his head. "Never, eh? The body is wrapped in a shroud and nothing more . . . I am afraid the Persian word does not suffice here . . . Yes, yes. That is precisely how it's spelled in the code. D-A-R-C-A-H . . . I have no idea how it is pronounced. As it is written I would—"

Joanna abruptly reached for the phone in my father's hand. "May I, Watson?"

"Of course."

"Sir David," she began. "This is Joanna Blalock whom I trust you recall meeting at the museum . . . Exactly. The amateur detective. I wonder if I could intrude a bit more on your valuable time . . . Excellent. Now here is an important piece of information you must consider. The sender of the coded message was a poor speller and he may have misspelled the word that has confounded us. As you no doubt are aware, individuals with spelling difficulties often write words phonetically, and that may be the case here. For example, the letter *c* can be pronounced with an *s* sound as in *celebrate* or a *k* sound as in *silica*. Let us apply these two sounds and see where they take us. We shall begin with the *s,* which phonetically changes *darcah* to *darsah*. Are there any Afghan words of this nature? . . . No, eh? Then let us try the *k* sound, and the word becomes *darkah*."

Joanna's brow went up. "There is a word that is quite close in Pashto, you say. Please spell it . . . D-A-R-K-H-A, with the emphasis on the H-A. Very good. Now please tell me what it means . . . Ah, yes! That appears to be a good fit. Thank you, Sir David. You have been of considerable help."

Joanna slowly placed the phone down, then gazed out the window, obviously lost in thought. She remained expressionless and silent, with the only sound in the room coming from the traffic below on Baker Street. Moments later we heard a horn blow and brakes screeching, so my father rushed over and closed the window to mute the noise. Joanna seemed not to notice.

I could not restrain myself further and asked, "Have you deciphered the message?"

"In large measure," Joanna replied and turned to us. "According to Sir David, the word *darcah* phonetically resembles the Afghan word *darkha*, D-A-R-K-H-A, which means a share or portion. Thus, Charles Harrelston's last message to Christopher Moran reads, I NEED A SHARE AT ONCE."

"Brilliant! Absolutely brilliant!" my father praised. "You surmised he wrote it the way it sounded. DARK-HA! DARK-HA! Who would have ever guessed?"

I was again amazed at how Joanna could take totally unconnected clues, which most people would have neglected, and connect them in such a fashion that they solved a riddle. Who would have thought to combine Charles Harrelston's poor spelling with the Pashto language of distant Afghanistan? It was an extraordinary gift that she inherited from her father. At length I said, "You continue to astonish me with your deductive skills, Joanna."

"But these skills have not put a name on the treasure they were hiding," Joanna said. "That most important clue continues to elude us, which once again demonstrates Moran's cleverness. He invented a superior code and made it even more complex by inserting the key word in Pashto, the true meaning of which was known only to the quartet. Thus, even if the remainder of the code was deciphered, the word *darkha* would not reveal what they were concealing. It is the best of codes that was constructed by an evil mastermind. And it caused us to waste a great amount of time for little in return."

"It was not at all a waste of time," I objected. "For you have broken the code, which few could do, and now we know beyond any question why Harrelston and Levy were murdered. It was for their shares of the treasure."

"True," Joanna said. "But there is a worry here."

"Which is?"

"Moran must assume that we would soon break the code, particularly after viewing our notes on Sherlock Holmes's workbench. This will force him to act more quickly."

"In what form?" I asked.

"Against Derek Cardogan," Joanna said darkly. "His life is now in even more imminent danger than I thought."

17

The Intruder

By unanimous consent we decided to dine at Simpson's-in-the-Strand to celebrate our victory over Christopher Moran's secret code. It was Sherlock Holmes's favorite restaurant, and my father knew the menu well. At his suggestion, Joanna had the lamb, I the beef Wellington, and he the roast beef carved off the trolley. All was accompanied by Yorkshire pudding and washed down with a superb Médoc. We finished with Turkish coffee, for we had no room left for their delicious desserts.

Before taking Joanna home, we had to return to 221b Baker Street to fetch a shawl she had left behind. Sitting next to Joanna in the carriage, I had an almost irresistible urge to take her hand in mine, but obviously could not in my father's presence. Nevertheless, Joanna and I sat close enough together for our shoulders to touch and we both enjoyed the moment. As our carriage turned sharply onto Baker Street, it provided me with the opportunity to slide even closer to Joanna. With our bodies pressing together, a wave of enticing electricity went through me and through Joanna as well, I suspect, for I heard her utter a soft sigh. It required all my effort not to reach over and embrace this most enchanting woman. But I did manage to send her a warm smile, which she returned, and for now I realized that would have to suffice.

Our carriage came to a stop and, as we alighted, my father noted a glow coming through the curtain of his rooms.

"Did you leave the lights on, John?" he asked.

"I must have," I admitted. "Please forgive me."

"Not to worry," my father said jovially, for he had greatly enjoyed a rare evening out. "Come, let us retrieve Joanna's shawl and send her on her way before Sir Henry becomes concerned."

As we slowly climbed the stairs, we heard sounds emanating from my father's rooms. There were heavy footsteps, followed by thuds made by objects falling to the floor. We stopped, and moved Joanna to a position well behind us.

"Do you by chance have my service revolver with you?" my father asked in a whisper.

"Unfortunately not," I whispered back.

"What do you propose, then?"

"To deal with the problem head-on," I said, and wrapped a handkerchief tightly around my knuckles.

I removed my coat and quietly approached the cracked door, listening for the sounds to indicate if there was more than one intruder. The heavy footsteps were those of a lone individual. Taking a deep breath to ready myself, I kicked the door open and rushed in. Before me was a brute of a man, well over six feet in height, with broad shoulders and a stout build. But it was his head that drew my attention. It was huge and scarred, with an overhanging brow that gave him an apelike appearance. He was not the least bit moved by my sudden entrance, and stepped toward me with large fists, confident I was easy prey. That was his first mistake.

The brute swung wildly at my head and missed, causing him to lose his balance momentarily. To his surprise, I countered with a powerful straight punch to his mid-sternum, which I am certain resulted in a fracture of the skeletal plate that protects the heart and lungs. He crumpled in pain and dropped to his knees, which provided me the opportunity to move in closer. Two quick jabs to the jaw split his lips and drew blood, making him stagger. In a split second, I opened my hands and slammed my palms against his unprotected ears, and this produced a sudden intense increase in the middle ear pressure. He howled at the discomfort, but was somehow able to rise to his feet. The look on his face was one of anger, mixed with a thin smile, for now he had an open switch-blade in hand. The blade was at least six inches in length and gave him a clear advantage at close quarters. He licked his bloody lips as he slowly moved in for the kill. I had no choice but to back away toward Sherlock Holmes's workbench, all the while looking for a defensive weapon. Then came the swish of the knife and I felt a sharp, stinging pain in my upper abdomen, followed by the warm sensation of blood on my skin. I quickly retreated, again desperately searching for anything to protect myself. All I saw was the microscope on Holmes's workbench. It was of no use, and now my back was to the wall.

Suddenly the brute let out a loud cry of pain, for Joanna had swung an iron stoker at the lateral aspect of his kneecap. He dropped his knife and grasped for his knee, then spun around to face Joanna. This move gave me a perfect target. I threw a vicious punch to the brute's high lumbar area where his kidney would lie. He staggered once more and screamed in agony. Now over-matched and in pain, he hurriedly limped out the door and tripped over my father's outstretched leg. The brute scrambled to his feet and scurried down the stairs.

My father dashed over to my side and, seeing the blood, cried out, "You are wounded!"

"I think it is superficial, Father."

"Allow me to examine the wound." My father opened my shirt and carefully examined the stab. It was approximately three inches in length, with even edges, and barely deep enough to break the skin. Still, it bled briskly. "You are fortunate. A bit more force behind the knife and it would have entered your peritoneal cavity."

"Do you have your suturing material, Father?"

"Of course," he said, and paused to examine the wound once more. "A few sutures will close it nicely and stop the bleeding."

Joanna waited for my father to go into his room, then came over close to me and breathed, "You were magnificent!"

"I almost ended up quite dead."

"Only because the animal had to resort to a knife." Joanna glanced at the wound and used a fresh handkerchief to stem the bleeding. "And I must say that was a wonderful last punch to the kidney area. He will be more than a little upset when his urine turns to blood."

"He will be even more upset when his knee swells to the size of a melon."

Joanna nodded happily. "That was a lovely blow, wasn't it?"

My father returned and, after cleansing the wound with antiseptic, closed it with four sutures and applied a gauze bandage. "We must keep an eye out for infection."

"I will watch it carefully," I said, and glanced around the parlor. The intruder was most interested in the area where Sherlock Holmes did his investigations. Files were overturned and scattered about, while texts and notes and papers were thrown onto the floor in a haphazard fashion. Even several bottles of reagents had been knocked over, although I doubt this was done intentionally. "This was not the work of a common thief."

"By no means," Joanna agreed. "It was done with a single purpose in mind and orchestrated by Moran."

"He believes we are closing in on him, does he not?" I asked

"And he is correct," Joanna said.

I waved my hand at the clutter and disarray that my father was attempting to deal with. "Was all this done simply to determine whether or not we had broken his code?"

"Oh, he wishes to know much more than that," Joanna answered. "He is aware that we are still investigating the deaths of Charles Harrelston and Benjamin Levy. He may have even gotten details from the gardener we questioned who could not wait to tell Moran's chambermaid of our visit. And she would eagerly pass the information to Moran in hopes of some reward. Remember, members of the working class tend to form cliques and love to inform each other of what transpires in the neighborhood."

"And the manager at the Athenian Club no doubt supplied Moran with the details of our visit there," I added. "As you mentioned previously, Moran will read the actions of Toby Two as if it was a book."

My father called over from Sherlock Holmes's workbench. "All of our notes and papers on the code are gone."

"Even the last letter we obtained from Sir William?" Joanna asked.

"That too."

"I made some notes following our visit to Moran's secretary. Are they missing as well?"

My father searched through the scattered papers on the table and floor. "Gone. And the newspaper articles on the deaths of Charles Harrelston and Benjamin Levy are not to be found either."

Joanna strolled around the parlor and gazed into each room, including the bedroom previously occupied by Sherlock Holmes. "Clumsy," she said.

"What?" I asked.

"The attempt to make the burglary appear to be the work of an ordinary thief," she replied. "Drawers have been opened and some of their contents spilled out in the other rooms, but there was no real effort made to search for valuables. This is more evidence that this is the work of Christopher Moran."

"Now Moran will know exactly where we stand in our investigation," I remarked.

"And more importantly, he will try to use this information to stymie us further."

"Oh, goodness!" my father cried aloud. "Where is my brain? What has happened to my memory?

How could something so important escape my thoughts?" He reached for a thin file and shook his head dispiritedly. "This could prove to be such an integral part of our investigation, yet I could not recall it."

"What is it, Father?" I asked with concern.

"The name Moran," he replied. "I had some vague recollection of it from the past, yet could not retrieve it from my memory bank. But our thief left one box unsearched and it contains some of Holmes's most memorable cases, one of which revolves around a scoundrel named Sebastian Moran."

"Another criminal named Moran?" Joanna asked at once.

"Not simply a criminal, but a master criminal," my father said, now reading from the file. "He had served as a colonel in the First Bangalore Pioneers and distinguished himself in the Second Afghan War. He was quite senior at the time, in his late fifties, but was called upon to participate in the war because of his strategic brilliance. In any event, he returned home, only to go bad under the wing of London's most notorious criminal, Professor Moriarty. Sebastian Moran was an esteemed officer who ended up on the gallows because he chose to match wits with Sherlock Holmes."

"What was his offense?" I asked.

"The murder of the Honorable Ronald Adair,

who was shot with an expanding bullet from an air gun."

"Astounding," I said. "One would never expect that from a distinguished officer."

My father smiled at some past memory. "Holmes would tell you that some trees grow to a certain height and then suddenly divulge some unsightly eccentricity, and that often occurs in humans. Holmes believed in the theory that the individual represents the whole procession of his ancestors, and that such a turn to good or evil is from some strong influence that comes from the line of his pedigree. The person thus becomes the epitome of the history of his own family."

"Are you saying that criminal behavior is under genetic control?" I asked.

"It appears to be so here, for Sherlock made a notation in his file that Sebastian had a single son whose name was—"

"Christopher Moran!" I shouted.

"The very same. It is in his blood." My father shook his head again at his memory lapse. "And I could not recall such an important case. My brain obviously suffers from the consequences of old age."

"Your brain is fine," Joanna said. "All of us have difficulty with distant memories."

"True. But it is more marked at my age," my father said.

"Do not underestimate your value to us,"

Joanna said. "Your experience is of great importance here, and if it requires an unexpected incident to awaken your memory, so be it."

"You are kind," my father said gratefully.

"I am also very honest. Now tell me everything you recall about this Sebastian Moran, for his son may be following in his footsteps."

As you are following in your father's footsteps, Joanna, I thought. But of course I kept this secret to myself.

My father referred to the file once again, then furrowed his brow while taking his memory back over the years. "The murder victim, Ronald Adair, was killed after playing cards with Moran."

"Like Charles Harrelston," Joanna noted.

"Colonel Moran had cheated Adair during the game."

"Another remarkable similarity."

"Adair was shot through a window."

"Again death centers around a window."

"And once Sebastian Moran discovered that Sherlock Holmes was on his trail, he tried to kill Holmes."

"By what method?" Joanna asked at once.

"That escapes me."

"Please do your best on this point," Joanna urged. "Our lives could be at stake."

While my father delved into the recesses of his memory, I continued to be astonished by the brilliance of Sherlock Holmes. How could he be so aware that the traits of good and evil might well be carried on genes and passed from one generation to the next? Sebastian and Christopher Moran were prime examples of this phenomenon. And so were Joanna Blalock and her biological father, Sherlock Holmes.

My father's eyes suddenly widened. "It occurred outside. The attempt on our lives took place at night in a thick fog. But all I can recollect is being pushed to the ground."

"Was it a shot, such as the one Sebastian Moran used to kill Ronald Adair?" Joanna asked.

"I cannot be sure," my father replied in a sad voice. "It happened so many years ago."

"Why not review your file on Colonel Moran for this incident?" Joanna suggested.

My father thumbed through a stack of pages and studied each one carefully, but found nothing of the attack. "It is not mentioned."

"Are you certain it occurred?"

"I believe so, but then again my distant memory leaves much to be desired."

"You have done splendidly, Watson. The connection of Sebastian Moran to his son is of immense importance," Joanna said. "And there is no reason to strain further on this far-off memory. Chances are it will come to you given the appropriate stimulus."

"Let us hope the recollection comes before the attempt," my father said solemnly.

I accompanied Joanna back to the Blalock mansion later that evening. Alone together for the first time, we talked and touched in the closeness of our carriage. As we rode through the darkened streets of Belgravia, our bodies were drawn together by a magical force that neither of us could resist. Then we kissed tenderly and I experienced a most wonderful warmth that I had never felt before.

"You are beyond beautiful," I whispered.

"And you beyond handsome," she whispered back.

"We make a fine pair, Joanna."

"Indeed we do, dear John."

Our carriage slowed and turned into the well-lighted avenue on which Joanna lived. We smiled at each other and shared a final, warm kiss and gentle embrace. Despite the enchanting moment, I could not hide my concern over my father's gradual physical and mental decline. We agreed that it happened to all who live long enough for the years to take their toll. But still, it was most sad to see in a loved one.

"You are fortunate to have had your dear father so long," Joanna said in my arms.

"I know."

"And we are fortunate to have him help guide us through this criminal maze."

"I am aware of that as well," I said, and drew her closer. "He has pointed out the remarkable similarities between the Morans to us, and how that may bear on our case."

"Quite so."

After a long pause, I asked, "Do you truly believe Christopher Moran will attack and try to do us bodily harm?"

"Do you believe Sherlock Holmes's concept that the elements of good and evil can be passed down through the generations?"

"I do."

"There is your answer."

18

An Unexpected Death

My wound was causing considerable pain the next day, but I worked through it because of the heavy schedule. I had just completed an autopsy on a most interesting case that had riveted my attention. It appeared that a very nice woman in Brixton decided to poison her husband with strychnine. The man's face had shown severe, tetanic muscle contractions that resulted in a devilish grin, and his skin was deeply cyanotic, for such patients die of asphyxiation due to paralysis of the neural pathways that control respiration. All of these were typical signs of strychnine poisoning. As I was writing my final note, a pathology clerk hurried into my office with an important message.

"Sir, I am sorry to intrude, but your father awaits you in a carriage at the entrance."

I was caught by surprise, and asked, "Did he mention the purpose of the visit?"

"He requested that I tell you that the game was afoot," the clerk replied. "That was all he said, sir."

"That was quite enough," I said, and reached for my coat.

I rushed down the wide corridor of the pathology department, wondering what had now occurred in this almost unbelievable criminal maze in which I was involved. Was it another break-in or more murder that necessitated such an unexpected visit from my father? My best guess would be the sudden demise of Derek Cardogan, who represented the final piece of the puzzle. Before I could dwell further on the thought, I was intercepted by Professor Willoughby, who was his usual disagreeable self. Again his ill-fitting coat and stained tie were his most notable features.

"Leaving again before your time, I see," Willoughby grumbled.

"The Charles Harrelston case still requires my attention," I answered, with a half truth.

"Is there some new development?" he asked, suddenly concerned.

"There have been no significant changes, but a few loose ends need to be tied."

"So my report stands?"

"Without contradiction thus far," I replied. "But if anything of consequence comes to my attention, I shall bring it to yours."

"Excellent. Be on your way, then."

Hurrying along, I continued to think of Willoughby's arrogance and how it colored everything he did. His autopsy findings of death by trauma to Charles Harrelston's body were correct, but he repeated the word *suicide* over and over in his report. He should have only used the word *fall,* but his pomposity would not have allowed this. He had to show everyone how brilliant he was in determining not only cause, but motive behind Harrelston's death. Of course when the truth came out and a new inquiry reconvened, Willoughby would again be questioned. I looked forward to watching him attempt to squirm his way around his mistake.

I jumped into the carriage and found Joanna and my father bundled up against the very chilly noon.

"You say the game is afoot?" I asked my father.

"Most assuredly."

"What has transpired?"

"Moran's secretary is dead."

I let the unexpected news sink in and immediately wondered how and why. "And the circumstances?'

"Most suspicious."

"Is it the method you refer to?"

My father nodded. "And the timing."

Martin Morris had been bludgeoned to death late last night while returning home from a nearby pub. The obvious motive was robbery, for his wallet and personal possessions were missing. There were no witnesses to the crime.

"It is the work of Moran," Joanna said.

"How are you so certain?" I asked. "Do you have evidence to confirm your suspicions?"

"No," Joanna replied. "For I have not yet examined Morris or the crime scene."

"Then, at this point, all we have is suspicion."

"What we have here is very strong inference that cannot be easily dismissed," she explained. "Remember the chain, John. Moran is at one end and the treasure at the other. Anyone who stands in between meets a most unfortunate death. And Martin Morris was definitely in between. His demise is not a coincidence, but a revealing fact."

"Which is?" I asked at once.

"That Martin Morris was much more involved than we ever imagined."

"Perhaps he just learned of something?" I argued.

"While he was in the midst of packing?" Joanna countered. "That would be most unlikely."

"So you are saying that Moran wanted Morris dead, for his secretary knew far too much?"

"That is the only plausible explanation."

As we rode along, the air became even more frigid and our exhaled breaths turned frosty. Joanna and I drew closer together to enjoy each other's warmth and touch, which my father noticed with a brief smile before looking away. I pulled up my blanket to cover more of us and this provided an opportunity for our hidden hands to come together and hold. The pain from my stab wound, which had bothered me so much earlier, magically disappeared.

A half hour later we found Inspector Lestrade leaning over the battered body of Martin Morris. The victim's head was bashed in, crown and back, with bone and brain exposed. There was a large pool of clotted blood that extended from his neck to the curb of the sidewalk.

Lestrade tipped his derby to me. "Nasty business here. We suspect that Mr. Morris knew his assailant, for the head wounds were meant to kill. The robber did not wish the victim to live and later identify him."

"A rational line of thinking," Joanna said. "But not correct in this instance."

"And why not?" Lestrade asked.

"The position of the head wounds," Joanna pointed out. "The vast majority of trauma is evident in the rear and occipital area of the skull, which indicates that the vicious blows were delivered from behind. I suspect that Mr. Morris never saw his assailant coming."

"Perhaps the murderer walked by Mr. Morris, then turned on him," Lestrade responded quickly. "That being the case, Mr. Morris would have surely seen him."

"Perhaps, but unlikely. An assailant approaching a prospective victim late at night would cause alarm, which is the very last thing the assailant would want."

"So you believe the assailant followed Mr. Morris home, then."

"It is more likely that the assailant lay in wait for Mr. Morris. Following someone undetected late at night when the streets are empty is no simple matter." Joanna turned and surveyed the nearby buildings. She motioned to a narrow alleyway between two rowhouses some twenty feet away. "That would be the ideal hiding place at night. It would be dark and nothing within could be seen from the street or sidewalk. I will wager that is where the assailant perched himself and waited for Martin Morris to pass."

"You could never prove that in a hundred years," Lestrade challenged.

"Let us have a look and see." Joanna strolled over to the alleyway, but did not enter. She studied the mud-covered ground just off the sidewalk and counted to herself. "Six."

"Six what?" Lestrade asked.

"Stubs of cigarettes," Joanna answered. "Which strongly suggests our assailant waited here for at least an hour before his prey arrived. It requires ten to fifteen minutes for even an anxious smoker to finish one cigarette and light another. Thus, our murderer stood here and smoked for an hour or more."

"Maybe there was more than one," Lestrade said.

Joanna shook her head. "I see footprints in the mud made only by the same shoe. A size twelve, I would approximate, which indicates our assailant was a quite large man."

"Blimey! Next you will tell me what the man looked like."

Joanna moved into the alleyway and studied the footprint and cigarette stubs at length, then searched the brick wall behind the stubs. Standing on her tiptoes, she plucked a black thread from a jagged-edged brick. "The soles of his inexpensive shoes show he is a member of the working class, as do his cigarettes, which are of the cheapest variety. He is a large man indeed, for the depth of his footprint says he must weigh two hundred or more pounds. His height would be six feet as evidenced by the length of his stride and by the area of the brick wall he rested against while waiting. Here," she said and held up a black thread, "is a thread from his coat that caught onto a jagged brick, where he leaned back. His coat was black and made of coarse wool. We know he was a very heavy smoker so we can assume he has a chronic cough, yellow teeth, and yellowing of his fingers where he grasps his cigarettes. Several of the stubs have a speck of blood on them so he may well have poor dental hygiene or an injured lip from a fall or fight. Finally, Inspector, you may wish to question the nearby pub and ask if a man fitting that description was in the establishment at the same time as Morris."

Lestrade pressed a hand against his brow and

shook his head at the same time. "My brain is in a whirl, madam. How is it that you make so much from so little?"

"It is because I have observed, and you have only seen," Joanna replied. "There is an obvious difference."

"So I am learning," Lestrade said. "Now please allow me to ask what makes you believe that our assailant was in the pub?"

"No thief worth his salt would wait in last night's rain on the chance some worthwhile victim would pass by. No, that would never do. More likely, our assailant was in the pub, watching Morris, so he could set the time and place of his assault."

"Then I shall inquire if such a man left the pub shortly before Morris departed."

"Not shortly before, but at least an hour in advance of Morris's departure," Joanna corrected. "And do not forget that the assailant was a stranger in this middle-class neighborhood. He would stand out among the clientele that the pub usually served."

Lestrade gaped in amazement at Joanna's insight, while my father and I simply exchanged knowing glances. After all, we were thinking, one would expect nothing less from the daughter of Sherlock Holmes.

"Would you care to examine the body?" Lestrade asked, gathering himself.

"We should have the younger Dr. Watson perform the examination, for this is his area of expertise," Joanna suggested.

"Very well," Lestrade said. "But we must hurry because the body will soon be transported to a nearby funeral home in preparation for burial, the expense of which the good Dr. Moran has graciously consented to cover."

A thin smile crossed Joanna's face. "Moran, you say."

"Dr. Moran himself, for Mr. Morris has no family left in this world. I had called Scotland to determine if the remains should be shipped north for burial. The officer in charge of the small town informed me there were no relatives and no funds, for the family has always been poor as church mice."

"Did you inquire further about Morris's past history?" Joanna asked.

"Oh, yes. The officer I spoke with was a long-term resident of the town and knew the family's story well. Mr. Morris was an orphan raised by a couple who were always down on their luck. As a lad he was quite bright and eventually received a scholarship to a nearby college where he fell in with a bad lot. He was arrested several times for unlawful entry and thievery, and jailed briefly before being dismissed and leaving town altogether."

"Never to return?" Joanna asked.

"Never, to the best of the officer's recollection."

"Then he shows up on the doorstep of Dr. Moran and becomes secretary to a distinguished physician."

"So it would appear."

"That is a rather strange route, would you not agree?"

Lestrade shrugged. "Sometimes the bad reform themselves. In any event, Dr. Moran had no complaints about Mr. Morris's work habits and considered him a good employee who was liked by all. And he was trusted as well. For health reasons, Mr. Morris decided to retire and move to Spain where he would look after Dr. Moran's house on the coast near Barcelona. From this we can conclude that Mr. Morris was a trusted employee indeed."

"Inspector, does it not strike you as odd there are so many deaths surrounding Dr. Moran?" Joanna asked. "First, Mr. Charles Harrelston, then Mr. Benjamin Levy, and now Martin Morris?"

"All easily explainable, with no evidence of any connection," Lestrade said, with a shrug. "Mr. Harrelston took his own life, Mr. Levy accidentally choked to death, and Mr. Morris met his end as a result of a brutal robbery. I see nothing to tie these unfortunate events to Dr. Moran."

"Just a coincidence, then?" Joanna asked.

"In my professional opinion, yes," Lestrade said authoritatively. "I would put it all down to coincidence, for there is no evidence whatsoever to implicate Dr. Moran in these deaths."

"You have done a most thorough inquiry, Inspector," Joanna said. "The details on Martin Morris are very helpful."

"Thank you, madam."

"There are one or two points I would like to be sure of, however. You say that Mr. Morris's family was poor."

"As church mice, I was told."

"So there were no real estate holdings or other such assets in the family?"

"Most definitely not," Lestrade assured. "The town had to take up a collection to bury the couple and prevent each from being laid to rest in a potter's field."

"And finally, when was Mr. Morris's move to the delightful coast of Spain scheduled to occur?"

"That was a sad part of the story, madam. According to Dr. Moran, the movers had come for Mr. Morris's goods several days ago, but refused to perform their work unless paid in advance. The shipment to Spain was of considerable expense, which Moran had graciously agreed to pay, as a parting gift I was told."

"How generous," Joanna said.

"Very generous indeed. However, Dr. Moran had unexpectedly been called away from the city and in his rush had neglected to leave a check for the movers. Thus, the move had to be rescheduled. Dr. Moran was most apologetic for this oversight, and vowed to rectify it. He was very distraught over his forgetfulness when he was at the crime scene earlier, for had the move proceeded as scheduled, Mr. Morris would still be alive today."

"I would suspect that Mr. Morris was quite upset at the delay."

"Not to any great extent, for last night Dr. Moran came by to drop off the check to the waiting movers, then the two went to a nearby pub for a farewell toast."

Joanna's brow went up. "Did they make an evening of it?"

"Oh, no. Just a pint and then Dr. Moran had to be on his way, for he had another engagement that very night. But the doctor assured me he left Mr. Morris in good spirits."

"Very illuminating," Joanna said, more to herself than to the inspector.

Lestrade took the comment as a compliment. "Thank you, madam."

"You are very welcome," Joanna said, then turned her attention to me and the corpse. "Have you found anything revealing, John?"

I arose from my kneeling position and brushed the dust from the knees of my trousers. "The head wounds were more horrid than we initially thought. They are massive, particularly in the occipital area, where the fractures extend down into the mid-brain. The blows were delivered with a blunt weapon, either a bludgeon or similar type sap, and were clearly meant to kill."

"Delivered from behind, no doubt."

"Most certainly, and with great force. In addition, I think we can safely conclude that Mr. Morris was no stranger to violence, for there is a well-healed scar on his neck that was poorly sutured and extends from his ear to his larynx. Someone with a terrible grudge once slit Mr. Morris's throat."

Joanna nodded and looked over to Lestrade. "This type of wound is not the sort that occurs to a petty thief."

Lestrade had to nod as well. "There is a violent past here. I wonder if Dr. Moran was aware."

Joanna smiled ever so slightly because to her the answer was self-evident. Then she came back to me. "Is there anything else noteworthy?"

"Nothing that I could see without stripping the corpse and performing an autopsy."

"It would be no problem for us to postpone the burial," Lestrade offered.

"No need," Joanna declined. "Mr. Morris's body has told us quite enough."

"So you would agree that this portion of the investigation has been successfully concluded?"

"I do indeed. But there are one or two other matters that may be of some importance."

"Such as?"

"I take it that the movers collected all of Mr. Morris's goods last night?"

"They did and I suspect they have reached Southampton by now. His goods may in fact already be on their way to Spain. When they reach their destination, Dr. Moran will have an employee unpack the boxes and turn their contents over to a local charity. I thought that that would—" Lestrade stopped himself in mid-sentence and blinked rapidly. "Do you believe we should have those boxes searched?"

"I think that would turn up very little, but I do recommend you thoroughly search Mr. Morris's rooms."

"That is presently being done."

"Then let us go to the pub that Mr. Morris and Dr. Moran visited last night."

"For what purpose, may I ask?"

"To discover the assailant, of course."

We walked at a brisk pace down Edgware Road, with Lestrade taking the lead. The noise from passing cars and carriages was enough to drown out any conversation and I did not wish to talk above it, for my words were not meant for Lestrade's ears. The inspector rounded a corner and now was completely out of sight and earshot.

I moved in closer to Joanna and whispered, "Morris is as big a liar as Moran."

"But not nearly as deadly," Joanna whispered back.

"How involved do you think Morris was?"

"Right up to his teeth."

We entered the pub called the Rose and Lamb and found it very busy. The barstools were all occupied as were the tables and booths. A chubby, big-breasted barmaid was dashing about and shouting drink orders back to a rotund barkeeper whose most outstanding feature was a red, bulbous nose.

Lestrade showed the barkeeper his credentials and said, "We have questions for you regarding Mr. Martin Morris."

"Ask away. guv'ner," he said, showing no unease.

"Were you on duty last night?" Lestrade asked.

"I am on duty every night and every day, for I own this pub, you see."

"Good. The lady here has some questions for you."

As Joanna stepped forward, the barkeeper chuckled to himself and asked derisively, "Would you like a nice cup of tea before we begin?"

"See here," Lestrade said sternly. "The lady is a consultant to Scotland Yard and you will show her the proper respect."

"I meant no offense," the barkeeper said, but he continued to grin.

"Let us be clear," Joanna said, and pressed the point. "I would like the truth and, if it is not forthcoming, the inspector will march you out in handcuffs. No doubt you will wish to leave that peculiar smile on your face behind."

The barkeeper's grin disappeared immediately. "Very sorry, madam. I truly am."

"I am not interested in your apologies, but only want to hear what you know for a fact and can answer to in a court of law. Do you understand?"

"Yes, madam."

"To start, did you know Martin Morris?"

"Oh, yes. He was a regular and came in at least twice a week."

"By himself?"

"Almost always, for he was a confirmed bachelor and told everyone he preferred to remain so."

"But last night was the exception."

"He came in with a gentleman of some standing and each had a pint of Guinness dark."

"How long did their visit last?"

"The gentleman departed after his pint, but Martin stayed on for a good many more."

"How many?"

"Five, by my count."

"So he was in good spirits."

"He seemed very happy because he was on his way to live in Spain. At least, that is what he told us."

"There was another man in here last night whom I doubt you have ever seen before. You would quickly notice a stranger to your pub, would you not?"

"From the second he entered."

"There was a large man, tall, over two hundred pounds in weight, who smoked one cigarette after another and probably had a wheezing cough. He would have stood off to the side, for he wished not to be noticed."

The barkeeper thought back briefly, then said, "I do remember him. He positioned himself off by the far wall, yet always faced the bar itself."

"Can you describe him for us?"

"I cannot, madam, and that is the truth. He stood in a darkened area and I did not see him up close, for he ordered his drinks from the barmaid. She had a better look at him and even mentioned he was a mean-looking bloke. I didn't pay it much attention because, if you cause trouble in here, you shortly find yourself in the street. Shall I call her over?"

"Please."

"Janie!" he cried out and waited for her to approach. "These people are from Scotland Yard and have some questions about that mean-looking bloke you served last night."

She recalled him instantly. "He was the type that you wanted to stay clear of."

Joanna asked, "Can you describe him?"

"Ugh!" Janie made a twisted face. "He had a big, apelike head, with a split lip, and he kept coughing over everything. He only bought one pint and didn't bother to leave a farthing extra behind."

I tried to hold my composure, for the man the barmaid was describing was almost certainly the brutish intruder I had fought the night before.

"How long would you say he remained in the pub?" I asked.

"Thirty minutes at most," Janie said. "Then he hurried out."

"Did he have a normal gait?"

She shook her head. "He had a bad limp, but it didn't stop him from scurrying out."

The barkeeper leaned over the bar and asked in a most serious voice, "Do you think that bloke had something to do with what happened to Martin Morris?"

Joanna shrugged indifferently. "We are only looking into all possibilities. Thank you for your assistance."

Outside, Lestrade could not wait to announce, "That mean-looking bloke is our assailant. In this very pub, he picked out Martin Morris as a likely target and followed him home."

"Spot on, Inspector," Joanna said.

"I shall put out a description of this man over all of London and can only hope he will show his face again."

"I am afraid he is long gone with his ill-gotten goods."

"We shall see."

Lestrade strode happily away, with his new but hopeless mission. We all knew that, unless the assailant walked into the very halls of Scotland Yard, he would never be seen again.

"Lestrade is half correct," Joanna said. "The assailant was not in the pub to choose a victim; he was there waiting for Moran to point the victim out. It was all nicely planned. Moran planted the murderer in the pub, then invited Martin Morris for a friendly, parting drink. Now the murderer knew how Martin Morris looked, where he lived, and what route he would take home. It was a perfect setup."

"And of course the assailant is none other than the brute who broke into my father's rooms last night," I added.

"Beyond any doubt," Joanna said with a sweet smile. "And asking the barmaid about the brute's gait was a very nice touch, John. His obvious limp was the icing on the cake."

"With any luck, he will limp the rest of his life," I hoped.

"I struck his knee with that in mind," Joanna said without inflection. "But now let us return to Martin Morris, for everything he told us was an out-and-out lie, which he may have rehearsed prior to our visit. He did not go to university, but to a local college. He did not leave to enter a business venture, but was dismissed because of criminal behavior. There was no family real estate in Scotland, for they were poor as church mice. And he did not inherit that house in Spain, which belongs to Dr. Moran, from any dead uncle. Lies! All lies!"

"But why deceive?" I asked.

"Because he is involved and does not want his true past known."

"But why? Is it because of fear of further criminal charges?"

"It is that and more, for Martin Morris assisted in the murder of Charles Harrelston," Joanna said. "He was the accomplice lying on the couch in Moran's parlor who pretended to be Charles Harrelston."

"I say!" my father cried out. "What proof do you have of this?"

"Allow me to draw your attention to the account of events given by Mrs. Lambert," Joanna went on. "She distinctly told us that, apart from Charles Harrelston, there were only two visitors to the Moran house that morning."

"The two ill patients," I interjected.

"Each of whom she escorted *out*," Joanna emphasized. "And recall that Mrs. Lambert zealously guarded both doors to the house so no others could gain entrance. That leaves Christopher Moran, Charles Harrelston, and the accomplice as the only occupants in the residence. Now pray tell, how did the accomplice enter the house under Mrs. Lambert's watchful eye?"

My father and I gave the matter careful thought,

then shrugged at each other, for there seemed no apparent way for the accomplice to enter the house without being discovered by Mrs. Lambert.

At length I suggested, "Perhaps Moran secretly left the tradesman's door unlocked."

"That would be far too risky," Joanna countered. "The housekeeper may well have found it as such and relocked the door. In addition, there was always the very real possibility that ever vigilant Mrs. Lambert would see the stranger entering and all would be lost. Keep in mind that our Dr. Moran is a very cunning fellow who will not take unnecessary chances nor commit stupid mistakes."

"But the accomplice had to make his way in somehow," I pondered.

"He came through the front door," Joanna said. "For, as I pointed out, the accomplice and Martin Morris were one and the same."

"But Morris had departed for a prolonged lunch when the murder occurred," I argued.

"By whose account?" Joanna challenged.

"Christopher Moran's and Martin Morris's."

"Both liars."

"But Mrs. Lambert is not, and she vouched that Martin Morris was gone at the time of Harrelston's fall."

"Pshaw!" Joanna said dismissively. "The housekeeper vouched for an empty desk and assumed Martin Morris had left for lunch. So

311

I implore you to do the arithmetic. By Mrs. Lambert's honest account, all visitors had exited except for Charles Harrelston, which indicated he alone was in the home with Christopher Moran. Yet an accomplice who had no way of entering suddenly appeared. This sequence does not fit the facts we have before us. The only possible explanation is that the accomplice entered the house much earlier and would raise no suspicion, for he had a familiar face. Thus, all the evidence points to Martin Morris. He no doubt made a rapid exit while the housekeeper was fetching a glass of water in the kitchen."

"So, despite Christopher Moran's coaxing, it was after all Mrs. Lambert who provided the important clue here," I remarked.

"Indeed," Joanna said. "The guardian at the gate is always the best counter of heads."

My father seemed lost in thought for a moment, then his eyes twinkled and he asserted, "Martin Morris was quite nearby when the murder occurred. He actually helped dispose of the body."

"From what do you draw this conclusion?" Joanna asked at once.

My father smiled slyly. "Why, I used your very splendid deductive skills. Charles Harrelston was killed while at the Chubb safe, was he not?"

"He was," Joanna agreed.

"And Charles Harrelston was a big man, almost as large as Moran, was he not?"

"He was."

"Then how did Christopher Moran move this heavy body up a steep flight of stairs to the roof? Remember, this was dead weight and had the body of Charles Harrelston been dragged up the stairs, which would have been a most difficult feat, we would have seen scuff marks from his shoes on the steps, which were not present. So the corpse must have been carried up."

"By Moran and Martin Morris, who lent a hand to this dastardly deed!" I exclaimed.

My father nodded, with the most pleased of expressions.

"Brilliant, Watson! Absolutely brilliant!" Joanna took his hand and gave it a gentle squeeze. "You have outdone yourself. And never speak to me again about your brain going soft."

I clapped my father on his back. "Even Sherlock would applaud, Father."

As I gazed at his happy face, I remembered the words he had spoken early in this story. When asked why he continued to see visitors seeking Sherlock Holmes's advice, he had replied, "I am merely an old man trying to remain relevant." Well, here he was, being very relevant indeed this day. And he knew it.

At that moment Lestrade ran up to us and paused to catch his breath. His face was flushed with excitement. "Look what one of my men found hidden under the floor in Martin Morris's closet." He reached for a wide manila envelope and extracted a thick stack of ten-pound notes. "A fat cache of one thousand pounds!"

"A fortune for a man on a secretary's salary," I commented.

"Now we know what the thief was after," Lestrade said.

"I wonder how a secretary could accumulate such a large sum," Joanna mused, and gave me and my father the subtlest of smiles.

"A very good question, which crossed my mind as well, madam," Lestrade said. "Rest assured we shall investigate the matter thoroughly."

The three of us exchanged knowing glances, for the source of the money was abundantly clear. It was payment from Christopher Moran. It was blackmail!

19

Derek Cardogan

Near noon the following day we set out to interview the man who represented the final piece of the puzzle.

"How did you obtain Derek Cardogan's address?" I asked.

"From the window tax records," Joanna replied.

"Surely you jest." The window tax was a fee levied on all dwellings in London and was based on the number of windows in a house. The greater the number of windows, the greater the size of the house, and thus the higher the tax. "I know for a fact those tax records are sealed and remain strictly confidential."

"Not if your father-in-law was once Chancellor of the Exchequer," Joanna said.

"Did you dare use his influence?"

Joanna smiled craftily. "He was of some small assistance."

As we continued our journey through the Knightsbridge area, I gazed out at the pricy shops and restaurants and the finely dressed patrons entering them. Derek Cardogan had to be quite wealthy to live in this neighborhood, yet he still desired his share of the hidden treasure, which no doubt was illegally obtained and thus had to be concealed from the public eye. But I kept remembering Joanna's statement that greed was a strange transformer of the human character.

As our carriage turned onto Sloane Square, my father broke the silence, saying, "I am surprised Mr. Cardogan agreed to be interviewed."

"He did not agree and has no idea of our impending visit," Joanna said.

"Then he will most certainly refuse to see us unannounced."

"Oh, he will see us promptly."

"Why are you so confident?"

"Because I will present him with a very persuasive message."

Our carriage pulled up in front of an impressive four-story brick home, with window frames that were painted a sparkling white. Its door was solid mahogany, the brass fittings polished and gleaming. All drapes were drawn, save for those on the second floor. I saw a face peeking out, but could not define its features.

We rang the bell of 510 Sloane Square and waited. The butler took his time before answering and promptly refused our entry.

"Mr. Cardogan is indisposed and is not receiving today," he said haughtily.

"I am certain Mr. Cardogan will wish to see us," Joanna persisted.

"Perhaps another day, madam."

Joanna reached into her purse for a sealed envelope, and handed it to the butler. "Please deliver this message to Mr. Cardogan. It explains the urgency of our visit."

The door closed, and we waited in bright sunshine.

"What is in the envelope?" I asked.

"A message that states we are here to discuss his share," Joanna said.

"That should rouse his attention."

"Particularly since it was written in their secret code."

A moment later the door opened and the butler informed us that Derek Cardogan had consented to our visit. He led the way into a spacious library, which was expensively furnished and had bound books lining all the walls except for the one that contained the windows. With its hanging tapestries and oil paintings, there was an opulence to the library, but it still seemed old and tired. The air held the unpleasant, musty odor of the sick.

Derek Cardogan was slouched down in a large, cushioned chair and did not rise to greet us, nor did he offer us seats. He appeared to be a wasted man, thin and jaundiced, with hollowed cheeks and hair that looked as if it had not been washed recently. He wore a thick, red robe which seemed far too large for his small frame.

"I am very ill, and do not wish to be bothered," Cardogan groused. "So make your visit brief."

"We regret the intrusion, Mr. Cardogan," Joanna told him. "But I am afraid you have a choice to make. Our intrusion, or your sudden death. Please choose."

"Are you referring to death by malaria?" Cardogan asked in a hoarse voice.

"I am referring to death by murder, such as occurred to your friends Charles Harrelston and Benjamin Levy."

Cardogan flicked his wrist dismissively. "Harrelston died by suicide, Levy by accident."

"How convenient their sudden deaths were," Joanna said. "Is it not strange that two of your partners left this world within days of each other and under such unusual circumstances?"

"These things happen."

"Yes, they do. Particularly when the deaths greatly benefit those remaining behind."

Cardogan narrowed his eyes. "I see no benefits from their deaths."

"But Christopher Moran did. Now he will keep their shares."

"Wh-what shares are you referring to?" Cardogan asked defensively.

"The share I mentioned in my message to you that gained us immediate entry into your library."

"I was merely curious regarding what you meant by the word *share* in your note."

"Come, come! You are not doing well at all here. In my note, I did write the word *share,* but I jotted it down in code known only to you and the other members of the quartet."

Cardogan stared back at her in silence, having no answer.

"Moran has no intention of giving you your share of the treasure. He will murder you for your share, as he murdered Harrelston and Levy for theirs."

"Ridiculous!" Cardogan raised his voice in protest. "We were all comrades in arms, and trusted each other with our lives during war. Christopher Moran is not a murderer, and it is scandalous that you even suggest that he is."

"It is the truth, whether you wish to accept it or not."

"Where is the proof of these accusations?"

"Right before your eyes if you will only see it. Think for a moment about the circumstances of your friends' sudden deaths. Harrelston, a stout-hearted fellow, jumps to his death over a debt that he knows his share of the treasure will easily cover. And Levy chokes on drink while asleep! These events do not ring true in any natural order. And add to them, the most recent murder last night of Martin Morris, Moran's former secretary."

Cardogan's eyes flew wide open. "Morris, dead?"

"Quite. With his head bashed in during an apparent robbery."

"A robbery! There you have it. Morris was not killed by Moran."

"But it was planned by Moran, who staged the robbery to cover the murder."

"Again, where is your evidence?"

"It is being collected and evaluated by Scotland Yard at this very moment."

"How would you be aware of this?"

"Because I am a consultant to Scotland Yard and am privy to what they do and what information they have." Joanna gave Cardogan a long, serious look and said, "We are here to save your life, the end of which is quite near. You must act now or suffer the consequences."

"I am steadfast in my trust of Christopher Moran, and none of your inferences or unproven evidence will sway me."

"It will only require simple precautions to prevent your murder."

"Bah! I need no protection from my dear friend Christopher Moran. He was here only yesterday to assure me all is well."

"All is well with your share? Is that what he meant?"

Cardogan's face closed. His mind was made up.

Joanna glanced at my father and gave him a subtle signal to continue the conversation as planned.

"Mr. Cardogan, my name is John Watson and I am a physician quite familiar with malaria."

"Watson? Dr. John Watson?" Derek Cardogan seemed to come to life. "The John Watson who chronicled the Sherlock Holmes adventures?"

"The very same."

"I am honored to meet you, sir."

"It is my pleasure," my father said warmly. "May we put aside our talk of murder and instead speak of malaria, in which I have considerable experience. I am afraid my medical curiosity has taken hold of me, but if you wish not to discuss your case, I will understand."

"Not at all," Cardogan said, now at ease. "All expert opinions are welcome."

"May I inquire where you contracted the disease?"

"In Afghanistan, during the Second Afghan War."

"I see. But while a member of the military, were you not given tablets of quinine to ingest as a precaution?"

"We were indeed, sir. And the quinine tablets worked wonderfully well. But then we were taken prisoner by the Ghazis and were forced to live under the harshest of conditions. Our supply of quinine ran out and I was most unfortunate to contract malaria."

"Did the others as well?"

"Luck was with them until they came down

with enteric fevers that nearly killed them," Cardogan recounted. "Their diseases eventually subsided, but mine remained."

"Even with quinine treatment?" my father asked.

"At first it worked nicely, but then over time I grew resistant to the drug. Now it has little effect at all."

"What about the newer forms of quinine?"

Cardogan managed a weak smile. "Ah! I see you are truly well informed on this disease. The French have discovered the most effective form of quinine, but apparently it carries risks that can be quite serious. For that reason I was hesitant to allow the treatment while in Paris. But now, my malaria has worsened even more and I am left with little choice but to undergo therapy with an injectable form of quinine at St. Bartholomew's Hospital."

"There is a very fine specialist in malaria at St. Bartholomew's named Stephen Marburg," my father advised. "Perhaps you should see him."

"I have already, and it will be Dr. Marburg who supervises my therapy tomorrow."

"Will he be responsible for your overall care while you are hospitalized?"

"He, along with my very dear friend Christopher Moran."

"Let us hope all goes well for you."

We bade Derek Cardogan good-bye, and

stepped back out into the bright sunlight. It being such a fine day, we decided to walk about the fashionable area and gather our thoughts. Shops were busy with English and foreign patrons, the restaurants full, with long waiting queues. Traffic was heavy and noisy in both directions as one expensive carriage after another passed by. We strolled on the edge of Sloane Square, where the crowd had thinned and we could not be overheard.

"I cannot believe that Derek Cardogan is so dense that he does not see the danger Moran represents," I said.

"Cardogan is not dense," my father stated. "He is a former soldier who trusted his life to a devoted, loyal friend during a fierce war. Remember, it was Moran's medical skills that spared the quartet from the knives of the Ghazis. So to Derek Cardogan, Moran is a faithful, brave compatriot who saved his life. It is very difficult to envision a man who once saved your life now deciding to take it."

"But why kill Cardogan? The poor man looks half dead from malaria now. Why not wait just a bit longer?"

"Because he may survive and improve with the new treatment."

"But if Cardogan does survive, why does not Moran simply give him his quarter share and send him on his way?" I asked.

"Greed," Joanna answered. "For you see, Moran is now concerned that Cardogan will demand half of Harrelston's and Levy's shares as well, if he has not already done so. After all, Cardogan will surely believe that he and Moran should share equally. Moran of course will think otherwise."

"But Cardogan is already a wealthy man," I argued.

"Greed has no end," Joanna replied. "It is like a bottomless well that cannot be filled. And at times the wealthiest are the worst offenders."

"It also affected Martin Morris," I surmised. "For he no doubt demanded more and more from Moran, and that cost him his life."

"That and the fact that he had a loose tongue," Joanna said. "Recall how vividly he described Moran's temper and deceit. He was cleverly covering himself in the event Moran was discovered. Moran, being the scoundrel that he is, would try to incriminate Morris to save his own skin. Were that to occur, Morris would proclaim his innocence and point back to our interview with him, in which he was so honest and helpful."

"I never gave Martin Morris credit for that much cleverness."

"Do not underestimate criminals, John. When it comes to survival, they can be as slippery as snakes."

"Oh, I almost forgot," my father interjected.

"Inspector Lestrade came by this morning with some additional, interesting information on Martin Morris. On further inquiry, it seems Morris was arrested ten years ago in Liverpool for assault with a deadly weapon. He pleaded guilty and spent five years in Dartmoor prison. It was during his imprisonment that he no doubt learned to speak French. You see, his cellmate was born and raised in France."

"It was at Dartmoor where I suspect Morris got his throat slit," Joanna commented. "I daresay he was much more than a petty thief who had graduated to blackmail."

"He and Moran were truly birds of a feather," I noted.

"Of the most vicious variety," Joanna said, then came back to my father. "Were there other interesting tidbits?"

"Oh, indeed there were," my father went on. "Scotland Yard looked further into Martin Morris's finances. He had recently opened a banking account for an amount of over two thousand pounds. Such a large deposit aroused the interest of the bank manager who questioned Morris regarding its origin. Would either of you care to guess where Morris stated the money came from?"

"The dead uncle who left him the house in Spain," Joanna answered.

"The very same."

"When was the large deposit made?" Joanna asked.

"Two days ago."

Joanna nodded. "I would assume that the thousand pounds found in Morris's closet was the first blackmail payment. The recent bank deposit was the second."

I nodded back. "Morris must have doubled his blackmail demand."

"And that cost him his life."

"There is one further piece of information that I believe you will find fascinating," my father said, and rubbed his hands together gleefully. "This will close the circle of all concerned. A moment ago I mentioned that Martin Morris spent five years in Dartmoor, which houses some of England's worst and most violent offenders. Would you care to try your luck on who was Morris's cellmate while he was imprisoned there?"

Joanna and I exchanged quizzical looks.

"A most violent chap, named George Girard. He is described as six feet one and weighing two hundred pounds, with a distinct apelike face."

"The intruder!" I exclaimed.

"Precisely," my father said.

"But why then would Moran bring Girard to the pub?" I asked. "Morris would certainly recognize his former cellmate."

"That was my mistake," Joanna admitted. "I

initially thought Moran had planted a thug in the pub to point out Morris. But now we know the thug was George Girard who had shared a cell at Dartmoor with Martin Morris. There was no need for Moran to show Girard who his target was, because Girard already knew Morris quite well."

"So why was Girard in the pub?" I queried.

"There is only one plausible answer," Joanna replied. "He was there to protect Martin Morris."

I shook my head in puzzlement. "You will have to explain how you reached that conclusion."

"It is somewhat convoluted reasoning, but it fits all the facts we have at hand," Joanna said. "We can all agree that Morris introduced Girard to Moran, so Moran could hire the thug to search Watson's rooms. Hence, all three men knew one another. And like all thieves, there was no trust between them. Thus, when Moran failed to show up to pay the movers, Morris became concerned that Moran would not hold up his end of the agreement. At this point, Morris began to fear for his life because he knew how vicious a blackmailed Moran could be."

"So Martin Morris hired Girard to protect himself from Christopher Moran," I deduced.

Joanna nodded. "And that is why George Girard was in the pub."

"But why did Girard kill Morris?"

"Because Moran paid him handsomely to do so," Joanna went on. "Once Moran noticed

Girard in the pub, he understood why the thug was present. He was there for protection."

"Or perhaps Moran thought that Morris and Girard planned to kill him, so they could gain possession of the contents in the safe," my father suggested.

"I doubt that," Joanna said. "If that were the case, Girard would not have made himself so noticeable in the pub. In all likelihood, Girard was there to protect Morris, and when he stepped outside the pub he was approached by Moran and given a large sum to do the killing. It was the perfect double-cross." Joanna smiled briefly to herself. "I tell you this Moran is a real beauty."

"Do you think George Girard will ever be apprehended and verify your suspicions?" I asked.

"I do not think we will ever see or hear of George Girard again, for I believe he is now dead or shortly will be. You see, Christopher Moran does not like loose ends, and George Girard was the only living witness to his last evil deed."

"With this new information, even Lestrade has become suspicious now," my father told us. "And the last thing we need is Lestrade snooping around and alerting Moran further."

"Were you able to throw Lestrade off course?" Joanna asked concernedly.

"I did my best," my father replied. "I suggested

he double-check the story of Morris's family poverty and search for any hidden real estate transactions that may have occurred in Scotland. Also, I thought it worthwhile to look into the local gambling houses and see if Morris had had a run of good luck. And finally, I attempted to dissuade him from questioning Moran further on this matter."

"How did you manage that?"

"By telling him that the good Dr. Moran had already suffered enough distress with the loss of two close friends and a valued secretary. I thought that other, more likely avenues should be investigated first."

"Well done, Watson," Joanna said. "That should throw Lestrade off the trail until we have brought our work to a finish."

"And how does this finish come about?"

"We have to set a trap that will be irresistible to Moran."

"But he will surely see through it, being the clever devil that he is."

"If it is done correctly, he will not see it as a trap, but as a perfect opportunity."

"Is this trap already in your mind?" my father asked eagerly.

"Only sections of it," Joanna answered. "For I require more detailed information to put it into play. If it is not constructed perfectly, it will not succeed."

"Will you obtain this necessary information from your books?"

"Books will be of little value here," Joanna said. "This information has to come from the most reliable of sources."

"Which are?"

"Our colleagues."

20

The Staging

Grand rounds were held every Thursday in a large amphitheater at St. Bartholomew's Hospital. There was rarely a vacant seat, for at this conference the most difficult cases were presented for either diagnostic or therapeutic consideration. This day the patient to be discussed was Derek Cardogan and his drug-resistant malaria. As was the custom, senior staff occupied the front rows, while those of lesser rank filled the benches farther back.

I purposely seated myself near the very rear, so I could be within whispering distance of Joanna who had secured a space directly behind me. She was dressed in a starched nurse's uniform, but it did not stand out because there were other nurses in similar attire around her. At the podium below was Dr. Stephen Marburg, a world-renowned expert on malaria, and standing next to him was Christopher Moran. Although the men were engaged in earnest conversation, Moran appeared to periodically scan the audience and on one occasion I had the distinct impression he was staring at me.

"Cardogan looks even more dreadful today," Joanna whispered. "His jaundice has deepened to the point he no longer appears to be Caucasian."

"It is the lighting in the amphitheater that projects a yellow glow on the fairest skin," I whispered back. "But you are correct in that he is obviously sicker than when we saw him last."

"They had better hurry with their new treatment or they will not have a living patient to treat."

"I am sure they are aware."

Joanna lowered her whisper further. "And if he dies, we will lose our bait for the trap."

"So, all is ready?"

"Not quite. I still require two more vital pieces of information."

"When and from where will this information come?"

"It will come now and from Dr. Stephen Marburg."

As if on cue, Marburg brought a heavy hand down on the podium and the amphitheater immediately quieted. He was a tall, distinguished physician, with salt-and-pepper hair, sharp features, and a commanding voice that even those on the very last row could hear well.

"The topic today is drug-resistant malaria which, as many of you know, is becoming more and more prevalent," Marburg began, then went on to describe how Derek Cardogan had contracted the illness while serving in the Second

Afghan War. He emphasized that had Cardogan been able to secure quinine tablets during his captivity by the Ghazis, he may never have been afflicted with the disease. Upon his release, Cardogan was treated with quinine, but the response was modest at best, and over the years the parasite responsible for malaria grew resistant to the drug.

"And the effects of drug resistance can be clearly seen in Mr. Cardogan," Marburg said to the audience, then pointed out the jaundice and other physical features of the disease, including an enlarged liver and spleen.

Joanna leaned forward and whispered, "I am surprised that Cardogan would submit to being placed on display."

"He had no choice," I replied in a whisper. "It is Marburg who makes the rules here, not Cardogan."

"Cast your eyes on Moran, who is observing the proceedings so intently," Joanna said. "He is the wolf measuring its prey."

"Are you convinced he will carry out his act here?"

"Oh, yes. It is the perfect setup. Cardogan is held captive while Moran has free rein."

"But here? In a hospital with Moran under constant observation?"

"Do not underestimate Moran," Joanna warned. "He is a very clever physician and

St. Bartholomew's is his home turf, which gives him the advantage."

The clinical discussion at the podium now turned to the treatment of drug-resistant malaria. According to Marburg, two French researchers, Pierre Pelletier and Joseph Caventou, had discovered the form of quinine most effective in treating malaria. The drug was always given orally until the French found that some patients did not absorb quinine from the gastrointestinal tract and thus none entered the bloodstream. In these patients, the failure of quinine to control the disease was not due to drug resistance, but rather to the failure of the drug to be properly absorbed into the patient's system. It was hoped that Derek Cardogan fell into the latter category and could be successfully treated with quinine administered by intramuscular injection.

For reasons I did not know, Joanna was most interested in this portion of the discussion and moved to the edge of her seat so as not to miss a word.

"Unfortunately, the side effects of large doses of intramuscular quinine can be quite dangerous," Marburg was saying. The expression on his face indicated he was not going to downplay the dangers because of Cardogan's presence. "By far the most serious adverse reaction to the drug has been cardiac arrhythmias that can be fatal. These abnormal heart rhythms range from ventricular extrasystoles to complete cardiac arrest, with ventricular tachycardia being the most common."

"How often do these severe arrhythmias occur?" asked a voice from the audience.

"Approximately ten percent of patients so treated developed serious arrhythmias," Marburg reported.

"That is quite a high percentage."

"We shall try to avoid this adverse effect by preparing the patient with a cardiac-soothing drug."

"How much time elapses between the injection and the occurrence of the arrhythmias?"

"All of the cardiac abnormalities have come to the fore within four hours."

"As the drug level peaks in the circulation."

"Exactly."

Another voice asked, "When you mentioned the ten percent figure, is that referring to fatal arrhythmias?"

"For the most part."

There was an audible gasp from the audience. The ten percent figure was high indeed. It was so extraordinarily high that most physicians would never consider using such a large dose of intramuscularly administered quinine. It flagrantly violated the most important law of the Hippocratic oath, which starts, "First, do no harm." But in the case of Derek Cardogan, there was little choice, I thought grimly. Either take your chance with the drug or die.

"Obviously the patient will require constant and careful observation once the quinine is injected," Marburg went on. "This will include close cardiac monitoring."

"Certainly there can be no side effects more drastic than those affecting the heart," Christopher Moran said from the front row.

"Not as deadly, but nearly as terrifying," Marburg said. "A few of the patients suffered deep comalike somnolence, others confusion and convulsions, all within the four-hour time frame."

"Were those fatal?"

"Only in a single instance."

A young physician sitting next to me stood and asked, "What of the nausea and vomiting that at times accompanies even the smallest doses of quinine?"

Marburg and Moran looked up at the questioner before Joanna could completely conceal herself behind me. Moran continued to stare at me and I am certain he recognized my face. But whether he spotted Joanna was not clear.

"Some nausea and vomiting occurred, but it was not severe and brief in nature," Marburg replied.

"That is surprising since nausea is quite common at the lower doses."

I had to resist the urge to jerk the young intern down by his coat sleeve, for he continued to direct Moran's attention to our position. Joanna was slouched behind me, but could not go lower or she would have slipped off the bench and surely caused a stir. I could only hope that Moran had not noticed her. The last thing we needed was for Moran to be on even higher alert.

Marburg was skillfully explaining that the nausea that often accompanied quinine ingestion was in part due to gastric irritation, which was avoided when the drug was given by injection.

Another questioner farther down inquired about the actual dose to be used.

Joanna asked in a low whisper, "Do you believe Moran recognized me in my nurse's garb?"

"I think not, but I cannot be sure."

"It would be unfortunate if he did."

"Let us hope that was not the case," I said softly from the side of my mouth. Now the doctors were examining a lesion on Cardogan's face. "This would be a good moment for you to depart unless there is a compelling reason for you to remain."

"I have what I came for," Joanna said, and quietly slipped away.

The conference lasted for another half hour, with most of the questions and comments on dosage and side effects of quinine. A heart specialist in the audience offered advice on cardiac monitoring during the procedure, while an ophthalmologist warned of possible adverse effects on vision from large doses of quinine. Finally, the grand rounds ended and a sullen Derek Cardogan was wheeled away. As the audience filed out, I walked down to the podium carrying a copy of Stephen Marburg's latest monograph on malaria and its various presentations. Moran watched my every step and made no effort to conceal his interest.

I approached Stephen Marburg and congratulated him, "Very nicely done, Stephen."

"Thank you, John," he said, and extended his hand to shake mine. We sat together on several committees at St. Bartholomew's and thus were familiar with each other. "I have not heard recently from your dear father. Does all go well with him?"

"For the most part. Of course he suffers from some of the infirmities that accompany the aging process."

"There is no avoiding those."

"True enough. But his mind remains sharp and he maintains a keen interest in malaria."

"I recall our discussions and his vivid recollections of malaria during his Afghan days. I am delighted that he is keeping up on the subject."

"Oh, it is more than simply keeping up. He reads every new advance and has an extensive file on malaria that he continually adds to. As a matter of fact, he has recently purchased your latest monograph on the subject and requests that you be so kind as to autograph it."

"It would be my pleasure," Marburg said. "And I shall insert a bit of a note as well."

I handed him the monograph and turned to Christopher Moran. "I trust things have finally calmed down on Curzon Street."

"They have, but of course there are people who continue to make needless inquiries," Moran said blatantly.

"That will soon end," I said. "For I have heard that Scotland Yard has officially closed the case of Charles Harrelston."

"And well they should have. The poor Harrelston family has suffered enough."

"I agree."

"And some people are meddling in the accidental death of Benjamin Levy as well."

"The newspapers say there are questions remaining that need to be answered."

"The death was *accidental* and now that Levy is gone and buried, no one can dispute that."

We exchanged knowing glances, both quite aware where each of us stood. He knew we were close on his trail, and I made no effort to hide it. As Joanna had predicted, Derek Cardogan would tell Moran every detail of our visit to his home yesterday. Joanna had also predicted that Moran's arrogance would not allow him to shy away from the accusations leveled against him. He considered himself too clever to be caught. And Scotland Yard was stymied as usual, and too amateurish to be concerned about the crimes in front of their eyes. Thus, Moran would not alter his plan to kill Derek Cardogan.

"Here you are," Marburg said, and handed the signed monograph back to me. "Please give your father my fondest regards."

"I shall."

As I climbed the steps I could feel Moran's stare at my back. Had my back been more sensitive, I might have also felt the hatred that accompanied the stare. For a brief moment, I wondered if we had miscalculated the cunning of this very clever killer. He seemed so confident and so unconcerned about those who opposed him. Did he have some plan that we had not yet considered? Was he in fact playing us rather than we playing him? Shaking my head, I quickly dismissed these negative thoughts and hurried along to the departments of cardiology and dermatology. Those two specialties had no idea how important their roles would be in placing a noose around Moran's neck.

21

The Players

Mrs. Helen Hughes was a short, stout, no-nonsense nurse who was in charge of the special care unit at St. Bartholomew's Hospital. She and Joanna had been close colleagues at the hospital and had remained friends after Joanna's departure from the nursing profession. We invited Mrs. Hughes to 221b Baker Street under the pretext that my father was chronicling yet another Sherlock Holmes adventure and needed her expertise to assure that all descriptions of St. Bartholomew's were accurate. She was more than willing to assist, for she, like most Londoners, was an avid fan of Sherlock Holmes.

"But Dr. Watson," she said to me while sipping from a glass of fine Madeira, "surely you and Joanna have the experience to supply the information your father requires."

I had a rehearsed response ready. "But for the most part, I am locked away in the department of pathology and Joanna has been absent for several years, so we may not be up to date on any recent changes at St. Bart's."

After a moment's hesitation, she said, "There

have been some modifications to the special care unit."

"Which is precisely where Sherlock Holmes was a patient," my father joined in.

"Oh, goodness! What disease was he stricken with?" Mrs. Hughes inquired, genuinely concerned.

"A feigned illness," my father said evasively. "But pray tell, what are the modifications you spoke of?"

"The special care unit is now sealed off from the remainder of the hospital, with strict requirements for entry. There is a clerk stationed at the door whose job it is to make certain only doctors, nurses, and hospital personnel can gain entry."

"A wise precaution," Joanna said. "As I recall there is only a single door into the unit, which, I assume, still consists of one large room."

"Yes and no," Mrs. Hughes said, and held her glass out for a refill of Madeira. "There is only one door in, but a side room was constructed for supplies and additional equipment."

"Could you please describe the equipment?" Joanna requested.

"It is mainly the cardiac monitoring machines that instantly produce electrocardiograms. These are of course needed in the event the patient's heart is adversely affected. There is also a respirator to assist breathing, and several wheelchairs and gurneys."

"To the best of my recollection, the unit has a single, large window."

"Which is always securely locked."

"As it should be."

My father asked, "Is the monitoring of patients done exclusively by nurses?"

"With only rare exceptions," Mrs. Hughes replied. "We are of course trained to take and record the patient's vital signs, and to quickly set up the electrocardiogram and respiratory-assist machines."

"But doctors periodically check on their patients, do they not?" Joanna asked.

"They do indeed. And in most high-risk cases, their visits are far more frequent."

"Say, every five or ten minutes?"

Mrs. Hughes shook her head. "Every half hour or so, but again only in the most difficult cases."

"This is most helpful," my father complimented while jotting down notes. "In the story, I have the nurses attired in their usual uniforms. Does that hold true for the special care unit?"

"The nurses always wear their highly starched uniforms, which is a requirement. But in the event the patient is plagued by vomiting or diarrhea, the nurses protect themselves with aprons and gloves."

"I would think the gloves could interfere with the nurses' giving injections," Joanna said.

"It is always the doctors who give the injection in the special care unit."

"For what reason?"

"To avoid any possible error, so they say."

"Do the doctors measure out the dose of the drug to be given as well?"

Mrs. Hughes nodded, with a grin. "Although we look over their shoulders while they are measuring."

"Oh, I forgot to ask," my father said. "Is there any type of alarm system in case someone attempts illegal entry?"

"None that I know of. But that would be quite unnecessary, for the clerk at the front desk is most vigilant."

"And I suspect he will be very vigilant tomorrow, when Mr. Cardogan undergoes quinine-by-injection therapy," Joanna said.

Mrs. Hughes narrowed her eyelids. "How did you learn of this?"

"We attended grand rounds this morning where the case of drug-resistant malaria was discussed," Joanna answered.

"A treacherous disease," Mrs. Hughes commented. "With a treatment that is nearly as treacherous. We will all have to be on our toes tomorrow."

"Has the nursing schedule already been established for this case?"

Mrs. Hughes nodded. "For the entire twenty-four hours he will be in the special care unit. This will require the use of three nurses, each working eight-hour shifts."

"And those will be very experienced nurses, I would assume," my father said.

"Our *most* experienced nurses," Mrs. Hughes said.

My father wrote down a final note, then said, "You have been of considerable help and you have been most generous with your time, but I have another great favor to ask of you."

"I shall try my best."

"Excellent." My father offered her more Madeira, which she declined. "As you must be aware, in my stories I must have absolute accuracy or they lose believability. Thus, I need to know the staff's expressions, voice tones, and gestures while they go about their professional duties. Would it be possible for Joanna and my son to carefully observe the proceedings on Mr. Cardogan tomorrow morning? They could take notes that they could later transmit back to me."

Mrs. Hughes hesitated. "I am afraid that would be most unusual, Dr. Watson."

"But my son is on staff at St. Bartholomew's and Joanna is a qualified nurse," my father persisted. "And their conduct would be in every way professional."

Mrs. Hughes sipped more Madeira as she

reconsidered my father's request. "It could be allowed, but you will require the consent of Dr. Marburg, who will be the physician in charge tomorrow."

"He has already given his consent," Joanna said. "However, he clearly stated that we need your permission as well, for the moment-to-moment activities will be under your supervision."

Mrs. Hughes slowly nodded. "Of course you will have to stand outside the unit itself so as not to disturb the patient."

"Agreed," Joanna said promptly.

"Then I believe we can arrange something suitable."

"Excellent!"

"I am most grateful," my father said. "And as a way to repay you for your generous help, I propose to include your real name in the Sherlock Holmes adventure, which is something I rarely do. Of course, I will only do so with your permission!"

"Oh, sir! I am flattered," Mrs. Hughes said.

"So you have no objection to your name being included?"

"None whatsoever."

"There is a condition," my father told her. "You must not breathe a word of this to any staff, for the word will spread and they may begin to act unnaturally, which is exactly what I wish to avoid. They must proceed with the same professional behavior that they always demonstrate."

"I shall not utter a word," Mrs. Hughes vowed. "Not even to my husband."

"Then we are agreed," Joanna said. "We shall see you first thing tomorrow morning."

"Oh, how exciting!"

"Indeed."

At the door, the women hugged each other farewell. Once the nurse was safely in her carriage, we gathered around a cheery fire and toasted our success with another glass of Madeira. Our first move was now in place, but it was simple and easy to perform. Subsequent moves would be far more difficult.

My father asked Joanna, "Have you truly spoken to Stephen Marburg?"

"No," Joanna replied. "But I shall."

"He may resist," I cautioned. "He is a stickler for exactness and protocol, which makes him a very fine physician."

"I know a person of authority who can convince him."

"And if he continues to resist?"

"Then he places Derek Cardogan's life in the direst of dangers."

As I was about to pour another Madeira, my stomach growled audibly, for it was mid-evening and I had skipped lunch to prepare a medical school lecture. "Shall we call on Miss Hudson to prepare one of her sumptuous meals?"

"It is her evening out," my father said. "I suggest we walk down to Gennaro's for a relaxing dinner."

"Is it Italian?" Joanna asked.

"It is, and the food and service are equally superb," my father replied.

We bundled up in topcoats and shawls for outside the dark evening had turned very cold. The chill was exaggerated by a heavy fog that shrouded everything and even dimmed the streetlights. We strolled half a block down Baker Street before deciding to cross. On the other side of the street we could barely make out the illuminated window of the small Italian restaurant.

"Careful now," my father warned as we stepped off the curb. "There is some unevenness in the cobblestones which one can trip over."

I took Joanna's hand in mine and gave it a gentle squeeze. Her return squeeze was gentler yet, and caused a wave of affection to sweep through every fiber of my being. At that moment I considered myself to be the luckiest of men, for beside me was the most enchanting woman I had ever encountered. And despite the strange set of circumstances that brought us together, we were a perfect match. It was a certainty I would love her forever, and that was sealed in my heart and mind.

"I do hope that one day you will be mine," I whispered to her.

"There is no need to hope, dearest John, for I am already yours," she whispered back.

We heard the sound before we saw its source. There were hoofbeats thundering against the cobblestones, which were combined with the distinctive noise of fast-turning wheels. In the dense fog we could not see the rapidly approaching carriage. Acting on pure instinct, my father pushed Joanna and me off the road onto the sidewalk, then fell upon us just as the carriage passed, no doubt saving us from serious injury or even death.

Catching our breaths and swallowing back our fright, we listened as the sounds of the horse and carriage faded into the night.

"That was no accident," Joanna said, her voice surprisingly strong.

"It had to be Moran," I agreed. "This would be the style of a backstabber."

"He is worried," Joanna said. "He knows we are closing in on him. He feels us nipping at his heels."

"So he tries to kill us."

"Or injure us badly, for either would serve his purpose. He needs us dead or, at minimum, incapacitated."

"Which is a sure sign that he plans to act tomorrow," I concluded, then thought further. "Or perhaps he will attempt to kill Derek Cardogan tonight."

"Tomorrow," Joanna said with certainty. "The special care unit at St. Bartholomew's gives him the perfect cover and will remove all suspicion."

We turned our attention to my father who was leaning against the brick wall, gathering himself.

"Are you all right, Father?" I asked.

"Quite so," my father replied, and pushed himself off the wall. "My body is intact and so is my brain, for it now recalls an attempt on my life, as well as the life of Sherlock Holmes, that occurred so many years ago."

"It was a horse and carriage then?"

"It was, and the name of the murdering scoundrel behind it was none other than Sebastian Moran." My father shook his head and sighed deeply. "How could I have forgotten such a monstrous deed, for it all seems so clear now. It occurred on a fog-shrouded street at a time when my hair was only beginning to turn gray. A horse and carriage driven by a nameless driver came straight at us and only missed by a bare whisker. We were fortunate to escape with our lives. And I also remember Sherlock's vow after the incident. He calmly said, 'We shall repay Moran back in spades, Watson.' And, as God is my witness, we jolly well did."

"And we shall again," Joanna promised.

I went to my father and gave his shoulder a congratulatory hug. "So the old brain is working quite nicely after all."

"When the appropriate jolt is applied, it seems to come to life," my father said.

"And so does your body, for it was your quick action that saved Joanna and me from serious injury or worse."

"It was simply instinct," my father said, downplaying his actions.

"It was heroic," Joanna said. "You were willing to sacrifice your life for ours."

My father shrugged at the praise. "You make too much of it."

"I think not," Joanna insisted.

"Now tell us, Father, was it you who saved the life of Sherlock Holmes those many, many years ago?"

"It was," my father said, with a hint of a smile. "It was indeed."

With great care we looked both ways before crossing Baker Street. I watched Joanna take my father's arm and could not but help think, there walk Holmes and Watson again on the very same street where they lived. And once more I realized that the past was reappearing in the present.

22

The Special Care Unit

Shakespeare once wrote that all the world's a stage, and all the men and women merely players: they have their exits and entrances. Although he no doubt was referring to life in general, it applied most accurately to the drama that was about to unfold before my very eyes.

From my vantage point, I could see that the special care unit was exactly as Mrs. Hughes had described. There was a single bed in its center surrounded by cardiac monitoring equipment and two carts filled with various drugs and antiseptics. A slender, bespectacled nurse, with long auburn hair, stood off to the side.

Anyone entering through the large door saw the patient covered up to his chin with a white sheet. A wet washcloth was spread across his forehead and brow to give comfort from the periodic fever brought on by malaria. A portion of his face was still visible and showed the deep yellowing jaundice of his skin. The intramuscular injection of quinine had been given three hours earlier and thus far the only adverse effect was somnolence and an occasional extra heartbeat. The ever vigilant nurse was again taking and recording the patient's vital signs when the door abruptly opened.

Stephen Marburg entered and hurried to the bedside. "He continues to sleep?"

The nurse nodded. "Except to use the bedpan."

"And he is comfortable?" Marburg asked, lowering his voice.

"Quite so. Even his fever is down."

"Excellent. Are his vital signs stable?"

"They remain unchanged."

Marburg made certain the cardiac monitoring wires were firmly attached to the patient's arms, then switched on the electrocardiogram machine and studied the running strip it produced. "The rhythm appears normal and you will note that the extraventricular beats he had earlier have disappeared."

"A good sign," the nurse said.

"Very. But keep in mind that the blood level of quinine has not yet peaked, and that is when the terrible cardiac effects are most likely to occur. So you must be ever watchful, particularly over the next two hours."

"Shall I take the patient's vital signs more frequently?"

"Every ten minutes should suffice," Marburg said, and turned off the electrocardiogram machine. "If there is any change at all, you must notify me without delay."

"Of course, Doctor."

Marburg checked his timepiece. "I will be making rounds on my other patients here at St. Bartholomew's over the next hour, so Dr. Moran will be looking in in my place."

"An excellent choice, sir."

"Indeed."

I watched Marburg leave and tightened my grip on my father's service revolver. Merely the mention of Moran's name raised my alert level to its highest point, for I was certain his move was coming shortly. He would surely seize this perfect opportunity to do his murderous work. My eyes stayed fixed on the door, but, in my peripheral vision, I could see the conscientious nurse hovering over the bed. Perhaps because of the quiet in the room, time seemed to crawl by at an agonizingly slow pace.

The door opened once more and Mrs. Helen Hughes, the head nurse, walked in. She appeared to be calm and entirely professional, just as Joanna had predicted. Her uniform was so strongly starched that there was not a wrinkle to be seen.

She came to the bedside and took the patient's pulse, then announced, "His heartbeat is steady."

"Even his occasional extrasystoles have ceased," the bespectacled nurse noted.

"Let us hope they remain so."

Mrs. Hughes eyed the electrocardiogram

machine and said. "I trust you continue to provide the cardiogram strips every fifteen minutes as requested by Dr. Marburg."

"Precisely every fifteen minutes, sister," the bespectacled nurse replied, using the term *sister* by which nurses are formally called. "Have you been informed that Dr. Moran will be covering for Dr. Marburg over the next hour?"

"I have, and I have no doubt things will go well with Dr. Moran at the helm."

"I feel so as well."

"Now keep a close watch and call out for even the slightest worry."

Mrs. Hughes was about to secure the door when she reopened it for the hospital's phlebotomist whom she recognized instantly. "What brings you back so soon. Rodney?"

"We need another blood specimen, which is to be sent to France for study. Apparently the French can determine the exact level of quinine in the blood. and Dr. Marburg wants to know if the level correlates with any of the dreaded side effects."

"An excellent idea," Mrs. Hughes said. "But please be careful not to dislodge the cardiac machine wires taped onto his extremities."

As the phlebotomist took the patient's arm from beneath the sheet, he commented, "The man's jaundice does not seem as pronounced as it was earlier."

"It is the strong sunlight," the bespectacled nurse explained quickly. "The sun rays blazing through the window tend to whiten the skin. Dr. Marburg himself remarked on this very same point."

"Brilliant doctor, that Marburg, eh?"

"Quite."

After Mrs. Hughes and the phlebotomist departed, the intense silence returned to the room. The waiting again became interminable and this caused my anxiety to grow. And worst of all, doubts began to enter my mind. Would Moran decide not to show his hand? Would he see through our trap and hold off for another, more opportune moment to kill Derek Cardogan? Perhaps he thought it best not to murder Cardogan medically, for this might raise suspicion. It might be better to have the deed done as if by accident. Such as being hit by a runaway horse and carriage.

But my doubts were short-lived. Without so much as a rap on the door, Christopher Moran barged into the special care unit. He had a very determined look on his face.

He studied the bespectacled nurse for a long moment. "Have I seen you before?"

"I do not believe so, sir. I have only recently transferred from St. George's Hospital."

"Perhaps that is where I know you from. Which section did you work in?"

"Surgery," the nurse answered, and turned her head to cough loudly.

"Do you have a cold?"

"I am afraid so, but it is beginning to subside."

"Does a fever accompany it?"

"Yes. But it is low grade and without chills."

Moran studied the nurse once more and said, "It is not easy looking after sick patients when you yourself are sick, is it?"

"No, Doctor. But I shall manage."

Moran picked up the patient's chart and read the notes. "How deep is this somnolence?"

"It resembles a semicoma, sir," the nurse replied. "He barely stirs except to use the bedpan."

Moran glanced over at the patient. "If he has had fever, why is he covered with a sheet?"

The nurse answered without hesitation. "There were chills and he requested it. Then he lapsed into a deep sleep. Do you believe the cover is doing him harm?"

"I doubt it," Moran said, and returned to the chart.

The nurse yawned widely and quickly covered it with her hand.

Moran caught sight of the yawn. "You look very tired, sister."

The nurse stifled another yawn. "I believe it is my cold, together with the poor ventilation, that brings it on."

"Indeed, it is close in here," Moran agreed. "It might be wise for you to take a few minutes and refresh yourself."

"But I must stay with—"

Moran held up a hand, interrupting her. "I shall be glad to look after my friend for a few minutes."

"You are most kind, Doctor."

"Not at all."

The nurse walked out and closed the door, but she left it slightly ajar.

Moran hurried out to shut the door completely, then came back to the patient. Glancing around quickly, he reached in his pocket for a capped needle and syringe that was filled with a milky-white fluid. He shook it back and forth, then removed the rubber cap.

"And good-bye to you, Derek Cardogan," Moran said cruelly. "This will surely cure you of your malaria."

Moran jerked the sheet back and stared down at the patient, stupefied.

"How nice to see you again, Moran," I said.

Moran lunged at me and tried to inject me with the poisonous needle. But I was already off the bed and on my feet, and easily sidestepped Moran's rush. Now Moran had the needle and syringe up high and was about to plunge it down. But I grabbed Moran's wrist and held it firmly where it was. Around and around we went, knocking over a small nightstand and the bedpan atop it. I attempted to land a punch on Moran's jaw, but the wiring from the cardiac monitors and the tightness of my hospital gown prevented my arm from extending fully.

My father dashed in, but had to stay back because Moran and I were locked in a death struggle, going from one side of the room to the other, with the poisonous needle dangerously close to me. My service revolver was on the floor, completely out of my father's reach.

Now Moran and I were on the bed. Moran was on top, holding me down with his superior weight. The needle was only inches away from my throat and moving closer.

The nurse had reappeared and she quickly grabbed the metal bedpan and raised it high. Then, with all of her might, she brought it down on Moran's head. The blow caused a resounding *bong* to echo across the room.

Moran straightened up for a moment, then dropped onto the bed, facedown.

"Good shot, Joanna!" I congratulated her as I jumped to my feet. I carefully retrieved the needle and syringe that contained the milky-white fluid. I held it up to the light for closer examination. "Nasty stuff, I will wager."

Joanna quickly removed her spectacles and auburn wig, then reached for the syringe to study its contents. "It is what I expected."

Inspector Lestrade rushed in, with two constables close behind him. He glanced down at Christopher Moran, who was coming to his senses. "So this is our murderer, eh, Mrs. Blalock?"

"It is," Joanna said, showing the inspector the deadly needle and syringe. "And this was his weapon. He tried to inject Dr. Watson with it, just as he had done to poor Benjamin Levy."

Lestrade eyed the syringe, keeping his distance. "A poison, eh?"

"One of nature's most potent," Joanna said.

My father moved in for a closer look and ventured a guess. "An extract of some sort, I would think."

Joanna shook her head. "No, Watson. This does not come from a plant."

"Well then, from where does it come?" Lestrade asked.

"From India, most likely," Joanna replied.

Moran got to his feet, shakily at first, then he stood tall. "You attacked me with that needle," he accused me, as he fabricated a story. "And I shall press charges."

"Oh, that will never do, Moran," Joanna said easily, and pointed to the auburn wig and spectacles on the floor. "We have a number of witnesses, you see. Besides Dr. Watson and myself, we have Watson's father who was watching your every move through a crack in the side door."

"They saw only my back," Moran snapped. "You can prove nothing."

"I can prove everything," Joanna retorted. She raised up the needle and syringe and stepped toward Moran. "Allow me to inject you with the solution you intended for your friend Derek Cardogan."

Moran cringed and drew away.

"Not so eager, I see." Joanna lowered the syringe and carefully removed its needle. "We will analyze this poison and characterize it, and surely find traces of it in Benjamin Levy's blood as well. And that will stand up in any court, particularly after your performance today."

Moran suddenly lunged for Joanna, but two constables moved in quickly and restrained him.

"Who are you?" Moran demanded.

"I am a creation of Sherlock Holmes."

Moran blinked rapidly as the name of the famous detective registered in his mind. He glared at Joanna. "Holmes, the snoop!"

Joanna smiled.

"Holmes, the meddler!"

Joanna's smile widened, then she said, "And hopefully Sherlock Holmes will be there in spirit to see you hanged."

Again Moran tried to lunge at Joanna, but the constables had a firm grip on him and he barely moved.

Lestrade motioned to the constables and they

led Moran away. He then turned to Joanna and asked, "How did you know that Dr. Moran would attack the patient today?"

"Merely a lucky guess," Joanna said.

Lestrade grinned. "Oh, no, Mrs. Blalock. This is more than a guess."

Joanna shrugged. "Then call it an educated assumption."

Lestrade scratched his bald head. "What is at the bottom of all this, then?"

"A treasure, Lestrade," Joanna replied. "And the never-ending greed that came with it."

Lestrade looked at Joanna quizzically. "A treasure, you say?"

"It will all become clear if you would be good enough to obtain a search warrant for Dr. Moran's lodgings."

"I do not require a search warrant to look about the doctor's premises."

Joanna raised an eyebrow. "Then you would be breaking the law."

"I would not," Lestrade argued forcefully. "Because you see, madam, in view of the new evidence at hand, the Harrelston death must now be officially considered a murder investigation. And since he fell from his death from Dr. Moran's parlor, the entire house becomes a crime scene. Now, I do not need a search warrant to examine a crime scene, do I?"

Joanna slapped her forehead with an open

palm. "How silly of me, Lestrade. Thank you for keeping me on track."

Lestrade beamed and happily nodded to the others, delighted that for once he had shown himself to be in command of the investigation. He came back to Joanna. "Shall we proceed to Dr. Moran's lodgings?"

"Yes," Joanna said, heading for the door. "And, Inspector, we will require the talents of a safecracker."

"We have an abundance of those," Lestrade said. "Anything else?"

"We will need one more person. His name is Phillip Chapman, and you will find him at the London Zoo."

"What role will he play?" Lestrade asked.

Joanna smiled thinly. "He will help gather up evidence."

In our carriage, and with Joanna's assistance, I removed the yellow pigment from my face and arms, using a weak acid solution. I had obtained the pigment from a colleague in the dermatology division, with the promise it would come off quite easily. Which was not the case. It required some vigorous scrubbing. Finally cleansed, I, along with my father, lighted Turkish cigarettes to enjoy the moment.

"You were magnificent, Joanna," I said genuinely. "Your performance was flawless."

"Particularly when Moran asked about the patient being covered despite a fever," my father joined in. "Your quick answer saved the day."

"My part was simple," Joanna said. "It was John who faced the terrible danger."

"It was close," I had to admit. "Another inch or two and that needle would have been in my neck."

"And when I was finally able to reach my revolver, I could not get a shot off," my father said unhappily. "Moran never gave me a clear target."

"It is probably best you did not shoot," Joanna told him. "For if you did, you might have deprived us of the satisfaction of watching Moran hang."

I asked, "Will you attend the execution?"

"Weather permitting," Joanna replied indifferently.

The carriage raced through the slum area of St. Giles, with its squalid tenements and filthy streets. The air was polluted and heavy with the smell of horse dung. The carriage moved on and finally turned onto Regent Street, where there were fashionable shops and well-dressed people.

"I must confess," I said, breaking the silence. "I have no idea how you were able to predict Moran's behavior with such accuracy. It was as if you were reading his mind."

"I was reading his words and actions," Joanna said, staring out the window at some action that momentarily caught her interest. "They told us everything."

"They told you, not us."

"I beg to differ," Joanna said, turning back to me. "Let us begin with his weapon. You knew, as well as I, that Moran would use poison. Is that not true?"

I nodded. "Of course I knew poison would be his weapon. But I did not know how and when it would be administered."

"The how was simple," Joanna explained. "He would inject the poison into Derek Cardogan's neck, just as he had done with Benjamin Levy. Direct injection of a potent poison into the carotid artery guarantees death. Does it not, Watson?"

"Indeed," my father replied. "And Moran being a physician would be aware of this."

"And when Moran would do it presented no problem," Joanna went on. "He learned of Derek Cardogan's impending admission to St. Bartholomew's for treatment of his drug-resistant malaria. That gave Moran the perfect opening. I also reasoned he would not use a tourniquet to inject the jugular vein, for that would be time-consuming and he would have only the briefest of moments to act. Thus, he would choose the carotid artery which could be injected in seconds."

"Yes, yes," I said impatiently. "This is all quite evident. That is why we went through the charade at St. Bart's. There remain two questions, however, that I cannot answer. First, how does one kill a patient in the hospital—particularly one who is being closely observed—and avoid all suspicion? And secondly, how could you predict exactly when he would try to do it?"

"It took a while to untie that knot," Joanna conceded. "But Stephen Marburg helped me come up with an answer. While Lestrade and I were recruiting him into our little play, he again mentioned that one of the side effects from injected quinine was a deep somnolence that at times resembled coma. And that was how I knew exactly when Moran would strike."

"At the moment Derek Cardogan was completely defenseless," I said.

"Precisely."

I thought through the matter again. "But there would always be a nurse in the room."

Joanna waved away the argument. "Moran was a doctor, experienced in the hospital setting. He knew a dozen ruses that would encourage a nurse to leave. That is why I coughed and yawned and feigned fatigue. This would convey the impression I obviously needed to refresh myself. He leaped at the opening I gave him."

"And of course anyone receiving this drastic treatment was subject to severe side effects," I concluded. "So Cardogan's death would have been blamed on the injected quinine."

"And there you have it."

"Extraordinary, most extraordinary." my father said. "The trap you set for Moran was ingenious and perfect in every detail. I particularly admired your disguise, which allowed you to be constantly at Derek Cardogan's bedside. And, with Lestrade's help, you were able to convince Stephen Marburg and Helen Hughes to play their roles in your well-planned charade."

"Stephen Marburg was superb in every regard," Joanna said. "It was his idea to have Derek Cardogan placed in the side equipment room where he could be carefully monitored after receiving the quinine injection. That, in itself, was a brilliant move."

"Indeed," my father agreed. "And according to Marburg, Derek Cardogan survived the quinine therapy nicely and, with a little luck, should make a full recovery."

"I wonder how well his luck will hold when he's questioned at the inquiry," Joanna said. "You see, he will have to explain his role in this horrid affair."

"But he was uninvolved with the killing," I argued.

"But not with the stealing."

And with that comment, Joanna leaned back in her seat, her eyelids now drooping noticeably.

She remained silent as we rode on, staring out the window and occasionally mumbling to herself. For a brief period she moved her head side to side, as if distracted by some thought. Then her expression became quite somber and I wondered if she was sinking into one of her moods Sir Henry had described.

Ten minutes passed before Joanna spoke again. "I see by the concerned look on your face, John, that you fear I have fallen into the doldrums, which usually coincides with my losing interest. That is, when my brain gears down, so does my mood."

I shifted around in my seat. "I do wish you would stop reading my thoughts."

Joanna smiled warmly at me. "Not to worry. I was simply tidying things up into a neat package. There were a few loose ends that seemed out of place, but all is well now. Nevertheless, there remain some points in the case that I believe make it a rather unique one."

"I hope you will share those points with us," my father urged.

"In due time," Joanna promised.

"I take it this uniqueness revolves around the hidden treasure."

"Of course, Watson. Everything in this case revolves around the hidden treasure."

23
The Treasure

Inspector Lestrade was waiting for us in the parlor of Christopher Moran's lodgings. Standing next to him was a short, thin, unshaven man with very few teeth. His clothes were wrinkled and dirty and worn down to the threads.

"This is Nifty Ned," Lestrade introduced the man. "He can open just about any kind of safe."

"Including the very best Chubb," Nifty Ned added.

"What tool will you use?" Joanna asked.

"A putter-cutter."

Joanna nodded and explained to us that a putter-cutter was a drill clamped to the keyhole of a safe. It permitted a hole to be bored into the lock, and through the hole this lock could be manipulated and opened. "Do not bore all the way into the safe," she continued.

"There is no need to, madam," Nifty Ned said.

"This is all well and good," Lestrade remarked. "But I see no safe to open."

"That is because you have not been looking

in the appropriate place," Joanna informed him. She led us through the closet and into the secret room. "There is your safe, Inspector. In it are the answers to all your questions."

Lestrade moved over to the side wall where the steps were located. "And here are the stairs you mentioned, Mrs. Blalock. The very ones he used to carry the corpse to the roof."

"Correct."

"Nasty business, this."

Joanna motioned Nifty Ned over to the safe. "How long will it take you to open it?"

"Not long," Nifty Ned said, and reached for a bulky drill. "But it will be noisy. The sound of the drill cannot be muted."

"Do what is necessary," Joanna told him. "But remember not to open the safe after you have manipulated the lock. Leave it closed. Do you understand?"

"Whatever you say, madam," Nifty Ned said, then attached the putter-cutter and went to work.

Lestrade came back to the group and spoke above the noise of the drill. "Why drag Charles Harrelston to the roof, Mrs. Blalock? Why not toss him out of the window?"

"Because the street outside is narrow and the houses across the way very close," Joanna replied. "The neighbors might have seen the crime being committed."

"So Dr. Moran first lures Harrelston into this room and bashes his head in, then takes him to the roof," Lestrade concluded.

"Lure is the correct word," Joanna said. "Early on, I did not understand why Harrelston had followed Moran into a secret room. After all, there was nothing in here but a small safe. I carelessly overlooked its importance. And of course the safe was the answer, its contents the lure. I only became certain of that when I deciphered Harrelston's coded message to Moran."

"What message?" Lestrade asked.

Joanna glanced over to me. "Do you recall the exact wording of the message, John?"

" 'I need a share at once,' " I replied.

"And that, Inspector, is a phrase used when one is demanding his portion of the profits or bounty or treasure."

Lestrade asked, "Would you care to guess what is in the safe?"

"A treasure from India," Joanna said without hesitation.

Lestrade stared at her, totally mystified. "Please tell us how you reached that conclusion."

"We know they met and fought together in the Second Afghan War," Joanna recounted. "Moran told us how he saved Harrelston's life when they were captured by the rebels. He also informed us that Benjamin Levy and Derek Cardogan were captives as well. And that is how they all became close friends who together came across this treasure."

"But how did they manage to gain ownership?" Lestrade asked.

"They stole it," Joanna said.

"And what makes you believe that?"

"Because the war has been over for more than twenty years and they still had not divided the treasure," Joanna explained. "There was a stain on this treasure that they hoped time would wash away."

My father grinned at Lestrade. "You should give thought to hiring her."

Lestrade cleared his throat uneasily.

"So everything points to the treasure being ill-gotten," Joanna continued on. "I suspect they came by it when their rebel captors attacked the well-guarded caravan. It was no doubt a fierce battle, and I believe Moran and his friends happened onto the treasure while they were escaping."

"So the treasure belonged to the caravan," my father interjected.

"Or was being transported out of India by it," Joanna said. "But now the quartet faced a predicament. They had the treasure, but the countryside was mountainous and desolate, and no doubt filled with thieves. So they decided to hide it. And they came back for it later, during their recovery from enteric fever."

My father nodded. "They spent a great deal of time at the hospital near Peshawar and Moran said they did stroll about the countryside during their recuperation. That is when they went back for the treasure."

"Precisely."

"What a tale! What a tale!" Lestrade exclaimed. "And it might have all ended well had not Charles Harrelston demanded his share. What was his rush anyway, Mrs. Blalock?"

"The family had suffered severe financial reversals," Joanna answered. "Charles Harrelston wanted to come to the family's rescue."

"And it cost him his life."

"Indeed."

Lestrade asked, "Who will the treasure go to now?"

Joanna shrugged. "That is for the courts to decide. But I can assure you the true owners will never be found. They are either long dead or have disappeared into the mountains of that far-off land."

"No doubt the government will lay claim to it," Lestrade said. "You know, the spoils of war and that kind of business."

"You are probably correct," Joanna said. "But I think it safe to say that a portion of the treasure will go to Charles Harrelston's family, where it will be most welcome."

"But why did they wait so long to divvy up the

treasure?" Lestrade asked. "After all, the war has been over a good twenty years or more."

"I wondered about that as well," Joanna said. "So I posed the question, in an indirect fashion, to my father-in-law who was once Chancellor of the Exchequer. He told of a case some ten years ago in which a bejeweled statuette was stolen from a museum during the war. When the statuette came on the market, the museum sued and the British court found in their favor. I suspect the quartet decided to prolong their wait for this reason. You must remember these four men were all well-to-do, and were in no rush to claim their share."

"Until Charles Harrelston demanded his fourth," I added.

Joanna nodded. "That was the flame that lit the fuse."

There was a loud click.

Nifty Ned got to his feet and announced, "She is ready to be plucked."

"Shall we?" Lestrade asked, moving toward the safe.

Joanna held him back with a hand. "Not yet."

"What are we waiting for?"

"Mr. Phillip Chapman."

"I am here," said a big, heavyset man in his forties, as he entered the room. He was carrying a large satchel on his shoulder.

"And right on time," Joanna greeted him. "We

are in need of both your knowledge and your skill."

Chapman flexed his fingers repeatedly, as if he was about to perform a delicate task. "Tell me how I can be of service to you."

"First," Joanna began, "am I correct in assuming that the cobra is India's most venomous snake?"

"You are correct, madam."

"And am I correct in saying that a snake located in a dark place will be startled by light?"

"Quite so."

"And if he has been without food, will he strike?"

"The moment it senses your presence."

"Then be very careful when you open the safe, because you will find it contains two cobras."

Nifty Ned darted behind Lestrade and used him as a protective shield.

"Can snakes survive in such an enclosed space without air?" Lestrade asked.

"They do not require much oxygen when being fed infrequently," Joanna replied. "So opening the safe door periodically suffices."

Chapman reached into his satchel and removed a collapsible rod. He quickly straightened it and tested the wire loop on its end. "Please stand clear."

Everyone backed up against the far wall.

Chapman opened the safe and waited.

A large cobra slowly crawled out, then stopped and raised its hooded head. Its tongue flicked out to sense the nearby prey. In an instant Chapman had the wire loop around the snake's head and dispatched the reptile into a thick cloth sack. A second cobra was handled in a similar fashion.

"Expertly done," Joanna praised the herpetologist.

"No problem at all, madam," Chapman said. "What would you like me to do with them?"

"Add them to your collection at the London Zoo," she answered. "Compliments of Scotland Yard."

"Two fine specimens they are," Chapman said, and closed his large satchel. "I shall be on my way, madam."

"Many thanks to you, Chapman," Joanna said, watching the reptile expert leave. She turned back to the safe and extracted a wooden chest, then opened it for everyone to gaze at its contents.

"I say!" my father cried out.

"Blimey!" Nifty Ned said, eyeing the treasure greedily.

"There must be a fortune in there," Lestrade remarked.

The chest was overflowing with diamonds and rubies and emeralds. Most of the precious stones were loose, but some were mounted on gold bands as thick as a thumb. Off to the side, long strands of white pearls were wrapped around diamond-encrusted tiaras. Joanna brushed away the top layer of gems and this revealed even more hidden treasure. Now we could see breathtaking pieces of jewelry that were clearly of Indian design. There were striking head ornaments that showed flowerlike displays of jade and rubies, and beside them were dozens of brilliant blue sapphires, all resting on a sea of gleaming gold coins. The value of these magnificent gems was beyond calculation, I thought, stunned by their beauty and glitter.

Joanna closed the chest, saying, "And so our case is closed."

"Brilliant, Joanna," my father praised. "Absolutely brilliant. No other detective in the world could have put all those pieces together."

"Perhaps one other," Joanna said without modesty. "I have read about a chap in Paris who uses my methods, and they say he is quite good."

Lestrade scratched the back of his neck. "I have one last question, Mrs. Blalock. How in the world did you know the safe contained two cobras?"

"The dog told me," Joanna replied.

Lestrade looked at her oddly. "The what?"

"The dog," Joanna repeated. "Do you not recall that Moran had a dog?"

"But he had died," Lestrade countered.

"From what?"

Lestrade thought back. "He had hurt his leg badly."

"He had been bitten," Joanna corrected. "Remember the words of Moran's secretary. Here was a Jack Russell terrier, playful and happy before he entered Moran's parlor where he lets out a yelp. Then moments later he limps out with a painful paw."

Lestrade snapped his fingers as the answer came to him. "He had encountered the snake in the secret room!"

"Exactly," Joanna said. "And there he was bitten."

"But Moran indicated that a rat had nipped the dog's paw," Lestrade recalled.

"Pshaw!" Joanna said dismissively. "There has never been a rat that could outdo a ratter-terrier, one on one. And besides, a rat bite would not have caused such intense pain and swelling within minutes, and death within hours."

Lestrade nodded slowly. "And it was strange that Dr. Moran requested his secretary to buy only two rats for the terrier to train on. Two rats would hardly be a starter."

Joanna nodded back. "Exactly right, Inspector. Those two rats were meant to be dinner for two cobras."

Lestrade asked, "Are you telling me you knew from the beginning about those snakes?"

"I suspected, but was not sure," Joanna admitted, and then added, "but when I saw the syringe in Moran's hand I was certain. For I had seen that milky-white venom before when visiting Phillip Chapman at the zoo, while on a charity expedition with friends."

Lestrade shook his head in admiration. "Should I include your observations in my report?"

"Better not," Joanna advised. "Simply indicate that the injury suggested a snake bite."

"I take it you would prefer me not to mention your name."

"I would indeed," Joanna said. "Only state that you employed three anonymous consultants who proved to be helpful."

"Most helpful," Lestrade emphasized.

"If you insist."

"But I must say it would be tempting to report we were assisted by a person who trained under the famous Sherlock Holmes."

"I beg your pardon," Joanna said at once.

Lestrade quickly brought a hand to his mouth. "Oh, no! I have let the secret out when I promised Dr. Watson to keep my lips sealed."

"We had your word!" my father scolded the inspector, then turned to Joanna and attempted to cover up his earlier fabrication. "I was forced to tell Lestrade of your past experience with Sherlock Holmes in order to explain your remarkable deductive skills and to urge that you be allowed to remain as part of the investigation." He nodded to Joanna to accept the story and waited for her to nod back, but she did not. He hurriedly continued on. "I did not mention names, but only told of your involvement in one of our cases some years ago. Because you seemed so keen and interested in unraveling the crime, Holmes decided to take you under his wing and taught you his skills, which you have displayed for us today. I can only hope you will forgive me for revealing the secret you wished so much to conceal."

Joanna finally nodded back. "You are forgiven, Watson."

"And you have my word never to speak of it again," my father vowed.

"And mine as well," Lestrade promised. "Allow me to once more thank you for your most helpful assistance, Mrs. Blalock."

"You are welcome."

"Now I must bid you good day," Lestrade said. "For I have before me the task of taking inventory on this treasure, and then searching the premises for other plunder Dr. Moran may have hidden away."

"If the treasure can be traced back to India, I would like to hear of it," Joanna requested.

"And so you shall, madam."

On our way out we passed Moran's housekeeper who had a most puzzled expression on her face. It was obvious Emma Lambert had no knowledge of what was transpiring. We left the unpleasant task of informing her up to Lestrade.

Outside the weather was clear, with a blue sky

and a cool breeze. Fashionably dressed couples strolled down Curzon Street, oblivious to the evil that had gone on inside Christopher Moran's lodgings.

My father said to Joanna, "I trust you will understand the need for me to tell Lestrade of your fictitious association with Sherlock Holmes. After all, you did demonstrate many of his deductive talents. Thus, I covered it with you being a trainee of his."

"Thank you for that, Watson," Joanna said. "I am particularly grateful you did not tell Lestrade the truth, for he obviously has a loose tongue and would have been more than eager to spread the word that I am in fact the daughter of Sherlock Holmes."

My father and I were stunned speechless. We stood there with our mouths agape, like befuddled schoolboys, and wondered how she could possibly know.

My father swiftly turned to me. "Did you utter—"

"Not a word," I swore.

"Nor I."

"Then how?"

"Come, come, dear Watsons. You must give me at least some credit on this matter. When a topic interests me, I chase it to the very end, as I did with my lineage. It was not all that difficult."

"But all the documents on your adoption were

sealed," my father said. "By law, they could not be unsealed."

"There was no need to," Joanna said with a shrug. "My adoptive parents told me of my birthday and the place of my birth and nothing more. So I traveled to St. Mary's Hospital in Paddington and searched for the babies born on my birthday. There were four, three boys and a single girl whose name was Joanna Adler Norton. I had earlier read of my father's exploits in *A Scandal in Bohemia* and recognized the last names of Adler and Norton. Irene Adler was the woman who had famously outwitted Sherlock Holmes and Godfrey Norton was the man she married and fled to Paris with."

"But surely their trails were impossible to follow," my father interjected.

"Difficult? Yes. Impossible? No. But at this point, I must admit I had to use my feminine instincts. First off, you may recall that Irene Adler was not a vicious, hardened woman, but rather a sensitive, caring one who was badly used by the King of Bohemia. Such a woman would never give up her newborn for adoption, even under the strongest pressure from her husband. No, there had to be a very urgent reason. Something had forced her, and left her no choice. Could this have been a fatal illness? I wondered. If so, she would have been terrified that her daughter would become motherless. So I searched the death records at

St. Mary's on or about the day of my birth. My mother, Irene Adler Norton, died on the day I was born. So, one piece of the puzzle was in place. The following year I went to Paris on a holiday with my parents, and unbeknownst to them I hired a private detective to find the whereabouts of my listed father, Godfrey Norton. I was soon to discover that Norton was a worthless scoundrel who had abandoned my mother and moved to Italy with his mistress. Most importantly, he had died of alcoholism a year before I entered this world. Thus, he could not be my father, and so the seed for truth was planted."

"But surely nothing thus far pointed to Sherlock Holmes being your father," I interrupted.

"Not initially," Joanna replied. "But as I matured and time passed, I became aware of my intense interest in crime and detectives, whom I often matched wits against. I rarely lost. When I read Sherlock Homes's text on *The Whole Art of Deduction*, it was as if I had written it. The writer and I seemed to be of one mind. It was then that I truly began to wonder if I could be the daughter of Sherlock Holmes. But here was a loveless, cold man who had never shown the least tender affection to women. What were the chances he and my mother would have had a secret, romantic assignation?"

"Almost impossible," my father answered the rhetorical question.

"*Almost* is the key word here, Watson. Thus, it was not truly impossible. Surely you remember one of Sherlock Holmes's cardinal rules, 'Once you have eliminated the impossible, whatever remains behind, no matter how improbable, must be the truth.' So the thought that Sherlock Holmes might be my biological father stuck with me. The thought was reinforced when sometime later I overheard my parents talking of a friend who was retiring from the practice of medicine. A dear friend who had arranged for the adoption of their daughter. This dear friend was you, Watson. Now I was nearly certain that Sherlock Holmes was my father, but had no solid proof. However, as the years passed, my son, Johnnie, grew and took on features that did not resemble either me or my now deceased husband. It was then that I happened upon a photograph of a young Sherlock Holmes in an old detective monograph. It truly took my breath away, for my son and Sherlock Holmes could have passed for twins. And so the puzzle of my lineage was solved once and for all."

"And you no doubt noted my father's reaction upon seeing young Johnnie for the first time," I added.

"I did," Joanna said, with a grin. "I prayed Watson would not faint as he did when Sherlock Holmes reappeared after his miraculous resurrection from his watery grave in the Reichenbach Falls."

"I nearly did," my father admitted, then, taking a deep breath, said, "But what a story you have told! What a remarkable story!"

"Now I have a favor to ask from you both," Joanna said in all seriousness. "I wish for my lineage and connection to Sherlock Holmes to remain a hidden truth. I would be most grateful that under no circumstances were you ever to mention that I am the daughter of Sherlock Holmes and Irene Adler. For were it revealed, it would bring fame and notoriety, neither of which I seek. These two intruders can destroy any family and their private lives as well, and could adversely affect my dear Johnnie. Thus I have never spoken of my true identity to anyone and hope you will do the same."

"Were you aware we knew all the while?" my father asked.

"Of course. You arranged for my adoption to the Middletons and would have only done so with the consent of Sherlock Holmes and Irene Adler. They no doubt swore you to secrecy, for they would have understood the harm that could have come to me should my parental origin be revealed."

"But if I was pledged to secrecy how could you be certain that John would be told of your lineage?"

"Because the Middletons informed me of a secret trust my biological parents had set up for me," Joanna replied. "At my request, Lord Blalock, who was once Chancellor of the Exchequer, was good enough to search into the matter and learn that you, Watson, were the sole trustee. Now, with your advancing years, you would have to appoint a new trustee to eventually take your place. It could only be someone whom you trusted implicitly. It had to be John who was told of the trust and its benefactor, the daughter of Sherlock Holmes."

"But why did you not tell us of your true identity earlier?" I asked. "Surely we had gained your confidence."

"Indeed you had," Joanna said. "And that is the reason I am divulging the details now. But during the investigation, I thought it best not to do so. With the three of us separately holding on to the secret, I felt assured it would remain hidden. But were the secret shared, we might well begin to speak of it casually to one another and our words could reach unintended ears."

"Such as Lestrade's," my father said, nodding. "He could not wait to tell of your fictitious association with Sherlock Holmes after vowing not to."

"Precisely my point," Joanna agreed. "So I must again ask that my lineage never be revealed, for it is in my family's best interest that it remain sealed and hidden."

"I shall never speak of it again," my father pledged.

"Nor I," I promised.

"And you must consent never to write of this story, Watson, for the facts would eventually reveal my participation and then my exposure. Again, neither of these are wanted."

"The story will remain unwritten."

Joanna gave us a warm smile and said, "But I must say that if another perplexing case comes your way, I would not object to being asked to join you two for another adventure."

"That would be our pleasure," my father said, and took Joanna's arm. "Now that all vows and promises are signed and sealed, I suggest we ride to Simpson's-in-the-Strand for a well-deserved dinner."

"A capital idea, Watson!" Joanna said. "But pray tell, how did you read my mind?"

"From simple deduction," my father replied. "I noticed that you gazed at the restaurant across the way several times and ignored the other structures. And when the transport carrying the sign purveyor of fine foods passed by, you appeared to be very interested in it. You even involuntarily licked your lips. Thus, I reasoned that your appetite must be aroused."

"But why Simpson's?" Joanna asked.

"That is elementary, my dear Joanna. For you see, that is in your blood."

As the pair strolled arm in arm just ahead, I could not help but feel the thrill of the past unfolding before me. In my mind's eye, I could envision Holmes and Watson once more sauntering down Baker Street, the very street they lived on. They were no doubt chatting about some new clue in their current case and enjoying their favorite pipefuls. With effort, I brought my thoughts back to the present. Gazing again at the fine couple in front of me, I was reminded that my dear father, through the grace of God, remains on the face of this good earth. And that Sherlock Holmes, through the lovely presence of Joanna Blalock, is after all still with us.

CLOSING NOTES

I promised my father I would never write this story. But I have broken this promise because my wife, Joanna, has given me permission to do so. After all, it is truly her story, not mine.

Our son, Johnnie, attends a boys' boarding school near Oxford, where he excels in all subjects and has a keen interest in the art of deduction. The principal wishes to advance the lad to a higher grade, but Joanna has declined this offer, believing that Johnnie will always be ahead of the others, regardless of the class level.

My father has suffered a mild stroke that has left him with some weakness on the right side, but his mind remains sharp. He is recovering nicely and spends most of his time reviewing old files for his next Sherlock Holmes adventure. Johnnie Blalock often visits his new grandfather. They get along famously. There is clearly a special bond between the two.

Joanna and I now reside at 221b Baker Street.

ACKNOWLEDGMENTS

Special thanks to Peter Wolverton and Anne Brewer, superb editors, who managed to find the best novel in my manuscript.

Books are produced in the United States using U.S.-based materials

Books are printed using a revolutionary new process called THINKtech™ that lowers energy usage by 70% and increases overall quality

Books are durable and flexible because of Smyth-sewing

Paper is sourced using environmentally responsible foresting methods and the paper is acid-free

Center Point Large Print
600 Brooks Road / PO Box 1
Thorndike, ME 04986-0001 USA

(207) 568-3717

US & Canada:
1 800 929-9108
www.centerpointlargeprint.com